JOHN D. MacDONALD . . .

". . . an author who does the American mystery with more flair and possibly with more authentic voice than any working in this area today. . . . MacDonald plots are plots, not meanderings, well-devised, well-executed. His themes . . . are relevant."
— *LOS ANGELES TIMES*

"His books are narcotic and, once hooked, a reader can't kick the habit until the supply runs out."
— *CHICAGO TRIBUNE BOOK WORLD*

"MacDonald is a compelling storyteller; during the years I have been an ardent fan I have learned better than to start one of his books if I want to retire early."

— *DAN ROWAN*

"With his exceptional talents as a storyteller, there's no problem he can't handle and handle well."
— *REX STOUT*

"One of the most creative and reliable writers."
— *THE NEW YORK TIMES*

"A crime writer who never lets the customer down."
— *SATURDAY REVIEW SYNDICATE*

1

THE place Pidge had borrowed was a studio apartment on the eleventh floor of the Kaiulani Towers on Hobron Lane, about a hundred yards to the left off Ala Moana Boulevard on the way toward downtown Honolulu.

Riding in from the airport, I had found out why taxis cost so much in Hawaii. When you want to know something, ask. "What happens," the driver said, "the companies bid for exclusive. Like the Ala Moana Shopping Center. I could drop you there, but I can't pick up from there. You pay so much for exclusive, see; it's got to be passed on to the customer. Your first time here?"

"No. But I'm no regular visitor."

"Everything costs an ass and a half, sport, and it keeps going right on up."

It does, indeed it does, sport.

Even though I had phoned from the airport, and had used the low-fidelity speaker system in the cramped foyer, Pidge Brindle didn't undo the door until she had opened it a few inches, to the end of the safety chain. A round eye, a segment of wide smile, a squeak of pleasure. She slammed the door, and I heard the clinking and clicking of chains and bolts, and then she swung it wide and pulled me in, saving the obligatory embrace until she had done up the door once more. Then she stood tiptoe tall, reaching up to hug with strength and enthusiasm, saying, "I can't believe it, Trav. I can't, I really can't believe you're here, you came."

"You called, didn't you?"

"I know. Yes. But it is a long way to come."

Five time zones is a long way. Here it wasn't yet time for lunch, and back at Lauderdale, Bahia Mar was almost into the early dark of early December. I had me a case of jet lag. It turns your brain to putty and makes the edges of everything too bright and sharp.

But Pidge looked very good, very real, though far too pale. It had been a little more than a year since she and Howie Brindle, a few months married, had set off from Bahia Mar in the *Trepid* to take their sweet long time going around the world. There had been a few postcards. But there always are, when people leave. Marinas are transient places. They are big, elegant, outdoor waiting rooms.

Then the phone call, small and meek and scared. "Please? Please?"

And as Meyer had pointed out, though it was not at all necessary so to do, if I had to make a list of the people to whom I owed a Big One, it would have to include one dead man named Ted Lewellen, whose only child, Linda, had come to be named Pidge because when very young she had learned to imitate the throaty warble and coo of a city pigeon perfectly. Meyer didn't have to remind me about Professor Ted because I had already said yes to that small faraway voice. I had told her to stay put and I would make it as soon as I could.

And so I phoned an airline, went through my check-list of things to do when leaving the old houseboat for an indefinite time, packed, and took off, leaving Meyer to keep an eye on the store and hang onto any mail which might come. Everything I needed went into a bag small enough to go under the seat. I carried extra funds. Her voice had overtones of the deep miseries. Most solutions are available in your local shopping center, at high prices. The call had caught me about one week into another segment of my retirement. I had made score enough for a half year of it this time, so I had ample cash in the hidey-hole in the bow of *The Busted Flush*. I stocked the wallet handsomely and put the larger reserve supply in a safe place.

I learned about the safe place long ago from a man who had to carry four complete sets of identity papers in his line of work. You get hold of one of the longer Ace bandages for people with trick knees. I have one anyway, the left one. You divide the money into two equal stacks, fold each in half, wrap each stack in pliofilm, slip one under the bandage above the knee in front, one above the knee in back. No risk of losing. Nothing uncomfortable. Just a comfortable presence.

I bought my ticket amid the night people at the National counter at Miami. There are two ways to go—first and tourist. First is better. Everybody's life style is jam-packed with as many small arbitrary annoyances as the industrial-governmental bureaucracy can cram into it. So when you buy first class you buy lower blood pressure, because when it comes right down to nit and grit, they call more decisions your way if you have an F after your flight number. And for a man who's six four and a bit, with a 34-inch inseam, there is more sprawl room in F. I had a DC-10 to Los Angeles and found on arrival that, for reasons unknown, my connecting flight, originating in Chicago, had not yet left there. So I shopped the terminals in the first gray light of day and switched to Continental, to a 747, to the window seat in the rearward starboard corner of first class, leaving in an hour and a half. The bigger the bird, the more you feel like something being processed, and that feeling is enhanced if you sit forward in first on a long flight in the 747, because they will sure-God pull down the movie screen and then yank down the little slide that will cover your window. "But sir, it spoils the quality of the picture for the people watching the movie if your window lets any light in." And what crass person would spoil the movie for a small crowd of first-class clutzes thirty-seven thousand feet in the air?

Airplanes are empty three weeks before Christmas. There is a little lull in there. I think we had seven jolly girls flouncing about, servicing fifteen customers. After the unreality at the terminal of being served pineapple Kool-Aid by a couple of yawning ladies in plastic grass skirts, and the further unreality of the Inspection Before Boarding—a ceremony that any certified maniac could outwit—I caught a single tilted vista of Los Angeles in morning light, and the altitude and the sweep of the light gave it a strange appearance of total emptiness, a grid pattern of pale broken structures and rubble, long abandoned, a place of small dry vines and basking serpents. Moments later I got a second rearward look from a higher place, and it was no longer city, but stale pizza sprinkled heavily with chopped nutmeats.

As soon as they had unstrapped, the hearty girls set about getting us bombed on Marys, then nailed our feet to boards and crammed us chock-full of airline food, depending on the dual stupor of booze and food to drop us off to sleep. For the sleepless, the stereo high fidelity of the sterilized, repackaged headsets with a choice of umpty channels, or the sterilized, repackaged motion picture, would keep them from bothering the stewardess crew with any demands for service.

Halfway along, a great big stewardess, a king-size pretty, came back and stopped and looked at me in a troubled way. I wasn't eating, drinking, reading, listening to music, or watching the movie. I was sitting there with my eyes open. This was unthinkable! Would I like a drink? A magazine? A newspaper, maybe?

In A.D. 3174 the busy, jolly nosexicles on the planet Squanta III will sever our spinal cords, put us into our bright little eternity wombs, deftly attach the blood tube, feeding tube, waste tube and monitor circuitry, remove the eyelids quickly and painlessly, and, with little chirps of cheer, strokes and pats of friendship and farewell, they will lower the lid and seal it, leaving us surrounded by a bright dimensional vista of desert, a smell of heat and sage, a sound of the oncoming hoofs on full gallop as, to the sound of a cavalry bugle, John Wayne comes riding, riding, riding . . .

"No, thanks," I said. "I'm just thinking."

Pursed lips. Vertical lines between the dark brows. "Thinking? Hey, I've got a friend who's totally freaked on the contemplation thing, you know, how a person can do brain waves. I thought a person had to be all quiet and alone. I didn't know you could do it on airplanes. Is that what you're doing?"

"Yes. You can do it on big reliable airplanes."

"We're pretty steady this time on account of we're taking sixteen tons of plywood to Hawaii on account of some kind of strike."

"That would make it very steady."

"If I set you back by talking to you, I'm sorry. I didn't mean to mess up anything. You just go . . . right ahead, huh?"

She went away happy. I wasn't idle at all. I was no longer a symbol of stewardess failure. But her farewell at Honolulu International was full of that special warmth which meant she was glad to be rid of me. Meyer says that not only are the New People incapable of being alone and idle without cracking; they feel compelled to turn all loners into group animals like themselves.

Anyway, before seeing Pidge again, I had a chance to think about her. Swift, bright images of Pidge. Color stills starting ten years back when she'd been fifteen. That's when she had appeared around Bahia Mar, the motherless daughter of Professor Ted Lewellen. Ted's wife had died suddenly, and out of impulse born of grief and shock, he had taken a long leave of absence from the midwest university where he had taught for years. The cover story was that he was taking off to write a book.

I would hate to have to estimate how many genuine, authentic, priceless treasure maps have been offered to me. Sunken treasure along the Florida keys, off Bahama reefs, near Yucatan. I think there must be a printing plant in Tampa which turns them out on a production basis, shredding the edges and boiling them in tea.

Ted Lewellen had taken a sabbatical year a couple of years before his wife died and had spent that year in the old vaults and dead-storage rooms of the ancient libraries of Lisbon, Madrid, Cartagena and Barcelona. Because his colloquial Spanish and Portuguese were almost without flaw and his credentials as linguist, scholar, historian were perhaps more honored there than here, and because his project appealed to national pride and honor—being the tracing of the lesser-known voyages and forgotten heroes of the thirteenth, fourteenth and fifteenth centuries who had sailed from Western Europe—he was given full cooperation.

Long after he had decided he could trust me, he had told me about that year. Letters, ships' logs, statements of account. Great masses of material never adequately researched. Stilted formal tales of gold and blood, piracy and disease, tempests and greed. So, along with his scholarly project, he had kept a personal account of treasure clues. He had called it the dream book. He and his wife had made jokes about it. Some day, baby, ahunting we will go.

The next year, during summer vacation, Ted and his

wife had come to Florida, learned the rituals and precautions of scuba diving, visited the sites of a couple of the wrecks of the galleons which had sunk close to the Florida shore. He read the extravagant literature of the treasure hunters and, with a scholar's discipline, extracted the helpful facts and discarded the gaudy myths. From every available source, he compiled a master list of known or suspected treasure sites, and then he went through his dream book and wrote off those he had found on other lists, knowing that either they had been cleaned out long ago or they had eluded long and diligent search.

I met them, father and daughter, when they had first come down and were looking for a boat. Each trying to turn it into fun for the other one. Both trying to respond. They had heard I was selling a boat for a friend. I drove them up the Waterway to Oscar's Dock, where Matty Odell's *Whazzit* was quietly, politely moldering away. I remember I wondered at the time if he was another treasure freak. But he didn't have the gleam in the eye, or the elaborate and misleading explanations about why he wanted a sturdy old scow like the *Whazzit*. He did not make the usual buyer's mistake of pretending to know a lot of things he didn't know. I answered his questions. He was on a close budget. He had an expert go over it. Then he made Matty's widow a first and final offer and she took it. I forgot about it until I was over at the gas dock one day about two months later and the Professor brought the scow in for fuel. It was now called *Lumpy*.

More than the name was changed; I could only guess at how many backbreaking hours he and his daughter had put into that tub. The Professor was leaned down to strings and sinew and sun-dried cordovan hide. He asked me aboard, showed me the big rebuilt generators, the air compressor. I noted the oversized Danforths and the hawser-type anchor line. It was still a slow, ugly old scow, but now it was a *nice* old scow.

I asked him why he'd equipped it the way he had, and he said he had an underwater research project lined up. I asked him where Pidge was, and he said she was in school and adjusting well. He said she never had trouble making friends. I watched him take the *Lumpy* on out, handling it smartly in wind and tide.

A few months later I learned by accident that Lewellen had sold the *Lumpy* to a scuba club down near Marathon. I decided he had gone broke and gone home. Then I learned that somebody had bought the *Dutchess*. She'd been on the block for a long time at Dinner Key. Out of my reach, financially. A fantastic custom motor sailer with a semitrawler hull and a beam you wouldn't believe. She was about ten years old then. The hull had been made in Hong Kong. Mahogany and teak. The diesels and all the rest of the mechanical items had been installed in Amsterdam. Huge fuel capacity, desalinization, all navigational aids. She had been rigged with automatic winches and heavy-duty fittings so that one man could sail her alone.

The new owner was having a lot of work done on her. Then he brought her to Bahia Mar, to a big empty slip. I walked over when she came in and found Ted Lewellen and Pidge crewing the *Trepid*, as he had renamed her. You could take that thing anywhere in the world and stay as long as you wanted.

It is very easy to tell yourself not to get involved. Too easy. I told myself that about once a day until finally I knew I *had* to get involved. I picked a morning when Pidge was in school. We had our long talk in the main cabin of the *Trepid*, the rain coming down in torrents on the deck, a gusty wind pushing at the bare pole and giving all those tons of boat a gentle motion.

I said it was perfectly obvious to me that he had gone out on his own and found something very rich on the bottom of the sea, and if I could add it up that way, a lot of other people in the area could add it up just as easily, and when they did, they were the type to come aboard, beat the top of his skull flat, and search every inch of his great boat.

He did it well. Shock, surprise, consternation, disbelief. He had a long story about wills and trusts and estates and executors, and how it had taken a long time for his wife's estate to go through probate and for the distribution to be made.

So I told him that even if that was the truth, the dumb and ugly ones could come swarming aboard, and the ones who were a little bit smarter might check the probate records up north and find out if there was enough money left him to buy this much boat and do all this extra work to it. He thought that over and thanked me for thinking about him and warning him, and said he would take suitable precautions. When I realized he thought I was trying to cut a piece of his action, I explained just how my special little aspect of the salvage business worked. In case he might need my services. He didn't think he would.

Our relationship was one of guarded friendliness until, two years later, he decided he could trust me. Pidge, at seventeen, had suddenly acquired one of the great crushes of the western world. And she was fixated on me. It is difficult to imagine oneself as being a romantic image to a teen-age girl. When she looked at me, her eyes would go round and then get heavy. She would blush, turn pale, blush again. She would stop in the middle of a sentence, forgetting where it was going. She tripped and blundered into things and followed me like a dog. Had she been a knob-jointed gawk with chipmunk teeth and a tilted squint, it would have been one thing. But a tawny, limber, lovely, blue-eyed girl in the first full burst of ripeness is another thing entire. A total humble adoration is discomfiting. It alarmed and irritated her father and made me a figure of fun around the marina. There goes McGee and his fan club.

Pigeon's mission was very clear, very simple. She wanted

to be married to me right away, and whatever she had to do to make that happen was perfectly okay with her, and she was out to prove she was a grown woman.

When it got so intense I began to wonder about her sanity, I provisioned *The Busted Flush* and took off down the Waterway. I made it halfway down Biscayne Bay below Miami when I chunked into something floating almost totally submerged. It thumped the hull and then managed to come back up and take a whack at the starboard wheel, getting to it in spite of the hull being heavily skegged. There was so much vibration I had to cut the engine off. The *Flush* is not exactly nimble even on both little diesels, and I had a tide set and a steady hard breeze out of the west to fight. I crabbed along until I got sick of it, then looked at the chart and headed on across the bay to some no-name islands on the far side. At dusk I put down two hooks and got out the wheel puller and a spare wheel, all ready to make my repairs in the morning. I was fixing a big drink when Pidge came floating to the galley door, eyes huge and misty, a tender little smile on her lips.

"Hello, my darling," she breathed. "Surprised?"

I was. We talked all night. The only thing I managed to convince her of was that I did not want any child bride, or any child mistress, or even any quick joyful romp that she promised she would never never mention to anyone ever, word of honor. She booed and hawed and strangled until her face was a big red heartbroken bloat, and her voice a sickly rasp. I got a call through to her loving daddy at midnight and explained the situation. I sensed he could not make himself believe in the bent-wheel story. It was a hard one to sell. He said he had been on the verge of calling the cops. I gave him an estimate of when I'd be back. He said he would prefer it if I off-loaded her at Dinner Key. I said that was fine with me, which caused another fit of hawing, hiccuping and general leaky misery.

By dawn she was exhausted, spiritless, leaden. She

made terrible coffee. I moved the *Flush* to sand shallows, went over the side, pulled the bent wheel and put the spare on. I ran the *Flush* from the fly bridge, and she went way forward and sat out there on the bow hatch, huddled small and miserable. Even her round little behind in her white sailcloth shorts looked humble and defeated. But there was something in the curve of hip into waist, and waist into back and shoulder, that made a little stir of lech and regret. It is always a tossup with me as to whether I am sorriest for my misdeeds or the deeds undone. In a world intent on defusing sex, I had failed to do my part. I'd let a classic get away.

We got to Dinner Key at ten o'clock and I saw Lewellen pacing back and forth over near the gas dock. I took it over there and sent Pidge forward with her little blue flight bag and waved off any help with lines. I had no intention of tying up. I held it steady and she stepped ashore and trotted to Daddy. A little cluster of boat bums watched her with appreciation. I guess she had been planning it all the way to Dinner Key. She wheeled away from his grasp and spun and pointed an accusing finger at me, and in a high, clear, artificial tone, she said, "Daddy, do you know what he did to me? Do you want to know what Travis did? All night long, all he did was sc. . . ."

By then Ted Lewellen had read the scene, detected the revenge wish of the maiden scorned, and understood how it was a perfect affirmation of my innocence. I was boiling back away from the dock, widening the gap. He clamped a hand gently over her mouth just in time, and she collapsed into his arms. He gave me a half-shy grin, a shrug, and led her away toward the parking lot.

Pretty soon she was eighteen and had gone away to school.

And here, years later, five time zones away, the lady and I embraced. Then broke it up quickly and clumsily. Old restraints are a memory in the flesh. She had a faint blush, a half smile, and spoke quickly, "Just this bag? Is this all you have? Sure. I remember. You always feel oppressed by *things*. Hemmed in and all. I hope you didn't find a place to stay. But you couldn't have unless you made a reservation from California. Help me stop gibbering, please."

"Hush up, Linda Lewellen Brindle, dear."

"Thanks."

"Want to talk later? Or now."

"Now. Come over here."

She took me over to a window. She had me lean close to the glass. From there I could see a segment of the forest of spars in the Yacht Harbor. She showed me where to start counting. Six berths over. And there, eleven stories below us and a half mile away, was the distinctive bulk of the *Trepid*.

"Where's Howie?" I asked.

"Living aboard."

"And you're living here?"

"For a month so far," she said. "It belongs to my best friend in school. She's back on the mainland to be with her mother, who's dying of cancer."

"Let me guess. Am I here to save a marriage?"

She dropped onto an orange sofa and touched her throat. "Not exactly, Trav."

"Then?"

"It's narrowed down to just two things that could be happening to me. Just two things. I am losing my mind. Or Howie is going to kill me."

It was a mind-boggling thought. "Howie? D. Howard Brindle, for chrissake!"

She looked at me most solemnly, and I saw the two simultaneous tears bulge large on her lower lids, then spill over and make shiny little snail tracks down her cheeks in an edge of light from the window.

"I keep trying to make it come out that it's the first thing. I want to believe I'm losing my mind. But I can't believe it. Then I say that people who are crazy can *never* believe they are, and that means I probably am. I just can't . . ." And then came slow bow of the face into the hands, lowering of the hands, and head to the lady-knees, brown hair hanging long, gleaming with life.

She made a soft, snuffling sound. Okay, McGee, salvage expert, salvage the lady's life. Give her a choice. Crazy or dead.

Howie *Brindle? Howie?*

Come *on,* Pidge. Now really.

2

I WALKED out to the Hawaii Yacht Club at the end of the long pier. A fellow looked at my membership card from the Royal Biscayne and straightened perceptibly. Yes, of course, any member of the Royal Biscayne has reciprocal privileges, sir.

I said I was just looking to see if any Florida friends were in port. He sent me to the dockmaster, who showed me the big map of the protected boat basin on the side wall of his office and told me to take a look. The tags for stateside boats were fastened to the cork board with pale blue pushpins.

Nobody I knew well. Three big boats I knew, and one I didn't. The large money has the full-time hired crew to go with the large boat, and the rich have the crew make the long runs. They fly out later. Like old McKimber. Now dead. He used to keep a crew of six aboard the *Missy III*. One hundred and fifteen feet. Seven hundred thousand gleaming dollars afloat and a minimum hundred thou a year wages and running expenses. He'd send it where he wanted to go. Portugal, the Riviera, the Greek Islands, Papeete, Acapulco. Then he would fly out and go aboard and stay for a time, accompanied by one of those big, blond, jolly ladies of his. But he never cruised in the *Missy III*. It made him too nervous. He didn't like to wake up in the night and hear all that creaking and crackling and sloshing.

So I made a sound of pleasure at spotting the *Trepid* and asked the dockmaster if the Brindles were aboard, and he said that as far as he knew it was just the mister staying aboard her. I thanked him and went to say hello to Good Old Howie.

The *Trepid* was well laced into her U-shaped slip, stern to the pier, with husky stern lines crossed to the big bollards, bow lines to the pilings, and a pair of spring lines to big cleats on the narrow dock on the starboard. A short gangplank had been rigged, and I went to the dock end of it and yelled, "Howie? You aboard?"

He rose up from the far side of the trunk cabin, where he had a deck chair centered under the shade of a tarp. He stared at me for an uncomprehending second, and then his big face broke into familiar groupings of grin-wrinkles, teeth white against tan hide, brown eyes looking misty with pleasure.

"McGee! Son of a gun! What are you doing out here, man? Come on aboard."

I had planned my explanation so that it was neither too elaborate nor too vague. And entirely plausible. Hand delivery of a legal document, and get the certified check before turning it over. A well-paid favor for a friend of a friend.

He got me a cold beer from below. We sat in the shade of the tarp, amid boat smells and marina sounds. He wore faded red swim trunks. I had forgotten the size of him. Almost eye to eye with my six four, but a McGee and a half wide. About two seventy, I would guess. Practically no body hair. A soft slack look to the smooth tanned hide. But do not be misled. There is a physical type which has a layer of smooth fat over very useful muscle. Hard, rubbery fat. Big men, light on their feet, agile, and very tough. You find a lot of them in the pro football ranks. Linemen and linebackers. I had played volleyball with Howie on a Lauderdale beach. Set the net up in soft loose sand on a blazing day and some very good specimens crap out on you quickly. I fool with it only when I'm in top shape, which seems to happen less often these years. The regulars were glad to have a new fish in the game, and they tried to run him into the ground. But old Howie Brindle kept bounding tirelessly, sweating, laughing, yelping, making great saves and going high for the kill. He didn't even breathe hard.

Later, one night, the week before he married Pidge, he told me about his skimpy football career. Because of disciplinary problems, he had played in only three games out of nine his senior year at Gainesville. He was a defensive tackle. He wasn't anybody's draft choice, but the Dolphins gave him an invitation to camp.

There under the stars on the sun deck of the *Flush*, he said, "Those coaches kept chewing at me, Trav. They kept saying what a shame it was, somebody with all my natural equipment—and talent, I didn't have enough resolve. I wasn't hungry enough. What they want, you should keep getting up again and chasing that ball carrier even after you know you haven't a hope in hell of ever catching him. It just didn't make sense to me. Give me an angle and I could lay it on them a heavy ton, like I fell off a roof on them. It doesn't make a lot of difference now, I guess. I'll say this. It all seemed pretty bush for a bunch of pros to want that kind of nonsense from somebody."

So now he asked about Meyer and the Alabama Tiger, Johnny Dow and Chookie and Arthur, and all the Bahia Mar regulars. And then I said, "Where's Pidge? Off shopping?" Pidge and I had decided I might get a better reading if he believed I had not yet talked to her.

He looked down at one of his big banana-fingered hands, made a slack fist of it, then inspected the nails. "She's not living aboard," he said at last.

"Trouble?" I asked.

I was given a quick, troubled, brown-eyed glance. "Lots," he said.

"It happens. Snits and tizzies. You two guys will straighten it out."

"I don't know. It isn't the kind of thing . . . I mean . . . I just really don't know *what* the hell to do, Trav. I don't know how to handle it. And I don't even want to talk about it, okay?"

"What do you mean, is it okay? If you want to talk, I'm here. If you want me to go talk to her, that's okay too. Is she on Oahu?"

He grimaced, lifted a big arm, and pointed. "She's on the eleventh floor of that place over there; about half of it sticks out to the side of that brown building. Kaiulani Towers. Apartment eleven-twelve. Some girl friend from school, name of Alice Dorck. It's her place and she's away."

"What will I say to her?"

"I didn't say I wanted you to—"

He was interrupted by a hail from the dock. "Hey, Howie? I'm ready to unstep the big stick. Your muscles still available?"

"Okay, Jer. Coming," he called in a cheerful voice. He stood up and said, "This'll take maybe twenty minutes. You in any kind of a rush?"

"I'll be here."

He grinned and went padding off on his big bare brown feet. His streaked blond-brown hair was shoved back and cropped off square, just below the nape of his neck. He had lost the front third of his hair, all of it. It gave him a huge area of face, all of it a deepwater tan. Apparently he was a very obliging guy around the yacht harbor just as he had been around Bahia Mar. The muscles were always available.

I strolled the deck areas of the *Trepid*. I wanted the pleasure of a good, long, quiet look at her. It is so damned trite to say that they don't build them like that any more. They can still build them, if there's anybody left with money like that. The anticipated pleasure slowly faded and died. I did not enjoy looking at the *Trepid*. Let me explain about a boat person, one like me who is always a step behind or a step and a half behind the normal maintenance chores aboard *The Busted Flush*. The *Trepid* was sound and good, and she would have looked just great to a civilian.

Her lines are quite a lot like the forty-six-foot Rhodes Fiberglass Motorsailor, vintage 1972, but the *Trepid* has ten feet more length, six feet more beam, and in spite of a dead-weight tonnage nearly twice that of the Rhodes, actually draws a little less when that big beefy centerboard is wound all the way up into its slot in the hull. She is a husky boat, built like a workboat, and if you want to use a small jib like a staysail and go on diesels, she can give you almost three thousand miles at eight or nine knots, depending on the condition of her hull at the time.

What I saw was dry, corroding running gear and blocks which looked as if they might be frozen by corrosion. I saw pitted metal, flaking paint, smudges and stains, milky cracking varnish, oily spots on the teak deck, and a speckly green on the sail cover which could be the beginning of a fatal case of mildew. Everywhere I looked I saw hundreds of hours of undone labor, and very dull labor it is. The sea has no mercy, and there is no such thing as "maintenance-free." All you get near the water is either more maintenance than you can handle, or so much that you can just about stay ahead of it. The fee I pay for living aboard the *Flush* is a minimum of two hours a day for exterior housework every day I am aboard.

The *Trepid* was like a large, healthy, handsome woman

who had been forced to sleep in her clothes and go without comb, soap or makeup for a couple of weeks. She was still sound, but her morale had started to go sour.

Not like when she was Ted Lewellen's lady. Not the way she was treated when Meyer and I flew out and lived aboard the *Trepid* anchored in sheltered water in Pitchilingue Cove in the Bay of La Paz in Baja California. There were five of us aboard. Beside Ted, there was Joe Delladio, a Mexican electronics engineer, and Frank Hayes, a construction engineer and scuba expert.

Maybe Lewellen wouldn't have brought me into his action even then, but I guess that I was the only one he could think of when two of the minor partners in his venture decided they could no longer keep on pretending they were not afraid of sharks. And three men could not do all the work which had to be done before the good season changed. At my suggestion, Meyer became the other replacement.

It was in the big salon of the *Trepid* the evening of the day we arrived that Ted told us about his past, about all the research and about the treasure clues he had found in the old original documents, the ships' logs, officers' letters.

He explained what he was after this time. The information had come out of the archives in Madrid and in Amsterdam. Long ago a Dutch pirate ship had knocked off a series of Spanish galleons and had loaded herself down with more treasure than was prudent. She had been intercepted by Cromwell, who was also a pirate at that time, in command of two English vessels. They caught the Dutchman north northeast of La Paz Bay, which is near the tip of Baja California, on the sheltered side.

The Dutchman had not surrendered very quietly and, in the fuss, was holed at the waterline. Cromwell took the dismasted hulk in tow and tried to make it to the shallows, but she sank well offshore. Some of the Hollanders escaped to shore, probably not more than a dozen, and two eventually made it back to their homeland. Professor Lewellen estimated that the pirate ship had been laden with about twelve millions in gold and silver. He had used Spanish sources to get a reading. From English and Dutch accounts of the confrontation, he had prepared an overlay of a geodetic chart of the area, with the search area marked out.

He explained we weren't looking for some romantic old vessel resting on the bottom. Tides and currents would have shifted her and broken her up a long time ago. Somewhere in the shaded areas of the overlay, she would have burst herself open like a rotten sack and dumped the heavy metal. The area was silt and sand bottom, constantly shifting. We would be working at a depth range of seventy to a hundred and thirty feet.

"I believe the heavy metal would stay pretty well bunched, no matter what happened to the ship. I think that her cannon will be in the same area as the precious metals. All I'll say about the search method is that it involves exhausting, gut-busting labor. And we may never find anything. If you decide against it, I'll pay your fare back, no complaints, no questions, no pleading. If you decide for it, then the cut works this way. After we take the expenses off the top, fifty percent comes to me and the vessel. Of the remaining fifty percent, Joe and Frank get sixteen percent each, and you and Meyer get nine percent each. If we cashed in at two million net, that would be ninety thousand apiece for you. If we get nothing, you've been nonpaying guests, and manual labor."

I looked at Meyer. Meyer had pursed his lips, beetled his brow, and said, "How did you become owner of this fine vessel, Professor Ted?"

"Just lucky, I guess."

"Meyer's question is pertinent," I reminded Lewellen.

He stared directly at me, and I have a vivid memory of that look. He had seemed a mild and gentle fellow, professorial, meticulous and fussy. He looked out at me from under sun-whitened lashes and eyebrows. Once upon

a time I rescued a great blue heron. Some cretinous subhuman had busted his wing with a small-caliber slug.
After I had run him down and quelled him with my right
arm wrapped around the surprising lightness of wings and
body, my left hand holding that long lethal bill, he held
still and looked at me, unblinking. It was the predator
appraisal. How would I taste? Was I worth killing and
eating? A pale calm yellow stare, devoid of fear.

Lewellen shrugged and turned slightly, and the look
was hidden, but in that few moments he had become quite
another person to me.

"You have a right to ask for batting averages," he
said. "There were three sites in the Bahamas. Pidge and I
worked them, aboard the *Lumpy*. We were empty on
one of them. We got sixteen hundred pounds of silver
ingots from another. We took seven hundred pounds of
gold coin minted in Mexico from the third. We stopped
when some strangers began to take an interest—the new
government in Nassau has a nasty habit of taking a hundred percent as its cut. I researched the clandestine market
in numismatic rarities. It's of no moment to you gentlemen
how and when I can turn such finds into usable cash. All
you need to know is that I can do it . . . if we find anything. And I rather think we will. That gold, part of it,
made it possible to buy the *Trepid*."

Meyer sighed and nodded. So we went to work. Joe
Delladio had set up the cover story, marine geodetic
research under a foundation grant. The *Trepid* stayed at
anchor in the cove. The search area had been marked
with buoys. We worked from a heavy-beamed old scow—
an oversized skiff actually—which Delladio and Frank
Hayes had overloaded with a high-pressure diesel pump
and big diesel generator, as well as a gasoline compressor
to refill the scuba tanks.

We had a dozen twenty-foot lengths of high-impact
plastic pipe two inches in diameter, open at one end,
closed and pointed at the other. The procedure was to

clamp the hose nozzle to the pointed end of the pipe, then jet the pipe down through the sand and ooze until about a foot was left above the surface. Signal to stop pump. Call for electronic probe. Then slowly lower it down inside the pipe, down through the ancient shifting strata of sand and silt, while topside somebody monitored the dial, ready to give a tug on the signal cord if the needle swung in any significant way.

We kept as close as we could to a square pattern, sinking the holes thirty feet apart. And we tried to keep from thinking about the simple mathematical fact that the three-square-mile search area would need a hundred and twenty thousand holes to complete it. Five men were the minimum possible. Meyer and I were more handicap than help until we learned how to handle the high-pressure hose. Then, after a week, we got to the point where we could stop thinking about every move, and production climbed up to the prior level, before the other two men had quit. Rotating the topside and sea-bottom jobs, the crew—allowing for mechanical delays—could average five holes an hour, but we could not push ourselves past eight hours, so it came out to forty a day. Meyer remarked that on a seven-day-week basis, that was only eight years of work ahead.

We switched jobs every hour or every five holes, whichever came first. The weather held. It was such brutal labor, there was a tendency to forget why we were doing it. Just before dusk we'd buoy the location of the last hole, and then we'd read and mark the bearings of a shale cliff north of us, a giant boulder offshore to the south, and the entrance to the cove where the *Trepid* was at anchor, just in case something happened to the buoy. We took a lot of pains about that, and we argued a lot about it. One hundred and twenty thousand holes is enough without sinking a single one of them twice. And then we would go droning back to the cove, shower the salt off, build a big drink, eat like ravenous monsters, and sit in a stuporous yawning daze for a half hour before tottering to a bunk, feeling as if all the strings and tendons and wires and muscles had come unfastened from the joints and sockets.

We tried not to think about what would happen if we got a reading. We would buoy the spot and bring the *Trepid* out and use four hooks to fasten her over the spot, and then go to work with the monster pump mounted in the bilge. It was, in effect, a small dredge, with a four-inch cutting head that would suck up the goop and then spill it over the side of the *Trepid* into a catch basin of heavy steel mesh.

The sharks came around. Shallow-water types. Nurse, sand, hammerhead. I could have felt uncomfortable if we'd had to work in murky water. But there was a good tide current across the work area at all times except right on the changes, and you could work upstream from the hole you were sinking and be in clear water. I wouldn't want to spend too much time in the same water with the tiger sharks and leopard sharks, because the averages might catch up with you. But they work a lot further offshore than we were in those waters.

The sharks were cruising their range, as is their habit. They would come upon us, put on the brakes, turn and make a big circle, watching us all the while, and then take off again. No wild creature, except perhaps the cockroach, is an experimental gourmet. Unless the food supply has disappeared, wild things want to eat what they have always eaten. Something that does not look, sound or move like anything that has ever been on their menu is not about to be tasted. It might taste incredibly nasty. Why take the risk?

Barracuda would come in quiet groups and hang almost without motion in the clear water, giving us the big eye for an hour at a time. Curiosity, not hunger. All wild creatures especially well adapted to their environment have free time they do not have to use in search for food and shelter, or in fleeing from their enemies. This free time develops the sense of curiosity and the sense of play. Porpoises play. Monkeys play. Otters play. Seals play. Young mammals play. Barracuda stand around and watch, like old men at a construction site, until a pang of hunger sends them darting off about their business.

The eerie savage predators of the deep have gotten a very bad press. I met a man who used to don an old-fashioned diving costume and go down into a tank in Hollywood and be pursued by a horrid, deadly octopus with arms about nine feet long. Octopi are timid and gentle. Hank would sort of lean way back on his heels and put his hands up in front of him as if to ward off untidy death, and then would walk slowly toward the octopus and it would retreat just as slowly. Then they would run the film backwards.

When the good weather broke and began to make up in too threatening a way for us to risk the scow in offshore waters, even though they were semiprotected waters, we took a day off. There were provisions to pick up. Professor Ted, Joe Delladio and I were eager for a break in the routine. Meyer and Frank Hayes stayed aboard to nourish a chess feud. Meyer had discovered, to his dismay, that when Hayes played the black, he had worked out a variation of the Yugoslav sacrifice in the King's Indian defense which Meyer had not successfully countered in three tough tries.

We broke out the little Whaler, clamped the outboard onto it, and kept to the sheltered side of the cove and the bay, oddly eager to see strange faces and hear unfamiliar voices.

Joe Delladio knew the area. So we went to a place where he was known, a little fishing resort and hotel called Club de Pescadores. At the Club (pronounced Cloob) Joe was given a warm Mexican *abrazo* by most of the staff. It was a little before noon. He borrowed a pink Jeep with a canopy to go into town and get the supplies, saying that if we were along, they'd cost more. We set ourselves up, Ted Lewellen on my left, at a table near a little outdoor pavilion bar with a thatched roof, with canvas laced between the posts on two sides as a windscreen. There were wire chairs and a tin table, like in the faded photos of old drugstores. Gray scud went past at express speed, and the wind was hot and wet.

I drank tall ones with fruit juice and a local gin called Oso Negro, black bear. It is guaranteed to let you know you have been drinking. Touch a fingertip to the top of your skull the next morning and your head will fall open like a cleavered melon.

It was all very nice after having been prune-wrinkled by long immersion in the sea, then barbecued in the sun glare aboard our work boat. I enjoyed the bar, the drink, and even the company, though Ted was not one to use three words when one would be enough.

I could not understand why I felt so very damned good and said so. It was a different kind of good feeling from what I get when I am in good shape. I wondered aloud.

"Heart," Professor Ted said, and then explained that a man's heart shares to a certain extent that trait of the whale heart and the porpoise heart of slowing when they dive deeply, to give a maximum use of the oxygen in the blood, to make it last. "You develop a bigger, slower beat, Travis, so that topside you're getting more nourishment to the cells of muscles and brain and gut."

It made sense. I was wondering how to ask about our chances of getting rich when a small herd of sports fishermen from the States came trooping in. They were noisy. They were clad in the Real Thing—big game garments from Abercrombie, L. L. Bean, Herter's, all properly sun-faded, salt-crusted, spotted with oil and fish blood. As there was absolutely no chance of any of the boats going out in that blow, the outfits looked too contrived.

They clotted around the bar and ordered booze in broken Mexican and tried to all talk at once about old Charlie trying to harpoon that big sonofabitchofa leopard ray, and how that idiot boy, Pedro, had gaffed the striped marlin when it was too green and got a sprained wrist and some loosened teeth from the gaff handle, and how poor old Tom lost a three-hundred-dollar outfit to some big billfish nobody ever even got a good look at. And they whined and moaned and bitched about the weather that was taking a good hunk out of their expensive fishing trip.

They were aware of us sitting there and made their loud brags for our benefit, with the sidelong looks that tried to estimate us and figure out who we were, sitting so sedately in clean khaki slacks, boat shoes, T-shirts, wondering no doubt if we were of the great billfish brotherhood.

Finally, as could be expected, one of them came wandering over, smiling, glass in hand, and said, "Hi, you guys. Just get in? You must have come by boat. Nobody gets color like that except on the water. Come down from California?"

Professor Ted looked at him for a slow five-count and said, "No."

Nine out of ten would have wandered off. I wish he had. But he was like a friendly dog in a friendly neighborhood. He smiled and sat in one of the vacant chairs at our table and said, "Mind? Honest to God, I'm the jinx of all time, and you better believe it. I've been counting on this for years. What is today? Thursday? I left Florida last Sunday, and we got out there bright and early Tuesday and in two full days you know what I got? Three strikes and flubbed every one of them. Bunny Mills over there— he's my boss—in charge of the southeastern district out of Atlanta—he got a blue that went two hundred and thirty. I'm the only one skunked so far, and I got to leave Saturday, and Manuel tells us this is a two- or three-day blow. How about that? Say, my name is Don Benjamin."

He held his hand out to me. What can you do? He was about thirty, slender, dark-haired, with a reddened and peeling nose and forehead. I took his hand and said, "McGee. And Lewellen."

"Glad to meet you. You been doing any good?"

I mentioned the fake survey and the fake foundation. Ted yawned. He signaled the bartender for a pair of refills. Don Benjamin sighed wistfully and said, "You know sitting here like this, it doesn't seem possible that come Monday morning I'll be right back there in Suncrest, right back in the old routine, peddling insurance."

He looked expectant. One of the afflictions of a transient society is the do-you-know disease. I knew a few people in Suncrest. But I didn't want to play.

"Too bad," I said.

So Bunny Mills came sauntering over. Don's boss. Don introduced him. Beef and belly, and a broad and meaningless grin. A type. The nasal, slurred, high-pitched back-country Southern whine of one of the "good old boys." I could guess that he moved his insurance business in political directions, had a piece of this and a piece of that, tiptoed on the outer edge of tax fraud, whacked judges on the back, and leaned hard on the serfs who worked for him. He came over to punish flagrant disloyalty. Don Benjamin had taken unauthorized leave of absence from his role as junior ass kisser to consort with strangers—without permission.

Bunny Mills beamed at Professor Ted and at me and said, "This little ol' boy here come so close to winning this here trip on the company, I tooken pity and sprang for it outen my own pocket, and never did I see a boy so plain dumb fumble-handed around a boat and tackle. He's just plain in the way. He even damn near lost me my blue, right, Donnie?"

Don Benjamin was staring up at him, his expression strained. "Mr. Mills, the premiums and renewals and the new business put me in the upper—"

"Argue that with the home office, boy." The grin was still there, with the small mean eyes looking out from behind it.

"But the printed list had me—"

"You got a sorry way of rubbing me wrong, Donnie boy. Best you shut your mouth and come back over to the bar."

We hadn't wanted Don moving in on us in the first place. But I've never enjoyed watching the abuse of power. So, slumped deeply into the chair, I grinned up into Mill's grin and said, "Soon as we finish our private conversation, Fats, I'll ship him back over to you."

There are men whose passports should be stamped NOT VALID OUTSIDE THE CONTINENTAL LIMITS OF THE USA. The further they get from home, the louder, cheaper, and tougher they get. And the more careless. They rove the world in honky style.

If I'd been wearing the right clothes for billfishing, I would have been a good old boy too. I made a serious mistake. I underestimated his capacity for violence, and I had not seen the weapon. I didn't see it until he pulled it free. It was a fish billy, with a thong through the hardwood handle, the thong having been suspended from one of those brass belt hooks sold to men who like to plod about jangling with the tools of play. Fourteen inches of club with a wide bracelet of metal encircling the fat end, said bracelet studded all the way around with little pyramids of steel about a half inch high and a half inch apart.

His face had clenched instantly into a red something that looked more like a fat boiled fist than a face. He planted his feet, snatched the club free, and made his whistling, grunting, earnest effort to cave in the whole middle of my face. Maybe he had never made a serious attempt to kill anyone before. God only knows what angers and frustrations had built him into this abrupt deadliness. He was ready, and I was there. And he was far from home.

My reflexes were in fine shape. There was no time for any conscious thought. I caught a glimpse of the club flickering toward me, shoved hard with both feet and went over backward in the chair, not certain it would miss me until it had. I wanted to tuck and roll and come up onto my feet, but I gave my head a solid ringing crack against the flagstones, and in the roll I caught my feet over the arm of a chair at the table behind me. It was a very sorry performance. People were roaring and I was moving in slow, slow motion. Comedy routine. Mommy, watch the man with the red face crush the skull of the man on the floor!

He was tippy-toe quick, the way some beefy men are. I did manage to roll just enough so that the second blow clanked the stones close to my ear. But I saw that he was definitely going to get me with his third try. Very definitely.

He was bending over me, feet planted wide, club high, hesitating so as to get good aim and maximum impact. Everybody was too shocked to move. Except Professor Ted. There was only one way he could change the pattern of events in time. He said later he had jumped up as I had gone over backward and had come around the table as the second swing struck sparks off the patio rock. He kicked big Bunny Mills in the testes from behind. Though on the scrawny side, Lewellen was in good shape. And he had played soccer before, during, and after college. And he was in a hurry.

I did not know what had happened. I heard a heavy thud of impact. I got a quick glimpse of big Bunny's face as he stumbled across me, all wide eyes and round wide screaming mouth. My hazy feeling from banging my head on the stone was fading very quickly, and I got up. Mr. Mills was on his back, both knees jacked as high as he could get them, rolling gently from side to side, making sweet little sounds like a basket of kittens, gently clasping the spreading stains in the fine sportsman fabric of his crotch.

Then, as is customary, everybody who had not done one damn thing until that moment began to try to do everything at once. They began running into each other and shouting orders at each other. Finally they picked him up and carried him tenderly into the clubhouse without trying to unfold him. Don Benjamin trotted alongside. I wondered if he knew that his career with that particular insurance company had ended then and there. The fisherman fellows perhaps handled their good old buddy a little awkwardly. I heard him scream twice, far away.

Joe Delladio appeared about thirty seconds after the second scream. He got a quick briefing from us and then talked to the bartender, the waiter, and one of the owners of the place, all of whom had watched, with awe, the gringos at play. They retold the story with much emotion, with descriptive gestures.

Joe came back to the table, minus his earlier apprehension. "An unprovoked attack," he said. "Mills has been here before. He always gets tight and makes some kind of trouble. They'll swear he tried to kill you and your friend saved your life. There's no doctor here. They'll arrange to have him flown over to Guaymas. So let's have a drink, amigos. Professor Ted, you astonish me."

"But not as much as he astonished Mills," I said.

We drank until the buzz was exactly right, and then we ate the specialties of the house, cooked with tender loving care for their old friend Joe, for the tall gringo who nearly got killed, and for the tough old one who had doubtless gelded the fat animal. We had sea turtle, *caguama,* cooked in its shell with an odd spicy sauce, and *bacha,* the giant clam with the sweet, firm meat, broiled just enough. And bottles of that great dark Dos Equis beer. It looked as if it could come up rain, so we carried the stores down to the Whaler and got back to the *Trepid* a little past four, took a siesta, and woke to the sound of the wet storm wind shoving and snapping at the hull, noisier than the familiar drone of the generator.

That evening I said to Professor Ted, "I owe you a Big One."

"I was trying to keep my work crew intact, McGee."

"I still owe you."

"When I need it, I'll let you know."

"Fair enough. Your deal."

3

YES, we found the cannon and we found gold. We found the site ten feet below the floor of the sea in a water depth of seventy-five feet, on the tenth of July at eleven o'clock in the morning. We used the high-pressure hose to wash our way down to it. It had whacked the needle way over against the stop. Ted said the cannon was of the right period.

We toasted the find in warm gaggy whiskey, and we laughed a lot at very little. Joe Delladio planted his waterproof gadget close to the cannon. It was fail-safe, would transmit for a year on its battery pack, and could be picked up at three hundred yards on a transmitting frequency too exotic for anybody to stumble on it. We took sightings, then pulled the buoys and headed home to the *Trepid*.

By ten the following morning the *Trepid* was moored right over the spot, and Joe and I were below, fighting the dredge head, one man on each side of it clinging to a brace improvised from a spade handle, sucking a wide area around the target because the sand and muck were too loose to hold more than an 8- to 10-degree slope. We knew that if something of interest were sucked up and spewed into the catch mesh, the people up above would cut the big pump. Or if we had visitors they would cut it and we would go into our science-fantasy act.

By early afternoon, having rotated tasks on the half hour, we were beginning to wonder if some old pirate hadn't deep-sixed a busted cannon. Ted wondered if they hadn't jettisoned everything heavy to try to save the ship. Frank Hayes kept close watch on his big pump, mumbling about how hot it was running.

About three o'clock we uncovered the business end of another cannon, and then the dredge sucked up a pocket of miscellaneous junk. Ted and Meyer were on the cutting head, and when the pump was cut off, they came up to look at what we had. After all the chunks of shell, bushels of weed, pecks of sandworms, it was a pleasure to see some man-made objects.

We spread corroding chunks out on the deck. It is a truly fantastic experience to watch what happens to iron after it has been in the sea for a few hundred years. When the air first hits it, the iron is chunky and solid. As it dries, the rusting process is so weirdly speeded up it is as though some terrible acid were working on the objects. They turned to flakes and powder, then to piles of dark dust in just the gentle motion of the *Trepid*.

There was one prize. At first it was a chunk of corrosion in the shape of an old flintlock pistol. As it dried, most of it crumbled into flakes and scabs and powder, leaving some solid parts behind—an ornate brass trigger guard, green with corrosion, some brass screws, an ebony grip, a brass butt cover, and, untouched by the sea or the years, gleaming yellow and pure, two lacy, fragile pieces of gold, representing a curve of vine with small delicate leaves. Ted identified the two pieces as the gold inlay which had been worked into the metal on either side of the weapon, in the area between the trigger and the hammer. The art of putting a hole in someone was accomplished with a great deal more elegance in the olden days.

The second prize came at ten the next morning, a single gold coin. A big one. It was crude but mint-fresh. Joe Delladio was so excited he lost his English entirely. I saw a very slight tremble of Ted Lewellen's hands as he turned it this way and that. "Spanish five-peseta," he said calmly. "A beauty. Look at the sharpness of the die marks. Often, the first run of gold coins with a new die were presentation pieces, to be given to the king. If our luck is good, there'll be a lot of those down there. God only knows what they'd bring at auction."

Maybe there were a lot. They are probably still there. Joe and I were on the cutting head when the pump stopped. When we climbed wearily up onto the deck, they told us that the big pump had suddenly started sounding like a washing machine full of broken stone. Frank came up from below, sweat-soaked, with a fresh and ugly burn on his forearm. "Vibration cracked a fitting," he said. "Main seal ruptured. Sucked sand into itself. Scored everything all to hell. Blocked the cooling system and froze up a half second before I hit the switch."

"How long to fix it?" Ted asked.

After staring at him for at least five seconds, Frank said. "You've now got the biggest, ugliest anchor in Mexico."

So after the conference about ways and means, Meyer and I flew back to Florida, Joe flew back to Guadalajara, and Ted Lewellen and Frank Hayes set a course for San Diego and a better pump. We were going to hit it again, the five of us, when the new season began, when we could count on good weather.

But that had to be the year that one of the rare whirly ladies came stomping into that part of the coast. Most of them roam out into the Pacific and die. She started quickly, stayed small and intense, curved right into that area of the Mexican coast, and changed a lot of the geography of both the land areas and the bottom.

Ted Lewellen had given up on it before I got a chance to talk to him a year later, when the *Trepid* came gliding into Bahia Mar, showing the effects of long sea duty. Maybe I asked too many questions about how hard they'd looked for Joe Delladio's little electronic beeper. Finally he said with irritation, "For God's sake, McGee! You can't even *find* where the Club de Pescadores once stood. You can't find a trace of a foundation. One of the islands is gone. Just plain gone. So is that rock the size of a church. Joe's gadget could be halfway to Los Mochis, in twenty-five hundred feet of water, or the damned thing could be in the top of a tall tree near Chihuahua! Part of the bottom we surveyed is dry land now. Part of it is three hundred feet deep!"

"Okay, okay. I was just asking, Ted."

"There are other ones."

"Not like that one."

His grin was tired, wry, inverted. "Not exactly like that one, no. Some are smaller and some are bigger, and they are all out there for the finding."

Out of almost every experience comes something useful. Sometimes you don't know what it is until you have turned it this way and that and checked it against the light, hefted it. I had learned that not finding treasure is almost as good as finding it. I had been given that absolutely vivid memory of how the lacy gold looked in the Mexican sunlight. And the coin. They were with me in total recall forever. So was that strange, sick excitement of making the hit, finding the place, knowing you were going to suck it clean.

Meyer agreed. Ted Lewellen hinted that he might be going out again soon. We hinted of a casual interest in going along. He worked on the *Trepid* eight to ten hours a day. One afternoon he went over to the center of town to buy something he needed. He rode the little Honda he kept aboard the *Trepid*. As they tell it, a rain started to come down as he was heading back. It had not rained in a long time. After a dry spell, the first rain turns the roads to grease. Ted was hurrying along, shoulders hunched, when a small fearless dog ran yapping out to bite him in the leg. Ted swerved and the bike slid out from under him, and Ted and bike slid slowly under a giant-size transit-mix cement truck, one of the juggernauts of the Kondominium Kulture. Their massive bumpers are at decapitation height, and too many of them are driven by arrogant murderous imbeciles encouraged by a venal management to "make time." The one who squashed Professor Ted might not have even known it had he not caught a glimpse of man and motorbike sliding under him. He stopped, got out, took a look, and had the grace to require hospitalization for shock.

The semipermanent population of Bahia Mar takes care of its own. Sympathy may not be long-lasting, but when it is focused, there is a lot of it. Pidge got a lot, and it helped her through the worst of it. There was no one else. She was halfway through school by then, and she thought that she had someone else, but the boy revealed to her an essential coldness by taking the death of the daddy as an irritating inconvenience. Looking at him with unclouded vision, she saw the poseur, the charmer, the manipulator, and told him to skip the trip to Florida, and skip everything else as well. Arrangements were made. Lewellen was cremated, and there was a small service at Lauderdale and then a graveside service in Indiana, where his urn was buried beside the one which held the ashes of his wife.

Meyer researched the problems of money, estate, taxes, and red tape. Ted had moved his money business from Indiana to the First Oceanside Bank and Trust and made the bank the executor. After the Trust Officer, a Mr. Lawton Hisp, had accepted Pidge's instructions to let

Meyer know all, Meyer finally made a bemused report to me of the situation as Professor Ted had left it.

"When your work brings you into contact with shark-type sharks and two-legged sharks, you keep things neat," he said. "He was a neat man. She gets the *Trepid* free and clear. He's been audited every year for four years, and he is okay with the IRS. There's cash to take care of the estate tax. There's a very nice portfolio which won't have to be disturbed, all in trust for Pidge. The only change Hisp will make is to divert the income to her instead of plowing it back into the kind of thing he has been buying, which are good solid convertible bonds and convertible preferreds. The yield based on current market value isn't so great, like four point seven percent, but because it is computed on a current asset value of eight hundred and seventy-seven thousand, she'll get a little over forty-one thousand a year taxable income. Hisp and I talked about moving it all into tax-free bonds, and she would get about the same income without taxes to pay, but we both felt uneasy about putting a person so young into fixed-obligation stuff. He's invested in the convertibles of companies big in natural resources, so if inflation ten years from now makes a new Chevvie cost forty thousand, the increase in the value of the natural-resources common stocks will have pulled the convertible bonds and preferred up—not in direct ratio, but certainly into the six-to-one, eight-to-one range. We agreed she should pay taxes now and maintain her equity position. At twenty-one, which is very soon, she can tap the principal if she wants to, but no more than ten percent of the asset value in any calendar year. When she's forty, the trust is distributed to her and her kids, if any, in equal portions. If she dies before forty, her children get the income until the youngest is twenty-one, then they get the principal, evenly divided."

We could all understand why she didn't sell the *Trepid*. It was the most direct link to happier days. And living aboard at Bahia Mar, she felt as if she was among friends.

She had no desire to return to school. Whoever was handy helped her when she needed help. Pretty soon it was Howard Brindle who was taking care of the chores. He had not been around Bahia Mar for very long, yet he fitted in so well it seemed as if he'd been there a lot longer. He never scrounged. He gave full value in time and muscle for all favors.

When it became serious, the whole village nodded and said that it was probably a good thing. Meyer and I appointed ourselves a two-headed daddy and grilled Howie.

Meyer planted the needle beautifully. "What do you want to be, Howie? Who do you want to be? Or are you happy and satisfied just to fall into it?"

This was aboard the *Flush*. Howie looked troubled and thoughtful and said, "We've talked about that a lot, Pidge and me. It comes down to this. I just haven't got much work ethic. We talked it out. It certainly isn't going to bother me if both of us live off what her dad left her. It isn't as if it was money Pidge earned herself. If it was turned around so my dad had left it to me, it wouldn't bother me living off it and doing nothing. I mean, how can you prove that anything a man does is really *worth* doing? She says it won't bother her because there's more than she needs, the way she wants to live. So what we want to do is get married, get the *Trepid* geared up for around the world, and then, by God, go around it, even if it takes three or four years. But it isn't as if we're closing the door on anything else. We could get restless. We could see something we think is worth doing, and then we could change our minds. The options are open. But neither of us is going to feel guilty if we don't take any other option ever. We've talked this all out."

"Maybe," I said, "you might want to pick up where Ted left off."

"I thought of that. He was getting geared up to go after something. We can't find a clue. She told me she'd searched every inch of the vessel. He hadn't left his research records at the bank, in the deposit box. We went over the boat together. We took three days, three whole days. Nothing. It's just as well. What would I be doing looking for goodies in the ocean? What could I buy I haven't got already?"

So that made three searches, counting the one Meyer and I made that lasted from the time we heard Ted had been killed until dawn the next morning. Not for ourselves. For the daughter.

Howie was plausible enough, and it was easy to see how happy they were just to be with each other. So there was a wedding, and there was a lot of work done on the *Trepid,* and a lot of intensive study of charts and celestial navigation and a lot of instruction in how to maintain and operate all the navigation aids and servomechanisms aboard that would go *pockety-queek* all the time she was trudging across the ocean blue.

And this was the first time I'd seen the *Trepid* since we all watched her take off one morning in November over a year ago, moving out into the tide run, tipping to the first ground swell, aiming southeast once past the sea buoy, about 105 degrees, the farewell champagne still cold in the glass.

I roamed forward, squatted on a big cleat, and picked morosely at a clot of some kind of tarry guck stuck to the teak. When a boat carries you all those sea miles safely and well, she deserves better treatment. In the marriage row, the *Trepid* was the innocent bystander getting hurt. I wondered how much green beard was hanging from her bottom. I wondered if her engines would start without an overhaul. There was a good sting in the Hawaii sunshine.

Howie came back aboard and I stood up and walked aft. He was sweating heavily and had lost some hide off the top of his right shoulder. He said the two of them had gotten the mast down on Jer's boat. Sorry it took so long.

"You were saying you don't want to talk about your problem?"

He flinched. "Not like that. Hell. I suppose why not? It's just that it's weird. Trav?"

"Yes?"

"I don't even want to say it."

"Try hard."

"I think . . . shem wummul neminum." He sat, big brown arms resting across his round brown knees, and he was staring down at the deck, huge hands hanging loose from his wrists.

"I can't hear you, Howie!"

He lifted his head, contortion twisting his mouth, brown eyes agonized. "I think she's flipping! Losing her head! Falling out of her tree. Oh, God damn it all anyway."

He popped up with that surprising, flexible agility, ducked out from under the tarp, and stood at the rail with his back to me. He made a single, gulping sob sound.

After he settled down, he told me how it had begun. They had hopped the Caribbean islands on the way down, skipping some, hiding from bad weather, learning how much and how little they could expect from the *Trepid*, settling into the routines of who does what and when. Honeymoon voyage, masks and fins over the reefs, unnamed empty beaches, music tapes aboard, scream of the reel with the line being pulled out against all the drag one dared use, sail popping and tilting as a listless breeze freshened, salty, sandy lovemaking under improbable skies. Santo Domingo, Guayama, Frederiksted, Basse-Terre, Roseau, Fort-de-France, Castries, Bridgetown, St. George's, San Fernando; and from there they hopped the coast of South America westward; La Asunción, Puerto La Cruz, Carenero, La Guaira, with a run up to Willemstad, then west and down to Riohacha, Santa Marta, Cartagena, and then across the gulf to Portobello and Colón and the Canal.

Things broke and were fixed. Other things wore out and were replaced. Sometimes the bank had to cable money. Twice, he thought. Maybe three times, but he doubted it. He could remember just the two times. They had worked their way slowly up the Pacific coast of Central America, and I broke into his recital of the ports they had hit and asked again where the trouble had started.

"Well, quite a way back. Anyway, we stopped at Mazatlán and got everything in top shape and stowed all the provisions aboard and . . . came here. Mazatlán seemed like a good place to start from because it is almost the same latitude as Honolulu, which is about thirty-two hundred miles due west. We'd had a lot of practice in navigation by then. No sweat. We knew we'd hit it and we did. One storm made me wonder, though. It was one big rough son of—"

"Howie! Get *on* with it!"

"Okay, okay. The first thing that seemed weird—it didn't seem important at the time—all over the islands you've got these kids with rucksacks, guitars, and Granola, hitching boat rides. I don't have to tell you. Tie up in Puerto Rico and pretty soon they're at dockside with the sleeping bags, looking to go up to the Bahamas or over to the Virgins or down to the Grenadines. From the ones we used to get at Bahia Mar, Pidge and I know you have to watch it. Most are really great persons, but some of them, you'd be better off stowing nitro in the hold, or carrying lepers."

Again he was sidestepping the obligation to be specific about Pidge. I waited him out. Finally he got to it. At Frederiksted, on St. Croix, two blond girls wanted a ride down to Montserrat, where one of them had an older sister married to a lawyer in Plymouth. They'd been traveling with a boy who'd had to return to the States because of some kind of family trouble. Joy Harris and Celia Fox. They had the crew bunks forward available to loan the girls if they chose. The girls couldn't afford to pay for the passage or the extra supplies, but they said they would work, really work, any kind of work aboard. They were tanned and pretty and young, trail-toughened to a watchful and skeptical wisdom.

Pidge and Howie had talked it over and decided the girls were all right, and when they came back they would be invited aboard for the trip. Pidge made some jokes about exclusivity and about becoming one of the three Brindle women.

But only one girl returned. The Harris girl, the smaller and prettier of the two. She said that she and Celia had decided not to travel together any more. She said she thought Celia was going back to the States, but actually she could not care less what Celia did, or how she did it.

"We talked it over and it was still okay with me, but Pidge had a lot of second thoughts. She said two girls were okay, but one was something else. If it was one girl, she would be with us all the time, and dependent on us. Four was company, three was a crowd. I didn't see it exactly that way. There were enough chores to keep three people busy. I told her she was being silly about it. She said she happened to own the boat. That wasn't like her, to say something like that to me. I shrugged it off. Hell, if it meant that much to her, so be it. So we sailed without the girl. We didn't even let her know we'd decided not to take her."

I frowned at him. "I don't see anything especially weird about her reaction."

"I haven't come to it. She was very quiet for three days. I thought it was on account of the quarrel. Not really a quarrel, but close to it. Enough to shake me up. So that night at midnight she came and woke me up and I went up to the wheelhouse to take over. She was on pilot, rumbling along on the diesels. There was enough breeze to go onto canvas, and the direction was good, but it wasn't steady enough to count on and it seemed a lot of trouble. She leaned against the bulkhead, right beside me, in the darkness. There were the instrument lights and some light from our running lights. I said that the stars were nice, and she said I was a cheap, dirty, sick bastard and then she went on from there, all of it in a low voice. I didn't know what was wrong with her. I didn't know what she was getting at. I kept asking her what her problem was. Finally she said, 'Stop trying to kid me, Howard. How did you expect to get away with it? You smuggled that blond ass, Joy Harris, aboard, and she's forward and keeps the door locked and the hatch dogged down. I know about the food you sneak to her, and I know about you balling her, and I've heard you two whispering and giggling and groaning.' Those aren't the exact words, but that's what she said. So I asked her if she meant Joy was on board that minute, and she said I knew damned well she was. The way she said it, the back of my neck got all cold and prickly. We were so damned ... alone! You know how it is. And we weren't even *going* to Montserrat, where the girls wanted to go. I should have used reason, I guess."

"What did you do?"

"It scalded me. It really did. It hurt to have her think I could do a jerk thing like that. So I told her she was absolutely right and I was going to keep an extra piece stashed aboard wherever we went. So she went below. She was crying. Right away I was sorry I'd been smart-ass about it. I stayed on watch right on into the sunrise and past it. It was hot and calm. I'd figured out how I should handle it. I cut the power off and in minutes we drifted dead in the water. I woke her up and told her to take her time looking around. I told her all the keys were on the cork board in the lounge. When she was satisfied, she could hail me and I'd come back aboard. So I tossed a raft over—that little one there—jumped after it and climbed aboard, freed the little paddle, and went off a hundred yards and stretched out on my face and went to sleep. It took a lot of yelling over the bullhorn to wake me up. By then it was ten o'clock. I went aboard. She was very quiet and strange. She agreed we were alone aboard. She wouldn't agree we had been alone the day before. She was jumpy. She had a way of looking at me. She didn't want me to touch her.

"For a lot of days we were very polite to each other. It wasn't much fun. We tied up three days at Fort-de-France, and the third day when she came back from one of her trips ashore, she was really in a weird mood. She kept trying to grin, but her teeth were chattering. She wanted to hang onto me. She was a very scared person. But she wouldn't say why. I was glad to have her want to be close to me again. I didn't push it. In her own time she finally told me. I guess I should say she showed me. At Fort-de-France she'd found a place where she could get a roll of film developed and printed. Twelve prints. It was the last three prints on the roll that scared her. I didn't understand why at first. They were shots of the bow taken from aboard. Dumb pictures, really. Empty-looking. She said she had taken three pictures of that girl, of Joy Harris, two of them of her sunbathing and one of her standing, holding onto the bow rail. She was sure she'd had proof I'd brought the girl aboard. She wanted to . . . you know, wave them in my face and ask me to explain. But there wasn't any girl in the pictures. I told her there'd never been any girl aboard. I told her she'd had some kind of hallucination. I told her that what we ought to do was head back and get her a good workup. She said she was okay. She said nothing like that had ever happened before and it would never happen again. So . . . we kept on. And sort of forgot it. Tucked it away. And things were great again."

I pried the second episode out of him. It started during the run from La Guaira to Willemstad. He'd wanted somebody to work on the generator at La Guaira, but the political situation was such no mechanic would touch the *Trepid*. It was a ticklish problem just to buy stores and get them aboard. The generator was getting noisy. Lubrication didn't seem to help.

"We were under sail, and at dusk I turned on the generator and she like to had some kind of a fit. She kept asking me to listen. All I could hear was the noisy generator. She made me turn it off and on again. Every time it was off, there was no sound at all aboard. Every time it was on she could hear, sort of mixed in with the noise, that Joy Harris girl talking and laughing. Trav, she could really hear that. I know. It was hallucination. But it was so damn real to her she almost made me hear it too. All the way up to Willemstad I ran it as seldom as possible. The only way she could stand it was to shut herself in the forward cabin, with rubber plugs in her ears. She lost weight. She got very jumpy. At Willemstad I got some parts replaced on the generator. It quieted down. She couldn't hear the voices and laughing any more after that. But it had changed her somehow. It made her quieter. She doesn't laugh a lot the way she used to."

The third episode was murky because he apparently did not understand just what had happened. After coming through the Canal in a convoy of freighters, after going under the high swing bridge of the Pan American highway, they made the eight-mile final leg to Balboa Harbor. It was suffocatingly hot. A launch took the pilot and the Panamanian line handlers off the *Trepid*. It was an hour before sunset, and they decided to keep moving and so they headed out into the Pacific, dipping and lifting in the long slow swells. The chart looked clean. He figured the heading at 190 degrees after adjusting for deviation. That would give them good water down through the Gulf of Panama, staying well clear of Las Perlas, passing them well to the west. And that heading would bring them within visual range of the light on Punta Mala to the west of them, and he drew a line on the chart to intersect the 190-degree line and told Pidge that they should be directly abeam of Punta Mala at about four thirty in the morning, if the wind held, giving them eight knots, and then they would change to 230 degrees. By daylight he hoped to take visual bearings of the coast and set the new course for the long run to Puntarenas, tucked snugly into the Gulf of Nicoya.

Pidge went forward to make certain everything was secured. The stars were beginning to come out. He caught a glimpse of her as she went over the side.

With no hesitation he yanked a life ring free and slung it into the dark sea as she slipped by. "It was a fresh breeze, almost abeam, heeling us over to port. No time and no chance to get her onto power. God, you know how small the chances are! I turned to starboard and into the eye and smacked her around, trying to count time, estimate speed, draw the lopsided circle in the back of my mind, and use dead reckoning to come all the way around and up and lay the *Trepid* dead in the water at where she ought to be. It had to be right the first time because the boat wasn't going to stay there very long. You know how she's set up. Under sail you use that wheel back aft, in the forward part of the cockpit, and under power you can run her from there or the wheelhouse. I came back up, trying to be downwind from where she went over. I was counting time and distance, and then I took my shot. I headed into the wind and yelled to her, and tried to hear something over all the gear slapping and creaking and banging. I was straining to see while she was in irons. Then, as the wind started to push the boat backward, I saw the white life ring back off the stern quarter. I didn't know if she was in it at first. Then I could make her out. The *Trepid* was swinging about and the wind popped the main full and heeled her over, but there was no way on her yet, no answer to the helm. I ran up to the bow and threw a line to her and could just make out the way it fell across the ring. I made it fast to a bow cleat and yelled to her to make it fast to the ring. When I got back to the wheel, there was enough way on her so I could turn her back up into the wind, and this brought Pidge swinging in alongside near the transom. I got the line with a boathook and pulled it up, got hold of the line, pulled her up inside the ring, skinning her knee on the hull. I was laughing and crying. It was such a *hell* of a long chance. And we'd made it. Know what she thought really happened?"

"What?"

"She thought I was watching her after she went forward and saw her lean way over the rail to free a line, and I turned sharp to port to flip her overboard. She thought I came back around and tried to run her down, for God's sake! And then for some damned reason, changed my mind and rescued her!"

"She get over that too?"

"I'd have to say not completely. I'm sorry I have to say it. If she'd just . . . give me a chance. Or if she'd get professional help. But as soon as we tied up, she got the hell off and won't even talk to me. It's a month. I don't know what to do."

"What were you planning to do?"

"The next leg? It was sort of open. It's a hell of a jump from here. You've got to want three thousand miles of open ocean and be ready for it. We'd planned to drop on south—Tahiti, American Samoa, then maybe Fiji to Auckland to Sydney—and decide there if we wanted all the rest of it, or if we'd had the best of it. If so, then we thought we'd probably sell the *Trepid* there and fly home."

Perhaps I let too much show as I looked around the deck.

"I know, I know," he said. "I just haven't had the heart to do the chores. Everything has just been meaningless."

"Maybe you'd feel better if you turned to, Howie."

He sighed and nodded. "You're probably right. I guess I would. This is a nice machine, and she's beginning to look like a slum. Yes, I guess I'll do that, Trav. I shouldn't have needed somebody to tell me."

"Shall I look Pidge up and talk to her?"

He looked eager. "Would you? Would you give it a try?"

"Of course."

"And get back to me?"

"Why not?"

"I hate to say this. But you see if you think she needs help. If you think she does, maybe she'll listen to you."

"I'll let you know."

He walked with me down the long jetty, past all the boats. He knew a lot of people for having been there such a short time. Hey there, Howie. How's it going, fella?

At the end of the jetty, he made a short sound of laughter without mirth. "When things start to go bad, they really go," he said. "I've told you enough. You shouldn't hear it all from me. Something else happened when we were a week out from here. You let her tell you about that one, and draw your own conclusions. That's why she got off the boat and why I can't even talk to her."

I shook his hand. He didn't let go. He looked at me with his big dumb brown brute eyes, and they watered, and in a husky voice, he said, "What I really want is . . . I want her back . . . If you could just. . . ."

He let go and spun away. His voice had broken. He started walking slowly back out the jetty toward the *Trepid*. It was a listless and dejected walk. A big dumpy giant, sad in the Christmas-coming sunshine.

4

IT was late afternoon when I got back to Pidge's borrowed apartment. She seemed remote, ill at ease, and strangely indifferent to my reaction to whatever Howie had told me. She took me down to the ninth floor and showed me the little studio apartment she had borrowed. She gave me the key and said I could come up when I'd freshened up.

I said it had been a while since I'd done any hotel-hopping, so how about humoring me and going out with me. She brightened perceptibly. By the time she phoned down and said she was ready and would meet me at the garage level, she sounded almost cheerful.

She wore a handsome pants suit and had carefully applied a fiesta face. She found it easy to smile. She had the use of the white Toyota of the missing Alice Dorck, and said that she was getting almost used to the traffic, so maybe . . . ?

She sat very erect behind the wheel, with firm grip

and frown of concentration. She angled the little car through holes just before they started to close. She whipped around the indecisive and tucked herself away from the certifiable maniacs. She picked productive lanes and managed to locate, without hesitation, the last parking slot in the lot off Seaside.

It was a good night for strolling, the air balmy and soft. Along Waikiki the hotels have not yet had to adopt the Miami Beach hospitality routine of posting armed guards at doorways who demand a look at your key and, if you look kinky, escort you to the desk for official clearance. At Waikiki you can still walk in and buy a lady a drink. We worked the little cluster across from the International Market—the Outrigger, the Surfrider, the Moana, checking out the outdoor bars. Get the rum drink in the squat glass and you get a stick of fresh pineapple to stir it with. Get the Mary, which she was drinking with both care and thirst, and the stir-stick is a stalk of celery.

I steered the talk to safe places, back to Bahama seas and Florida beaches. She cheered up and freshened, and her voice broke free of the monolevel, moving up and down the scale of her emotions. Have a drink; take a walk; drink again.

In the most inconspicuous way, I was trying to get her well smashed. Yes, in vino there is veritas, if you can translate it, if you can figure out which side of the truth you are seeing. The International Market was closing. We roamed through a corner of it and I bought her one flower, the color of cinnamon, not quite an orchid, not quite anything else either. And then to the slightly airport flavor of the Princess Kaiulani Hotel, where I steered her, slow, smiling and smashed, through interlocking lobbies back to that place where the Chinese food is the very best of Mandarin, the tastes less separated than Cantonese, more heavily spiced.

We made wishes with chopsticks, pulling them apart, then arguing over who got the largest portion of the bamboo base where it split. She won both sets, and said she would think about the wishes. Her small, strong-looking hands were deft with the chopsticks. She ate with hunger, glancing across the candlelight, smiling, saying, "Mmmm." She would swing and shake her head in a certain remembered way to settle the brown hair back. Nice.

"And the two wishes?" I asked.

She took one more morsel of the squash, then dropped the sticks on the plate. She shook her head. "Oh, Trav, you know . . . if I could only have just one wish . . . how I need that one wish."

She jumped up and was gone. I waited ten minutes and then paid the check and tipped our waitress to look in the ladies' room. She came back and told me the lady would meet me in a couple of minutes in the lobby. The waitress had a sweet, worried smile. Lovers' quarrel?

Irregular formations of touring Japanese men moved through the lobbies with worried celerity, all their satin-black Nikons with the bulky nighttime headdress of rechargeable strobe. Why are their glasses frames always so shiny?

Pidge came to me, shy and damp-lashed, the nose red from blowing. "First date in forever, and I can't hack it," she said.

"Home?"

"To what passes for same. Yes. And a lovely, lovely time up until I went owly."

I drove back through practically no traffic, and she showed me where to duck into the ramp under the Towers, and where the car belonged. On the way up in the elevator, I heard her sigh over the whisper of machinery. At eleven, I held the door open by leaning against the edge of it and said, "We'll tackle it tomorrow?"

She studied me and turned, just a little uneasy on her tall shoes. "No. Come on. Damn it all. Come on, let's pick the scabs off." So I let the urgent doors hiss shut behind us, and helped her with the double-key arrangement to number 1112.

I made a mild joke, something about her friend Alice Dorck being some kind of security-conscious international agent. She said Alice had answered the door once for a man who said he wanted to replace the filter in the air intake. She let him in, and in the process of raping her he broke two ribs and three fingers on her left hand, tore her earlobe, and squeezed her throat so hard she had traumatic laryngitis for two weeks. She said that after that, Alice tended to be lock-conscious.

No more jokes, I decided. Once inside I asked for a drink and was assured to see her pour one for herself. Down to cases.

"Here it *is!* This is the camera. Instamatic. I've had it forever. I buy Kodacolor in twelves. You can usually get it developed almost anyplace."

"And these are the twelve prints."

"How many times do you—"

"Now tell me again, Pidge. These three pictures, the last three on the roll. You took them in this order?

"Y-yes. Yes, that's right."

"You looked through the finder and you took this picture. What did you see in the finder? Details!"

"Don't roar at me! I saw Joy Harris. I guess she'd come up through the small hatch, and she was stretched out on the bigger hatch cover. She was . . . on her side with her elbow stretched straight out and her head on her hand, and she was looking straight ahead. I thought about what a cute figure she had. Small but kind of lush. She had on bikini bottoms, faded blue or blue-green. The top was under her, on the hatch. Her blond hair was kind of damp-dark, like sweat or she'd washed it."

"She fitted in the frame?"

"Oh, sure. It takes in a lot. You hardly ever have to back off to get things in."

"And this one?"

"She hadn't seen me. Howie was asleep. I went back to the cockpit to see if we had moved too far off course. I'd put a loop over a spoke. It was okay, so I went back up the side deck on the starboard side and she had rolled over onto her face, so I got a little closer and took this one. See? The hatch is bigger. I was closer. I was thinking that I was getting real evidence. I wanted to get her face. I was thinking of yelling at her and taking it when she jumped up. It said 'eleven' through the little window, so I cranked it up to twelve, and that was the last one on the roll. As I was wondering what to do, she sat up and put the bikini top on. I backed off. When I looked again, she was standing at the rail. Right here. So I took the last picture of her. Her hair was blowing in the wind. She sensed it, I guess, because she turned and saw me before I could lower the camera. I ran from her. How about that? My boat and my camera and my marriage. And I ran."

"And you took these first nine on the roll?"

"Sure. These are all at St. Croix, the dock area and the other boats and so on. That one was a real nice trimaran from Houston, the biggest I ever saw. I didn't know they made them that big. See? Howie is in these two. Yes, I took them all at St. Croix."

"Then what about the film?"

"I told you before that—"

"More detail this time."

"Jesus, you are a terrible person. You know that? All right, all right. I went below. Once you finish a roll, you just keep on winding and it all goes over into the other side and you see little lines through the window. Then you open it here and take it out. That's what I did. I hid it in a place nobody knows about but me."

"You sound certain."

"I *am* certain. In my music box. You think you are looking right through it where the little dancer turns around and around, but you're not. It's mirrors in there, at angles so you think you're looking through. It's 'Lara's Theme,' and there's a certain place where I push the little nub to stop it. If anybody opened it when I wasn't there I would know because the music wouldn't start in my place, where I always stop it when I hide anything in there. Nobody got at that film, if that's what you mean. God, how I wish they had! After we were tied up at Fort-de-France, I took it out of the box and it wasn't out of my hand until I gave it to the man in the camera store."

"By then you knew the girl wasn't on the boat."

"I didn't *know* anything by then. I didn't know what to believe. When I got the film back and saw these three pictures and she . . . just wasn't in them, the whole world turned black. Black with little specks roaming around in it, and a roaring going on. Travis, I'm getting so tired of . . . "

"Let's go back to the voices you heard."

"Why? I heard voices. Everybody hears voices. All crazy people hear voices."

"Always the same girl?"

"Yes. Joy. I never could make out the words. The laugh was the same. It was Joy and Howie talking and laughing. Much more of this?"

"Quite a lot, I think."

"Then we need another drink."

She brought the drinks back to the sofa in the living room. When she touched glasses, she touched a little too hard, spilling drinks from both our glasses. She giggled and mopped it up.

She said, "To answer the question you haven't asked, Yes, the son of a bitch was trying to run right over me with the *Trepid*."

"And you think he could see you?"

"Why not? It wasn't black night yet. And I didn't have any trouble seeing him."

"He handled the boat in such a way, he made you fall overboard?"

"No doubt about it."

"But he threw you a life ring."

"I think he just didn't have the guts to do it. I think he knocked me overboard and then panicked and threw the ring. While he was working his way around and back, he got his courage up again and decided to run me down, and then at the last minute he veered off and threw me a line. Like the rifle."

"He didn't mention that."

"I can see why he didn't."

"He said there was something else, and you should tell me about it."

"It's the rifle my father bought for sharks. It goes in an aluminum case he bolted to the side of the instrument panel in the wheelhouse, sort of in the corner, barrel up. The case has pressure clips and a rubber lip. It would even float. Anyway, he taught me to use it when I went with him the first time. It's a Remington seven hundred. I forget what it shoots."

"Probably three-oh-eight?"

"Right! Sometimes they get funny about a gun and you have to let the customs people keep it for you while you're in port, but in a small boat usually it's okay. Which you already know. We were a week from Honolulu, dead flat calm, grinding along at about six knots, which is the best for stingy, on automatic pilot. I was sitting on the roof, forward, reading and drying my hair. BAM! Out of nowhere! I spun around and he was in back of me, not eight feet away. He had the rifle and he had a couple of empty cans in the other hand. He had a dazed look on his face. He said he thought he had unloaded it. He didn't know how it went off. Anyway, it was pointed almost straight up when it went off, he said. But I know how that thing sounds when it's straight up or out to the side or pointing away from you. It's more like *whack*. Or *smack*. Not like BAM. This ear *still* isn't right. It rings a lot. Trav, I think that slug was inches from my head."

"How did he act?"

"Really shocked. Like . . . almost too shocked. He cried. He threw up. That was later. He'd been going to ask me to throw the cans off the bow, out as far as I could. Then he was going to try to plink them from the stern as we went by."

"And you decided right then to leave him as soon as you docked?"

"Not right then. No."

"Something else happened that last week?"

"Oh, no. I mean I think I'd sort of decided even without the rifle part. Maybe without falling overboard, or the voices, or the girl who wasn't there."

"I don't know what you mean."

"Neither do I. Oh, God, Trav, I'm drunk. I can't say words right. I'm seeing two of things. You got me drunk."

"You mean that it wasn't going so well, as a marriage."

"Please let me sleep!"

"Okay. You can have a nap. I'll wake you up."

"I mean really go to bed. Please. And you go away, huh?"

"Not until we get through all of it."

"What in hell else can there be? You're turning me inside out on these things."

"You said you had to find out something. We're trying to find out."

"I've got to go wash my face and get out of these clothes. I get all sweaty thinking of how scared I got."

"Make it fast."

She came back in ten minutes with scrubbed face and brushed hair, wearing a shortie caftan in a big flower print. She was barefoot, and she was drugged and dazed by drink and weariness and strain.

She plumped down on a stool, fists between her knees, and swayed, yawned, and said, "Honest to God. Really, McGee. I just. . . . "

"Did Joy have moles?"

"Huh? What?"

"Moles, marks, visible scars, insect bites, any kind of flaw when you looked at her through the finder?"

"N-no."

"The laughter you heard. They were both laughing at you. Right?"

"Yes. Yes, they were."

"And you're no damned good in bed."

She peered at me. "Huh? Whaddaya mean? I was pretty much okay with Scott. You could say I was a lot better than okay. Chee, you jump around so."

I remembered Scott was the boyfriend who flunked out when her father was killed. "But nowhere near okay with Howie."

She reached and got her glass. The ice was long melted, the drink still strong. She drank and made a face. She told it piecemeal, the first pieces the most difficult. Good old Uncle Travis.

She had wanted every part of the marriage to be great. Howie was a strange person. You wanted to know him. He was like a little house with a door in the front and a door in the back. One room. He'd let you in his house and it was fun. Chuckles and games. No pressure. So you wanted to know him better and so you went through the doorway into what was going to be the next room of his personal house, but you found yourself back out in the yard, and the little house looked just the same, back and front. One room.

"Me, I'm a personal person," she said. She'd finished her drink. She leaned toward me and put her palms against the side of my face, cupping the sockets of the jaw. She slid forward off the stool, round knees bumping the rug, stood erect on her knees, and tugged at me until our noses were six inches apart, each of us well inside the other's living space, each breathing into the other's domain.

"Look inside of me," she said.

Well, so they were lady eyes, slightly inflamed, gray but so almost blue they would be blue at times, a tiny spangle of small pale tan dots in the left one, in the iris at seven and eight o'clock, close to the wet jet black of the pupil. They wobbled and then fixed full focus upon my eyes. They were lady eyes for ten heartbeats, and then something veered and dipped inside my head. There was a dizziness, then everything except her eyes seemed misted out of focus, and the eyes seemed larger. She became a special identity to me. Linda Lewellen Brindle? There had been a kid named Pidge who had a terrible crush. There had been a bride in white called Linda by the Man with the Book. She was an identity which had no name as yet, this new one. Pidge was a name suitable for the yacht-club porch at Bar Harbor, or doubles in Palm Springs.

"Hey, Lewellen," I said, changing the last-name tempo, turning it into a half-whispered name of a suthrun gal. Lou Ellen. Somehow right.

It startled her. She sat back onto her heels and frowned up at me, shaking her hair back. "Who told you that? That was my grandpop's idea. They all said it was flaky. They all said you couldn't saddle a kid with such a weird name. Lou Ellen Lewellen. I didn't even know until I was maybe ten, and hated Pidge and hated Linda, and called myself Lou Ellen for . . . oh . . . a couple of years. I almost forgot until now."

"It just seemed to fit."

"Are you going to call me that?" The strangeness that had started working at six inches was now working just as well at a yard away.

"Probably. Okay with you?"

"Perfect with me. Travis. This eye thing. What I wanted to show you . . . well, you know. It works for us. For you and me. I'm a personal person. What I was trying to say about Howie, you could look into his eyes eight hours a day, eight days a week, and they're pretty brown glass. You bounce off. They look back at me the way my dollies used to."

She was wiggling loose. Inquisition requires a kind of domination, a control of tempo and intensity. I pulled away from all the invisible strands she had looped around me so quickly.

"And you know why the voices were laughing at *you*, right?"

It jolted her back off balance. "I don't want to talk. . . . "

"Talk about anything that might be your fault, think about anything that might be your fault. You want to be perfect."

"W-why do you get so—so damned *mean*? What made you *say* that about being no good in bed?"

"Because it was a funny wedding, honey. No musk, no steam, no itch. A wedding of good buddies. A wedding of brother and sister. Remember the kiss after the pronouncement? The kind of quick peck the long-married get at airports."

So she got down to the clinical details. She said at first it was all her fault, not being able to respond. And as she explained her incapacity to respond, the picture of the sensuality of Howie Brindle emerged. Beef and sweat, quickly stimulated, quickly satisfied. Some days early in the voyage, an almost insatiable gluttony, a dozen episodes a day, in a dozen places on the boat. Apparently very little tenderness, emotion, romance.

"Like those damned chocolate bars," she said.

"Like what?"

"He keeps a locker practically full. He says he's a chocoholic. Right in the middle of plotting a course, or working out a position from the tables, or fixing the trolling lines, he'll pop up and go peel a chocolate bar and chonk, chonk, chonk, it's gone. Wipe his mouth with the back of his hand, lick his fingers, wipe his hand on his pants, smack his lips, and back to whatever he was doing.

When it was happening often enough, and I was trying hard, I could stay far enough up sometimes, in between times, to make it, but when you have to be worried about not making it, it isn't all that good when you do. And when you don't and you have to ask somebody to help you afterward, it's another kind of turnoff."

And by the time they had reached the Virgins, the edge was off his appetite to the point where he would take her at those times when he was awakening her to take the watch, or she went below to shake him awake. But it was not ritual. It was now and again.

"My father was gone and Scott turned out to be a terrible mistake, and when I finally could lift my head and look around, there was Howie, taking care of things, taking charge. And it seemed as if that might be a good way for life to be. Sort of safe and steady."

"You began to have very bad dreams?"

She cocked her head. "How'd you know that? Very foul and very vivid. They'd cling in my mind for days. Something wrong with me, usually. Like in one I looked down and there were two smooth holes in my chest. Somehow I'd gotten my breasts on backwards and the nipples were way inside there someplace. I was frantic to keep people from knowing it. It was so shameful. I kept hunting for round things I could hold there with my bra, but they'd fall out."

"Numb places on your hands?"

"You know, you're a weird person, Travis? Right along here, on the edges of my hands and around the base of my thumb. And I would get numb around my mouth sometimes too."

"And diarrhea?"

"Where'd you graduate from, Doctor? Constantly!"

"Now think back. Was there ever a time in your life when you felt as if you were utterly without any value at all, completely worthless and contemptible?"

"Yes. After my mom died. It didn't make any sense,

but I had the feeling it was my fault somehow, that if I hadn't been such a total nothing of a person, she wouldn't have gotten sick and died and left me. I sort of went down and down and down. I slept all the time, practically. Food tasted vile. I didn't want to leave the house. Daddy took me to a clinic, some kind of diagnostic thing, and they gave me every test known to man. Then they recommended some kind of special school. But my father got a prescription from them for something that made me feel edgy and jumpy. We had some terrible scenes. He yelled at me that I was letting him down, and I, by God, was going to learn navigation, small boat handling, marine engines, map reading, scuba diving. When he wasn't yelling at me, he was telling me what a wonderful person I was, how special I was. How smart and pretty and outgoing and all. And . . . I began to work hard, and I came out of it, and by the time we got to Florida, I was pretty much okay again."

"I've got one last question, Lou Ellen."

"Oh, it better be the last. My head is trying to fall asleep and my stomach is trying to throw up."

"Do you like yourself?"

"What the hell kind of a question is that?"

"Do you, Linda Lewellen Brindle, *like* Linda Lewellen Brindle as a person."

"How can people like themselves anyway?"

"Do you like yourself?"

She shuddered. "You mean really?"

"Really."

"Oh, God. No. I just don't think about myself if I can help it. I'm such a wormy kind of sneak. I'm a nothing, pretending to be something. Can't you see me? Fat thighs and dumb lumpy breasts and nothing-colored hair and weird-looking teeth. People are always talking about things I don't understand. I like real square dumb things. I got through school, almost. I just can't . . . respond to life because I don't know what is really going on most of the time. Why are you *doing* this to me? I'm practically dead!"

"I'm no doctor. I can't shoot you with sodium pentothal. I shot you with booze. This is a small group for group therapy. I've been pushing you. Lou Ellen, dear, you are, I think, an anxiety type. Sometimes I detect a whiff of it in myself. What is that bit about the neurotic? The psychotic says two and two are five and the neurotic knows two and two are four, and hates it."

"But I—"

"Listen for just a minute. Some of the classic symptoms of anxiety neurosis. The numbness, vivid and ugly dreams of something being wrong with your body, diarrhea, depression, self-contempt. There are others. Double vision, incontinence, and being always too hot or too cold, night sweats. . . ."

"There's another of mine."

I took her hands and pulled her onto the couch beside me and kept hold of her hands. "Listen, dear. Why shouldn't it happen to you? An only child. A lot of pressure on you to be the best child ever. Impossible goal, of course. Sense of failure at not making it. So your mother died when you were at peak vulnerability, and then your father died, and you never had a chance to prove to them you could hack it in this world."

"This is funny. I'm not really crying. It's just water running out of my eyes like this."

"So, out of a sense of being terribly alone, you marry a very large and sort of limited guy. Part of it was rebound from Scott. And revenge on Scott. And it was the pursuit of perfection. You have all the images and symbols working for you. Hold still! A great motor sailer, youth, money, time, honeymoon, tropic seas. But on board the *Trepid* we have two people who maybe can't make a marriage, can't make a honeymoon, can't make a future. Other people have all the excuses. Rotten jobs, cost of living, depressing neighborhood, meddling in-laws, babies too soon. What's the excuse when you can't hack it in paradise? So you lay it all on yourself, Pidge. Very heavy. And somewhere you start to make that funny little sidestep into another world, where it changes neurotic to psychotic, changes suspicion to paranoia."

She shook the mists out of her head, held my hands in a grip that dug her nails into me. Her eyes went wide and looked through me, looked back down the avenue of the months and months of cruising. I think she stopped breathing.

Suddenly she wrenched her hands free and left, running unsteadily, whamming the doorframe with a hip as she went into the connecting hallway to bedroom and bath. A door slammed. In the silence of predawn I heard her in there yawking and hawking and wheezing, and knew she was the sort who would rather break blood vessels than have her head held.

I leaned back, rubbed granular eyelids, then pushed the stud on the Pulsar. The red numerals glared up at me from the ruby screen on my wrist. 4:11. I held the stud down and the seconds appeared . . . 56 . . . 57 . . . 58 . . . 59 . . . 00. The 5 was constant, and the second figure changed to each subsequent figure in that odd, parts-saving method of digital design. I released it and pressed the stud again for an instant, and 4:12 glared at me for the second and a quarter, the specified recognition interval. I had checked it with the shortwave time signal from Greenwich a week after a rich lady had given it to me. Gift of a toy in return for making the right contact for her which enabled her to buy back the stolen, uninsured black opal ring her deceased husband had given her on his last Christmas on earth. An easy salvage, too easy to warrant charging half the value. A good rule is to levy the standard charge or nothing at all. So it was nothing at all, and the watch was a gratitude gift. And running two seconds fast.

Little red numbers to fit you back into time and place.

Going on quarter after four on Friday morning, December 7th, in Hawaii—where they have had some remarkable December 7ths.

Meyer made one of his Meyerlike observations about the Pulsar. He said it was ironic that this space-age, world-of-the future, computerized gadget was, in reality, a return to the easier and more relaxing and contemplative times of yesteryear. The wristwatch with dial and hands keeps needling you every time you happen, by design or by accident, to look at your wrist. Get on with it, brother! Life is running out the bottom of the tube! In gentler eras, if a man wished to know the time, he took out his gold pocket watch and snapped it open and looked at the hands. If he did not want to know the time, it never intruded. Time served man. The Hamilton Pulsar does not intrude either, until you decide you want to know the time, and you push the stud, and it tells you, then keeps its peace until next time.

It is, the booklet said, guaranteed to withstand a force of 2500 G's. But can McGee, who wears it, endure having his body weight upped to two hundred and seventy-five tons? I would cover the area of a tennis court to a depth of a sixteenth of an inch, and there in the middle of me would be the sticky lump of the Pulsar, ready to glare red-numbered accuracy at the next fellow to push the little stud.

I snapped out of a smoky doze as she came floating out, in a different and floor-length caftan, looking fifteen pounds lighter, three inches shorter and five years younger. She sat shyly on the edge of the couch.

"I just imagined those things," she said. "I know that now. You're right. Oh, I got so god-awful close to the edge. There's a funny thing about the edge. When you get close, somehow you . . . want to get closer. You want to look down. You might even want to fall over the edge."

"Has this past month been better?"

"Off the boat? I guess so. Yes. It has been better, but

then, when I kept phoning and phoning you and finally got the call through and then I couldn't say anything I'd planned to say, that was a low point. Believe me, that was a very low point. A feeling of . . . complete, total failure in everything."

"Who's watching? Who's keeping score on you? Who's grading your paper, honey?"

She looked puzzled. *"They* are. Whoever They might be. The ones who watch you."

"And who live inside your head?"

"They live somewhere."

"You can walk down ten thousand crowded streets in ten thousand cities of the world, and nobody will give damn one about whether you cope or can't cope, whether you live or die. The ones who notice you wonder if there's any safe way to use you, or they give you a part in the little fantasy theater inside their skulls. There is an estimated price on your clothes, shoes and purse, but the rest of you is just so much live meat. Pretty meat. No bonus for how well you perform the feat of living."

"That is so *goddamn* cold!" she said loudly.

"Scare you?"

"I guess."

"That's the way it is. Nobody grades your performance except you and your own ghosts. And you've gotten so anxious about the scoring, you hallucinated."

She sighed and softened, and in moments was nodding and yawning once more. Where the light touched her hair, it wove fine patterns of gold in spun threads, and her posture pulled the caftan tight to the round of left hip and flank.

So I got up and, with a small pat of affection, a quick kiss on the temple, I said good night and got out of there, all the scruples of my self-awarded medical degree intact. Guilt in one area, Meyer says, can lead to unexpected virtue in everything else. Also, it is unseemly for a sportsman to feed the tame deer a carrot and then shoot it dead.

In the borrowed bed on the ninth floor I was able to spend at least fifty seconds in somber thought before sleep took me. When people invite you to come into their lives and meddle, that is what you do, if you are concerned about them. Right? Right? Right. . . .

5

I WOKE up at eleven in the gloom of the draperied room, having just dreamed of being dead. I was dead on the stones of the patio of the Club de Pescadores, my skull mashed by the blow of the fish billy swung by Bunny Mills, the blue-tail flies already humming around the raw broken meat.

In my dream I had been mourning me. Dead is dead. Dead lasts long. The word is strange, like a tap on a slack drumhead. Like striking the key of a piano when the hammer mechanism is broken. I had been dream-mourning the rangy, knuckly, chopped-up, pale-eyed, wry-minded beach bum. Meyer was quite broody about losing me. The regulars at Bahia Mar would gather a few times and laugh at crazy memories, hoist the sentimental glass and get mournfully drunk. It would move them, I suppose. In each relationship there had been something of meaning, some communication beyond that inaccurate code-and-cipher convention of speech. Male or female, it would fit that Rilke quotation: *Love consists in this, that two soli-tudes protect and touch and greet each other.*

. . . That slip over there, that's where what's-his-name used to live aboard a houseboat named . . . damn it, how can I forget names so easy?

So suddenly, sitting on the edge of the bed, I began to laugh. Big hard laughter, clenching the belly and rough-ening the throat. The vision of lugubrious McGee, whining as he fondled his incomparable skull, was too much.

In the shower stall I thought about death in a definitely jolly way. Pidge had talked about Them. I have my own set. They gave me a little bit of space at the edge of the gaming table, and They gave me a few hints about the rules. I made the choice, as does everyone, about how much I want to bet and how often. I decide what I am willing to win and willing to lose.

The house takes a cut of every wager. So you can play a close tight game, work out little conservative systems, calculate the odds to several decimal places, and no matter what you do, sooner or later They will bust you, because the house busts everybody. The house percentage does it, sooner or later.

Or, if you want, you can bet the long shots, go for the hunches. You will give Them a chance to bust you sooner, but you will maybe live a little bigger and better while you still have a place at the table. Only children of all ages think they will play forever. The man who knows in advance that They are going to bust him should not start whining about it in advance. They will bust you with Big C, or a truck driver on uppers, or pilot error, or an Irish bomb, or a coronary occlusion, or gas in the bilge. Other creatures play on smaller tables, and they all get busted, from mayfly to possum to quick red fox.

By the time I began shaving, the shadows were not as heavy across the back of my mind. Dreams can change a day. I guessed that being aboard the *Trepid* had brought Bunny Mills back. Most probably he had never tried to kill anyone else, before or since. The time and place had been just right. A whole set of his internal cycles had peaked at the same time, making a killing possible, or even necessary. In the presence of professionals, my instincts would probably keep me alive. God deliver me from amateurs. Bunny had nearly gotten me, and maybe the mark it left was deeper than I had realized.

I had finished shaving when the door chime bonged once and then again. I knotted the big yellow bath towel around me and went to the door.

Pidge came plunging into the room, all manic intensity, with a smile that came and went so quickly it was like a grimace. She wore a little white dress. Her voice was fast and was pitched a half octave high. She gave the impression of trotting back and forth in the small studio room, like some kind of nervous goalie. She shook her hair back a lot. She made mouths of many different shapes. Yes, she had been up since eight—woke up abruptly, knew she couldn't sleep any more, knew I was right. Yes. It had all come clear to her.

"The big question, you see, is did I ever really love him. It is one thing to accept the idea you can really and terrifyingly hallucinate and think you are actually going crazy, and another thing to sort it all out and say, Do I go back to him and start again. Well, suppose all the hallucinating and so on hadn't happened. What would I be like now? I suppose I would be on the boat and maybe we'd be a thousand miles south of Hawaii, and everything would still be blah. It would be a big sack of absolutely nothing, because what threw me off the tracks was the way I was trying so hard to tell myself that it was all loverly. And it wasn't. Oh Trav, it just wasn't! And c-c-couldn't ever b-bb-b . . . "

"Blub?"

"Oh, God. And I put in so much time on my eyes. Look at me."

"I am looking at you."

"I don't mean look at me the way you're looking at me."

"If it's bothering you, go back out the door, take five and come in again and we'll start over, Lou Ellen."

"I'm in here now. It's a lot of trouble."

"You shouldn't have done that eye-to-eye thing with me."

"There's a whole list of things I never should have done."

"I've got a longer list."

"Oh, what the hell, Travis. What the hell, darling."

I remember that my mind, adrift and afloat amid our busy-ness, went all the way back to Biscayne Bay, to the time when I was toting her back to Daddy, when she sat huddled and miserable on the bow deck of *The Busted Flush* and I had felt a wistful lust when I looked at the shape of the lass in her white shorts. That and other memories of her were strangely merged with the sweet and immediate realities of her, the here-and-nowness of her, so that I seemed to live in the past and present all at once. After a little while she cried out, and after that there was no room or time for memories. All the old nostalgia became the immediate and heated nimbleness, the present need. She was a temptation out of the past, served up on some kind of eternal lazy Susan so that it had come by once again, and this time we had taken it.

We sighed and murmured slowly back from all that lifting effort, made ourselves comfortable on tumbled bedding, shifted weights and pressures. "Umm," she said. And, "Hey now." And, "Umm," again. She stretched and turned and kissed and sagged back again. Her eyes were very bright. "I was going to fake it anyway," she said.

"Run that through again?"

"I mean I decided that it would be only fair you should have the idea it really got to me."

"What do you mean, fair?"

"As long as I was using you."

"Premeditation?"

"Damn right. Except it took me practically three hours to work up enough nerve. You never had a chance, McGee."

"I didn't?"

"Of course not! I know how I am. Now that we both know something funny was happening in my head, you'd go back to Florida and I would probably think about getting divorced from Howie, and I would see him and probably move back aboard the boat, and we'd keep on cruising and I'd go all weird again. It's too scary. I can't go through all that again. Not ever. So there's just one thing that would keep me from going back to him. And we just finished that one thing, and it was really beautiful. I wanted to do it with you a thousand years ago and you wouldn't. You were pretty stuffy about it."

"I tend to get stuffy about statutory rape. It's one of my character defects."

I turned her, stroked the fine smooth curves of her, all warm damp with prior effort, and snuffed the natural perfume of her brown hair.

"Do you mind if I sort of used you?" she asked.

"I have a tendency to forgive you, lady."

"I can't go back to Howie after doing such a rotten thing to him."

"I suppose."

"You see, dear, I had to make absolutely *sure* I wouldn't go back to him. Do you understand?"

"I understand."

"Hey. What are you doing?"

"Proving I understand."

"What do you mean by that?"

"I mean that in a little while now, I am going to make you doubly sure."

"Good thinking," she said.

"And you approve?"

"If I didn't, would I be doing *this?*"

There may be better ways of spending the middle part of a Friday in Hawaii or anywhere else. If so, I find it very hard to think of any. It made a fine Friday. And Saturday. And Sunday.

On Monday I spent a half hour with Howie Brindle before Pidge drove me out to the airport.

The *Trepid* was looking a little better. He was transparently eager to have me notice the change and remark upon it. If he had had a tail, he would have wagged it.

I told him I had a long talk with Pidge, several long talks in fact, and we were now both convinced that she had been hallucinating due to emotional pressures.

"I didn't give her any emotional strain," he said, frowning.

"You did without meaning to."

"I don't believe that. How?"

"She was alone and she was lonely and you were there, and she married you. She doesn't love you."

"She certainly does!"

"No. That's her problem, Howie. Listen and believe. She has been trying to be in love with you, but she can't. She really can't. And that gives her a sense of failure. That makes her depressed, and she gets confused."

"But I love her! I really love her, Trav."

"There's no law that says it has to run both ways. If you love her, you'll do what's best for her."

"Which is?"

"Let her go."

"Maybe if she could understand that I understand the problem, then we could be together and it wouldn't—"

"No. Won't work."

"No?"

"Absolutely never."

He looked down. I thought it was a snort of sour laughter, and then realized it was half snuffle, half sob. I saw tears run down his round ruddy cheek. I felt like a coconspirator in a very rotten plan. This was a very simple decent guy. So, like a coward, I tiptoed offstage.

At the airport, there was time for kisses. But they had the slightly sour flavor of betrayal. She beamed at me and said that when she came back to Lauderdale she would decide whether to marry me or merely keep me. I said I would be on tenterhooks until she gave me the word. She had always wondered what was a tenterhook. I told her that a tenter was the frame on which they used to stretch cloth when they made it, so it would dry evenly, and the bent nails around the frame were tenterhooks. She said it sounded uncomfortable to be on tenterhooks, and I said that it probably would be, so hurry home, girl.

I closed my eyes at takeoff and opened them in the night sky over Los Angeles. I had about thirteen minutes to catch my flight to Miami. If I'd checked luggage through, it never would have made it. I hoped to go right back to sleep aboard the National DC-10, but the stirring around the Los Angeles airplane station, and a National stewardess who wanted to give me more service than I needed, left me bulge-eyed awake. The jets were yanking me back into my habitual time pattern, and it was as if scrambled brains were coming unscrambled. I thought back to the terribly cute words of the parting lovers in Hawaii. Keep me or marry me. All in a dizzy, guilty, quiverous condition, all in a lust that had not been quenched despite all the trying. A kid! The teenager who'd stowed away and been taken back to Daddy.

The farther the airplane took me away from her, the more incredible it seemed. I knew that I was going to leave that whole affair out of the record when I talked to Meyer. She had come looking, but that didn't mean she had to get what she sought.

I yawned until my jaw creaked. I fixed the pillow again. Five miles below me, sensible people were sleeping in beds. Take that young wife, McGee, and file her under TTF. Try to forget.

6

I TUMBLED back into the strange pre-Christmas world of Fort Lauderdale and surrounding area. It is the same every year. The unaffiliated, unfamilied, uninvolved make the obligatory comments about Christmas being the Great Retailers' Conspiracy. Buy now. You don't owe a dime until February. The Postal Service gets their big chance to screw up the delivery of three billion cards. Urchins turn the stores into disaster areas. Counter clerks radiate an exhausted patience leavened with icy flashes of total hate. The energy crisis is accelerated by five billion little colored light bulbs, winking on and off in celebration. Amateur thieves join the swollen ranks of the professionals in ripping off parked cars loaded with presents, in picking pockets, prying sliding doors open, shoplifting and mugging the ever-present drunks. Bored Santas jingle their begging bells and the old hymns blur loudly through the low-fidelity speakers of department-store paging systems.

Unreality was compounded this year by a long stretch of unseasonably torrid weather, comingling sweat and jingle bells. And all the merchants and hotel managers and saloonkeepers immediately violated all the rules of business management by turning on all the giant compressors and pulling the interior temperatures down into the 65- to 68-degree range, never realizing they are the unknowing victims of a long-term conspiracy.

When a new structure is built, the air-conditioning experts are encouraged by the architect and the builder to overspecify the project. If they specify an $80,000 system instead of a $40,000 system, the architect and the contractor each, in most cases, pocket an extra $4000. Trade periodicals harp on how customer traffic flow is increased by keeping the thermostat low. In the densely urban areas, the heat output of all the overspecified systems so raises the ambient temperature that the big compressors have to kick in more often to keep the store at 67 degrees.

The knowledgeable general practitioner and the specialist in respiratory diseases will both tell you that it is a total idiocy to subject the human animal to abrupt temperature variations of more than 15 degrees. He gets sick. He has more virus infections. He takes more time off from work. He feels rotten.

Were there a Florida law stating that all thermostats would have to be blocked so as to prevent a lower interior temperature than 75 degrees in all public places, all stores, all homes, all hotels and motels, Florida Power and Light would be able to give up their huge smoking plans for new power plants. We would all be healthier. We would be able to dress more sensibly.

So it was a reversal of the Christmas temperatures of the remembered childhood in northern places. Lauderdale was steamy hot on the outside, achingly frigid on the inside. This invited to town the new flu mutation, which began dropping the folk right and left.

It was a curious and restless time. It seemed to me

that I spent a lot of time getting in and out of automobiles, a lot of time traveling from places I did not care to be to places I didn't want to go, accompanied by batches of noisy people I did not know very well and did not care to know better. I heard, too often, the sound of my own voice going on and on, talking without saying anything and talking loudly to be heard over all the din, for reasons I could not remember. And there was a lot of getting in and out of boats, in and out of pools, and, in a daze of booze and indifference, getting in and out of beds, even though I had long since discovered that it is a habit which degrades the receptivity to sensation, coarsens selectivity, implies obligation, and turns off most useful introspection.

In that silly random season I found myself thinking of Lou Ellen, not in an orderly, consecutive, narrative way, but in very quick and vivid takes which were swept away as quickly as they appeared. She was just beneath the surface of my mind and was revealed in those moments when the light was just right.

Some very curious attrition was going on. Ruthie Meehan, one of the long-time waitresses, began to act strange and remote, drowned in the sea while swimming at night, was brought in through the Inlet by the tide, and was found floating in the bay shallows by an early fisherman. Some said she'd gone on sopors. There were rumors she'd left a note. People said we ought to *do* something, but there wasn't anything to do except go to the funeral, and nobody went because her sister in New Hampshire sent for the body.

Brud Silverman borrowed Lacey Davis's Charger and drove it out Route 84, destination unknown, and hit a big pine on the canal bank about a mile and a half west of Fern Crest. Estimated speed, a hundred and twenty. No sign of skid marks. A perfect hit, absolutely square. The car bounced back about seven feet from the tree, compacted to half its showroom length, and fried Silverman down to a child-size cinder.

And Meyer keeled over.

He said he felt very strange. Far away. A nice fast walk on the beach, a swim, some exercises, a shower, a steak, and he'd be just fine, he said. But when we walked up the slope of the beach after swimming, he stopped and looked at me and said, "I think I . . . "

I waited for the rest of it. He smiled, rolled his eyes up, and pitched onto his face in the soiled sand above high tide. He is as broad as a bear and as hairy as a bear. You think of heart. You think of something going bad inside that big chest. I eased him over. He had sand in nose, mouth and eyes. I laid my right ear on his wet, hairy chest and heard the engine going. *Tuh-PUM, tuh-PUM, tuh-PUM.* Too fast? But he'd been swimming hard. A fat, gentle woman filled a kid's sand pail with fresh water and cleaned the sand off Meyer's face while we waited for the ambulance. Ambulance service to the beach is very good. Four minutes this time. Resistance to my riding along, until I said I could tell the emergency room just how he had acted before he passed out and when he passed out.

Fast ride. Deft handling. Too damned cold in the emergency area. They got a blanket over him, steered me to the admissions desk, wheeled him away somewhere. I was a conspicuous figure, walking around in there in swim trunks. A tiny blond nurse, almost a midget, found me an XL robe before I froze. I upset several people in my search for Meyer by appearing in places I was not supposed to be. The medical industry is never ready for inquiry. They never used to like to answer questions. Now they have the excuse they could be sued. They overwork the excuse.

A saturnine, leathery doctor named Kwalty was supervising the workup on Meyer. I answered the questions I thought he ought to be asking and had to assume he heard what I said.

He wrote something on a form and gave it to a gray-headed nurse. An orderly wheeled Meyer away, with the nurse keeping pace.

"Where is he going now?" I asked.

"What is your relationship to the patient?" Kwalty asked coldly.

"I'm his sister."

Kwalty pursed his lips and stared up at me. "If you start trying to muscle the staff, fellow, you won't find out one damn thing."

"Would you like to put a little money on that, Doctor?"

He tilted his head. "Maybe not. Your friend has a temperature of almost one hundred and five degrees. And some fluid in the lungs already. It's a virus infection. He goes to Intensive Care. When the lab puts a name on the bug, we'll go to the antibiotics with the best record against it. It can kill him, leave him in bad shape, or he can recover completely."

I took a cab home to *The Busted Flush* and got clothes and money and drove back in my blue Rolls pickup and parked her five blocks from the hospital. That was as close as I could get and legally leave it there for a long period.

I did not mind hanging around. I had nothing pressing to do. I was sick of going to the places I had been going to. The hidden compartment in the hull of the *Flush* was stocked with enough cash to afford six or more months of very good living. So the hospital was fine. It was a project. Infiltrate. Ingratiate. Learn the kind of protective coloring that gets you past the places where they stop the civilians, and learn the kind of behavior which keeps the staff from using their authority to toss you the hell out.

There is no reason why a person cannot buy and wear a white, long-sleeved shirt-jacket. It does not look at all like a medical smock. A person can keep things in the pocket, pencil flashlight, several pens. A person can carry an aluminum clipboard. The pace is important—steady and mildly purposeful. Smile and nod at every familiar face because that is the way *you* become a familiar face. Do little favors. Look up the nice folk who took such good care of you the last time you were in. And the time before.

By the time they let Meyer out of Intensive Care, after four rough days and nights, I had goodies all lined up. I had a fine private room assigned to him, 455, on Four South, ten easy paces from the nurses' station. And that was a most agreeable station indeed because, rarity of rarities, the nurses on all shifts were cheery, competent and funny, and half of them were pretty.

I had become friendly with Kwalty after our bad beginning. He said that if I wanted to throw away my money, a private nurse just for the span from eleven at night to seven in the morning might be helpful, as Meyer was still a sick and a weak man. The day-shift gals on Four South put their heads together and came up with Ella Marie Morse, RN, thirty-something, tall, dark, graceful, husky and highly skilled, a lady who had married a wealthy patient who had died in a plane crash on a business trip to Chicago, leaving her financially comfortable and bored.

They wheeled Meyer to 455 and eased him from bed to bed at four in the afternoon of the day after Christmas, Wednesday. I had looked in at him in Intensive Care several times. He looked worse at closer range. The infection had eaten him down. He looked shrunken in every dimension. His hair was dull, and his face looked amber and waxy. After they took pressure and temperature, and got his four o'clock medication into him, they left us alone. Meyer gave me a slow, thoughtful, heavy-lidded look.

"Christmas . . . is really gone?"

"So rumor has it."

"The medication . . . fogs my brain. I can't handle . . . word games."

"Yesterday was Christmas."

He kept his eyes closed for so long I thought he had gone to sleep. He opened his eyes. "How was it?"

"Christmas? Well . . . you know . . . it was Christmas."

After he closed his eyes again, I gave him a chatty account of McGee's Christmas, about decorating the tree in the nurses' lounge on Christmas Eve, about bringing in a batch of presents for people on Christmas Day, about attending three different staff parties in the hospital Christmas afternoon and evening. When I was through I realized he was snoring softly, but I did not know when he had dropped off. I decided he had not missed anything of great moment.

Nurse Ella Morse arrived early, a little after ten. She was taller than I had pictured her, not quite as pretty as described, and had an unexpected—and attractive—flavor of shyness in her manner. It made her seem less mature than she obviously was. After she had checked her sleeping patient out and had greeted the girls on duty, she and I took coffee into the small visitors' lounge at the end of the corridor. She asked about Meyer. A semiretired economist living alone aboard his dumpy little cabin cruiser over at Bahia Mar. That doesn't cover it. Meyer is something else. She would find out. Meyer is a transcendent warmth, the listening ear of a total understanding and forgiveness, a humble wisdom.

I explained that Doctor Damon Kwalty had suggested that she be the judge of when Meyer could get along adequately without her help. With a trace of officiousness, she asked me how come I was able to remain in the hospital so long after visitors' hours. I said they had given up asking me to leave, probably because I was handy to have around.

Maybe it has a certain emotional importance, or significance, that all this was on the night before I got Pidge Brindle's letter. Or perhaps I am straining at a gnat, or, once again looking for some way to make myself into a better person than I am.

At any rate I hung around until just before the shift change and then, following a lady's detailed instructions, walked down the corridor and around the corner and shoved the stairwell door open and, without going through it, let it hiss shut to the point where a folded piece of cardboard kept it from closing all the way and latching. Just beyond the doorway, I slipped into the treatment room through another door and pushed it almost shut. I sat on the treatment table and waited. The reflected glow of streetlights came into the room, glinting and glimmering on the glass and stainless steel of the medical equipment.

I could not tell exactly how long it would take her, because if someone went down with her on the elevator, then, instead of getting off at three and walking to the stairwell and climbing one flight, she would ride all the way down, fake a trip to the rest room, and climb the three flights back up to four.

I waited about five minutes before Marian Lewandowski, RN, pushed the door open silently, slipped into the treatment room and carefully closed the door. The latch clicked and the bolt made a tiny grating sound. She was a slender white shape in the darkness, a whisper of professional fabrics coming toward me, a barely audible "Hi, darling" as she came into the clandestine embrace, to be held and kissed in the stolen darkness.

She had little body tremors of nervousness, and her whisper-voice had little edges of anxiety, and she had a talking jag. On the afternoon before Christmas, she had come to the lounge three times for a few minutes each time, to make sour jokes about being stuck on the three-to-eleven on that day, Christmas day and the day after. Lots of nurses were sick with the bug. A woman with a lovely, lively body, tons of energy, a face more worn than the body, blond hair tied tightly back, blue eyes a sixteenth of an inch too close together, lips a millimeter too thin. She kissed and trembled and said, "You know, I figure we were both kidding, talking a good game, neither of us going to show up, but all the time it was happening, you know, like getting carried along. It's just kidding at first. Then it's like a game. Like playing chicken."

"I know."

"Well, I talk a good game, but the way it is with me, Norman is on pipeline work in Iran, no place I would want to take my two babies, and so here I am living with Norman's mother again, and I wouldn't really have to work except it would drive me out of my tree trying to live in her house with her, and that rotten old woman is holding a stopwatch on me right now, you can bet your life on it, figuring I'm late because I took time on the way home to get laid. When somebody bugs you and bugs you and bugs you all the time about something you haven't been doing, you end up doing it, right?"

"I guess you do."

"I wouldn't know about this being a good safe place except for Nita, she's on vacation, my best friend practically—she sneaks it here with a cardiologist she thinks is some day going to get a divorce and marry her, but it never happens."

"I guess it doesn't."

"Mostly what is wrong with me, McGee, it isn't just that Norman is away for such a long time and the old lady bugs me so, and if I know Norman he's set up a shack job for himself, what is wrong with me, I guess, is . . . somehow the work is different being a nurse now. There are so many *old* ones coming in, coming in and *dying* all the time. It makes you think about time going by you, like you're on a train that never stops and you look out the window at things streaming by that you'll never see except that way. Dying isn't scary because they come in here and they are so confused and kind of dim they don't really know what is happening, and then all of a sudden they're in a coma and they got an I.V. going, and a catheter and a bag, and an oxygen clip on their nose, and they don't know a damn thing about living or dying anymore. That's going to be me and you sometime, bet on it."

"But not yet."

"Feel how I'm shaking? I don't know what's wrong with me. Nita says don't try to use the table, it's so high and narrow you could fall off and break somebody's back, she said there's a rollaway in here . . . there it is, I can just make it out, and the thing to do is open it a little ways and pull the mattress out and put it on the floor. Look, this is weird, the way I feel. I'm a *nurse*, damn it, and you know the reputation we got, and I like you a lot. I really *like* you, and I've been excited for hours thinking about you, but would it be a mean, rotten, dirty trick if— if I asked if we just skipped it? Would you get really sore?"

"No, I wouldn't."

"Maybe it's his mother there waiting and waiting. Why should I make such a big thing? It isn't a big thing anymore in the world. We've got the rights that only men used to have. Well, just hold me like this and kiss me like you did before, for a little while, and then I better be going, and I'm sorry. I'm really sorry."

And in about ten minutes we were on the mattress together. Her flesh was cool, and as pale in the darkness as the uniform had been. Her thick curls had trapped odors of medication and asepsis. I heard the muffled bong of the corridor call bell, a night shriek of city brakes, the thunder-roll of a jet, fast and high, and soon the more immediate *bumpity-thud, bumpity-thud* of Mrs. Norman Lewandowski's pale, pretty and earnest hips against the compressed kapok of the thin, hard, rollaway mattress. Thus we exorcized our private ghosts, leaving *old* and *dying* far behind as sensation rushed forward in the rich, frictive celebration of life and living.

I dozed after she was gone and awoke with a start, chilled to the bone by the air conditioning, which had dried the sweats of effort while I slept. It was only 12:11 by the little red Pulsar digits. I buttoned my shirt wrong on the first try, and when I did it wrong again on the second try, I seriously considered sitting down on the floor and crying a little.

I drove stately old Miss Agnes home through the tropic night, sitting at the big wheel in one of the deepest, saddest, most dismal postcoital depressions I have ever known. I was an absolutely trivial, wasted, no-good son of a bitch. I wanted to moan, tear my hair out and gnaw my hands raw. This had really been one great December. Point with pride, you dumb horny old scavenger. You zapped Pidge just because you missed her the first time around, and you're trying to make a perfect score, right? And since you got back, there have been a half-dozen casual availables, and if you put your mind to it you can remember four out of six of their names and maybe three out of six of their faces. And now this lonely nurse person. Like shooting fish in a barrel. No. More like using a shotgun to kill a minnow in a teacup. What is wrong with you this year, fellow? Should you be married, for God's sake? Should you look in the yellow pages for your friendly neighborhood monastery? Should you sign up for a double orchidectomy? You have to do something, because something is definitely wrong with a grown man who spends the idle hour ramming his rigid self into chance acquaintances, no matter how willing they might be, no matter how far away Norman is.

When have you been like this before?

I locked Miss Agnes and walked the empty dock to Slip F-18 and boarded the *Flush*. Tired as I was, I went through the motions of checking the little panel in the bulkhead to see if any uninvited visitors had been aboard in my absence. I cut the switch with the special key, let myself in and remembered to use the key again on the inside switch. That is where most security systems fail. Thieves wait for you to deactivate it on the outside, then jump from cover and make you take them inside. If you have a double switch on the alarm circuit, with a sixty-second delay, it can be wired so that if the inside one isn't deactivated in time, you get sirens, bullhorns, calliope music, anything you might want to hear.

I remembered when I had been like this the last time. The last time it had been a defensive reaction. I had suspected a far deeper involvement with a lady than I had wanted. And so I had tried to cure it with warm poultices of other ladies, or at least to muffle it, blur it, diffuse it.

Pidge? Lou Ellen? Oh, *no*, McGee! She's just a kid. Well, not quite. She used to be a kid, and not too long ago. She's not at the bottom of all this cut-rate Lothario routine. Couldn't possibly be. Use the acid test on her. Okay. Would I, Travis McGee, bring thee, Linda Lewellen Brindle, aboard this houseboat to live herein and hereon, with me, happily, so long as we shall all remain afloat?

Hell, yes!

I went to bed then, dismayed, not knowing I would get her letter the next day.

7

Darling,

*This feels like the tenth letter to you, and I have the
strange feeling you know what was in the other nine I
threw away, just like I picked up the phone all those times
and didn't call you. In all the letters I threw away I said
I love you so many times you have to be used to hearing
it from me by now. And you can't hush me up the way you
kept doing when we had that absolutely incredible weekend here together after I seduced you. That word looks
funny written out. I looked at it so long I had to go look
it up to see if it was spelled right. I found out I can lie
down and close my eyes and think about us, and remember exactly what it was like the different times and
different ways, and after a little while I feel all hot and
out of breath and dizzy. Do you think of me like that? Do
men ever do that? Can you get big just by thinking about*

me? I hope you can. Because it was a lot more than just games, wasn't it?

You are going to have me on your hands. I guess you know that by now. Or you've guessed it. I'm going to walk along the dock and walk aboard and find you and say Hello dear, here I am to spend a little time with you, like the rest of my life. Then what are you going to do? Nothing at all. It's ordained. Way back when I stowed away, it was all settled for us even then. I am very rich and I can cook. What do you want anyway?

But don't start looking for me tomorrow. I have this thing about neat. I want to wrap up this whole part of my life and seal it and put it away in a cupboard and never look at it again. When I'm with you I won't ever get freaky again because I don't have to think about things not being right, because they are right every minute, no matter what we are doing.

The Professor taught me that the worst thing you can do is run away from things, and it marked me. So I have things to settle first, and then I'll be heading toward you as fast as they can fly those birds. Two days after you left, I went and had my first long talk with Howie. He was really awfully upset. He didn't know how to take it. He just refused to believe me. I guess he's really in love with me, the poor ox. When he wads his face up, he looks just like a baby about to start to cry. It took a lot of long talks to make him see that if he loves me, he has to let me go. Could I ever let you go? I don't think I could, darling. I wouldn't be strong enough. Thinking about us gives me the strength and patience to talk nicely to Howie.

Now he's resigned to it. He's very morose, at least he was, but now he seems a little better. I guess it's because of the final cruise. You should see my poor hands! We've been working like maniacs to get the Trepid ready. Because it's too much boat for one person to sail a long distance, we agreed to sell her here. Howie is a really good salesman. That's what he should be doing, I guess. Any-

way, there is a man named Dawson who is very interested in her. And the price is okay, I guess. $130,000. He is being transferred from here to Pago Pago in American Samoa. He works for a land development company and he seems young to be so successful. He says that he'll be down there several years on a project, and that the Trepid is exactly what he wants. He says that he can get her surveyed there, and if she is as sound as she looks, he will be able to get a bank draft for the full purchase price, and we can fly home from there.

I am even sort of looking forward to the voyage, darling. I think Howie has the idea I'll "come to my senses" or some fool idea like that. But I will be alone on the beautiful sea, thinking of us. I couldn't stand him even kissing me. But I'll feel better for making the cruise because it will let him know that I am completely serious about divorcing him, and it will prove to me that I am not some kind of flippy person going around hallucinating at the drop of a—of a what? A spook? Already all that is a bad dream, thanks to you, darling. I am the most stable girl in the world. I am in love. That helps a girl a lot.

So now the Trepid is lovely again, looking fresh and proud and new. Everything aboard her has been checked over and over again, and as you know my father was a nut about fail-safe backup things, so no need to worry. I came back here to the apartment to pick up the last of my things and wander around and think of you and smile secret satisfied smiles at myself in the mirror. Remember when you came up behind me and put your chin on top of my head and we were like a funny totem pole in the mirror, making horrible faces? And to finish this letter which I started yesterday.

We have been working on the charts and figuring out time and distance, dear. We'll have about 3000 miles to go, and we are going to top off the tanks and really push it because even at standard cruise, there is still a tiny safety factor. With allowance for weather, the best we can do, *running all the time, is a hair under two hundred miles a day, so sixteen days should just about do it. It is a shame to miss some lovely islands, but they would mean nothing to me unless I shared them with you. It is a shame not to use the wind when the wind is good. But the man wants the Trepid as quick as he can get her, and I want to be out of this marriage just as quick. And so it goes.*

Darling, you took a flippy girl with weird teeth, lumpy boobs, fat thighs and nothing-type hair and you've made her feel almost beautiful. I hope you're satisfied. I mean I am going to make real sure you're satisfied.

So I will mail this on the way back to the boat and today is Christmas Eve, so God only knows how long it will take. We will be taking off early tomorrow morning, and I imagine we'll be tying up at Pago Pago no later than Thursday, the tenth of next year, the first year we are going to spend most of together. All the dumb lines of the dumb old songs have become wonderful. We don't have a song yet! Kiss Meyer for me. Say hello to everybody. Tell everybody that Lou Ellen is coming home. They won't know you mean me if you say that. You can use Pidge to outsiders, okay? But never to me between us alone. I am so damned incredibly happy! I looooooooooove you.

Lou Ellen McGee

PS: If you don't remember proposing, that's okay. You can always take care of the details later on.

Meyer's fever was up again on Thursday. Not dangerously high. High enough to make Kwalty irritable. He changed some of the medication and ordered more fluids. I sat in his room and when he dozed I read my letter again. I didn't overdo it. I don't think I read it more than fifteen times. Did I feel the stirring then of some terrible premonition? No. I was clam happy, with goof grin and a little song to hum, a foot to tap. Life had suddenly revealed to me its long-concealed and exquisite design.

When Meyer would seem to want something, I would go get a nurse to take care. He was dim and grumpy. He seemed to bring some of the dozing dreams out into daylight and a mild delirium of fever. Once he sat halfway up, face twisting, and said harshly, "No! Don't let him, Cable!"

I went to him and pushed him back. "Hey, Meyer. You're okay. All that happened a long time ago."

His eyes cleared and he looked up at me, then tried to smile. "Sorry. Sorry."

I sat again, knowing that in the brain warped by fever, Meyer had gone back in time to the Cypress County jail when Deputy Lew Arnstead had beaten him cruelly while Deputy Billy Cable watched. When you have been beaten to helplessness and still the beating goes on and on until you wonder if you will live, that is when the marks go deep.

I went to lunch and came back in through one of my newly discovered private entrances where I did not have to con my way past the Gray Ladies with their file of visitor's passes. Meyer was still on the no-visitor list, but Kwalty had given me verbal assurance that I was his exception. When I walked down the corridor of Four South I came upon Marian Lewandowski at the nurses' station, checking through the patient records. She glanced at me and said hello and I watched the pink blush move up out of the collar of the white uniform and up her throat, suffusing her forehead last of all. She swallowed and moved ten feet down the corridor with me, glancing nervously back to see if we were clueing her peer group.

"Anybody see you leaving?" she asked, barely moving her lips.

"No. How'd you make out at home?"

She made a mouth. "The usual. Nobody could ever be good enough for Norman. When she accused me other times, I get so mad I yell at her. So I had to get mad last night too. Listen, it was crazy. I wasn't going to do it, really. I did cheat before, but it was different. It was a big beach-picnic thing, blankets, everybody smashed, and Norm had gone off with a girl he used to go with, in her car, to get more beer, and he didn't come back soon enough."

"Marian!" somebody called from the station.

"I'll come to four fifty-five, huh?" she said, and spun and went striding back. I watched her. An alert, heads-up pace, little white cap, teacup size with blue edging, riding squarely atop the clenched blond curls, white shoes with rubber ripple soles, toeing in, the long stride swinging the hips. It was a difficult, almost impossible feat to relate that brisk professional image to the night creature of the rollaway mattress, so quickly sensitized that she jerked, flexed, gasped at each caress until, in response to the body language of tugging and reaching, I had rolled her under.

And now I could not conceive of ever wanting to take her one more time. And suspected that she too would like to avoid a rerun. This is one of the new relationships in a transient society for which there is no word or phrase in common use. Marian and I were not friends, because friendship grows out of mutual concerns and out of being together at many times in many places. We were not lovers, because there was little or no continuity of desire. We were not completely casual libertines, dissolute and uncontrolled. Each of us had fed a great many bits into our personal computers, at breakneck speed. Is he-she physically attractive to me? Is he-she clean and healthy? Will he-she be circumspect and private about it? It he-she seeking some kind of angle or advantage I don't know about? Is he-she likely to be kinky in some kind of vulgar, unpleasant or even alarming way? Could he-she be hunting some kind of long-range emotional security and personal involvement I can't afford? Are there so many shadow areas in the computer response to the questions that the anticipated pleasure is not worth the unknown risk?

For each of us the equation worked, but there was the element of risk, the element of the unknown that honed the edge of anticipated pleasure. So it was too tense to be entirely casual.

The Great Magician had called us up from the audience. He had wanted a man and a woman. Marian and I had come from opposite sides of the packed theater, accepting the risk of volunteering, and had been locked together in the magic box by the Magician, feeling vibrant and short of breath. The trick had worked. We had disappeared completely and had materialized back in the real world, no better and no worse for the experience. We had fattened our memory banks with information which might be of use someday. And in a mortal world, in the midst of all the dying, we had once again proven we were desirable, trustworthy and sexually competent.

Acquaintances perhaps? The encounter, though brief, struck too deep for that shallow word. Conspirators? There is no word for the relationship. It is a small, delicious and important risk which is being taken an uncountable number of times each day—two-person encounter groups making initial contact in the office, plant, supermarket, waiting room, banquet hall, country club, bus station, cocktail bar. Eye contact, speculation, appraisal. Run all the accessible data through the memory banks of experience and, after an hour, a week, or a month, set up the assignation. The more discriminating and fastidious the risk-taker, the rarer will be the taking of risk.

You can read all about it in the newspapers when the gamble goes really sour. Look under divorce decrees. Under hospital admissions. Under indictments for assault, rape, and homicide.

If it is a bad risk and there is just a small loss, it becomes a dreary episode, with petulance, regret and ugly words. The risk seems to turn bad when one of the players finds the partner is a compulsive player, a prowler, a collector of souvenirs of the hunt, a scorekeeper.

Ours had been an unexceptional event. Quite pleasant, leaving a residue of a mild and patronizing fondness. Good girl, there. Jolly good show, and all that. Nobody was a hunter. The contact had been accidental, the vibrations acceptable, the conclusion foregone.

She came to Meyer's room at four o'clock. With the gentle deftness of the very good nurse, she took temperature, blood pressure, pulse, and made notes to transcribe the information to his chart at the nurses' station. With a hesitant look and beckoning motion with her head, she drew me over to the window corner.

"So?" she said, half whisper.

Pride kept her away from any edge of commitment. I couldn't read her eyes, or the shape of her mouth. I said, "What I want to say is same time, same place—question mark. You know that."

"But you can't?"

"Same place. I can ask that. But I have to be out of here by ten tonight. No way out of it."

Face of disappointment, but genuine? "That's too bad."

"Earlier?" I asked, knowing well the answer.

"On shift? No *way*. Not even if we were quick as rabbits, and who needs it that way?"

I was beginning to be confident of my earlier guess, so I said, "It'll have to be Friday then."

"Wonderful, darlin'! Oh, dear. No. I just remembered. I'm off from tonight until when I get a shift change and come in Sunday morning at seven. Look, we're a girl short this shift, and we're full to the brim. If your friend is still here Sunday and if . . . we both still feel the same way, maybe we can work something out, okay?"

"Okay."

"And if we can't, well, we're still ahead of the game, McGee."

"Way ahead."

She grinned and leaned and gave me a quick kiss, a quick pat, and went swiftly to the door, hauled it open, and disappeared into the busy corridor. As the door slowly, slowly closed, I had a diminishing view of an old man with a walker going along the corridor. His head was canted way over so that his cheek was almost against his left shoulder. He would slide his left foot six inches forward and then lean forward, hands braced on the aluminum tubing of the walker until his weight was over the forward foot. Then he would lift his right shoulder and turn his body to slide and swing the right foot up even with the left. He would then shove the walker another six inches forward. I had watched him in the hallway. He had all the blind, dogged, stubborn determination of a half-smashed bug heading for the darkness under the sink. It was impossible to imagine what was going on inside his skull. The door snicked shut. I wondered how many Marians the old, old man had known. I wondered if he thought of any of them, or one of them, as he made his timeless journeys, each as valiant perhaps as the last five miles of the Boston Marathon.

"Got a new buddy?" Meyer said in so normal a tone I nearly jumped backward out the window.

I walked over to the bed. His eyes were bright. "The more I jolly up the nurse corps, the more nursing you get," I told him.

He felt for the buttons on the side of the electric bed and wound his head and shoulders higher, and cranked his knees higher.

"I am happy," he said, "that in my misery, in my torment, I have been able to provide you with a new little garden of posies, and a perfect rationalization for plucking one, if you feel the need."

"You are cured!"

"And you have an infinite capacity for self-deceit, Travis."

I sat on the foot of his bed. "What makes you think you can look at a whispered conversation about the condition of your health, Meyer, and come up with a diagnosis of my character flaws?"

"Fever sharpens the wits. And the hearing."

"Oh."

"Attractive woman. Good nurse. How long will I be here?"

I stared at him and shook my head in wonder. I had not really admitted to myself the chance that the Meyer I knew was gone forever. Too high a fever over too long can cook the little synapses in your skull. Were Meyer to become a very dull fellow, I would have seen to it that he had a pretty good life, considering. But it would have been a long gesture of thanks to the Meyer I had once known.

But this thing with the shrunken saffron face and the bright eyes was my friend, rising from the valley of the shadows. I went over and looked out the window to blink away, in quasi privacy, the stinging feeling in my eyes.

"You are a tough old bastard," I told him.

"The way I feel now, there is nothing tough left. I don't think I could survive a bad case of hangnail."

"Terminal hangnail is one of the challenges modern medicine must face." I moved toward Meyer and sat on a corner of the foot of his bed. "Let's stop talking about your problems and talk about mine. Like my infinite capacity for self-deceit. I believe you mentioned it. I want to say something, but all the words come out of terrible song lyrics. There is now one lady I want for keeps."

"That nurse?" he said. His expression was quizzical, unbelieving.

"No. Pidge."

"Pidge!" He was definitely startled. "Was there . . . did you . . . when you went to. . . . "

"Yes, yes, yes, dammit! One partridge in a pear tree,

and on a low limb, in a good strong light, and me with an automatic shotgun and number seven shot, standing six feet away. Pow."

He nodded and nodded.

I said, "What are you smiling at?"

"Me? Oh, it's just that I don't have to worry about you. I was worrying, you know, before I was struck down. You began to puzzle all your friends. You came back from Hawaii and began acting like a salesman at a convention. You were into Plymouth gin pretty heavy at all times, and you began hewing your way through the solid wall of doxies a determined man can find anywhere and especially in Lauderdale. I wasn't keeping score or keeping track, as you know, but I could not help notice two tourist ladies, the new hostess at the Beef'n It, one stewardess, one schoolteacher, and, God save us and help us, one Avon Lady."

"And a nurse," I said in a very small voice. "And you say that now you don't have to worry about me?"

"Oh, I can worry a little. I think you have been in too many beds, and you may have bounced your brains loose. But I would suspect that the efforts you have gone to in fighting fire with fire indicate that you have a very hot fire to fight. You've overcompensated."

"I've what?"

"You're thrashing around, boiling the water, trying to throw the hook. And, in the process, being something of a damned fool."

"Thrashing, eh? I'm through that phase. The nurse was the end of the line."

"Thus accepting the inevitability of the shared life?"

"You could cheer a little. Or clap."

He cocked his head. "Not quite yet. She's really very young for you, Travis."

"I keep telling myself that."

"With an entirely different set of values."

"I know."

"And, of course, she's still married."

"But wants out and will get out."

"And you have lived for a long time in a random pattern no woman could ever really accept. Can you change your pattern?"

"I keep thinking that other people have friends, and they talk about ball games and the weather and laugh a lot. What have I got? Ann Landers."

He smiled and closed his eyes. Thirty seconds later he was in deep sleep, mending.

8

WHEN I got back to Bahia Mar from the hospital that Thursday night, there was a dark bulk snoring in the deck chair on the aft deck of *The Busted Flush*. I came quietly aboard and moved to where I could bend over and get a look at his face in the half light. I knew him so well that it surprised me that I had to grope for the name. Frank Hayes. Construction engineer, scuba expert, mechanical wizard. I hadn't seen him since the diesel pump froze up, down in the Bay of La Paz.

"Frank?" I said softly.

The snore stopped. His eyes opened. He slanted his glance up at me, not moving his head. Two seconds of appraisal. Then he rolled up onto his feet and said, "How's Meyer making it?"

"He must be getting better. He turned mean."

"I asked around about you two."

I opened the doorway and hit the lights and ushered him into the lounge. He carried a duffel bag and a bedroll.

He wore safety shoes, faded twill work pants, a smudged white T-shirt and an old wool army shirt worn unbuttoned and outside the pants. He had a beard stubble that misted the heavy lines of his jowls.

"You're looking healthy, Frank."

He shrugged. "Less hair, more belly."

"Too late to go looking for a place to stay. You're welcome to stay aboard."

"Thanks. Suits me."

"Want to wash up?"

"If I go through here, I should come to the head?"

"Right. I can fix some eggs."

"I ate already, thanks. A little bourbon and water, half and half, no ice."

I fixed drinks. I wondered what was on his mind. I knew I couldn't try to pry it out of him. Frank Hayes had to do everything his own way, in his own time.

When he came back into the lounge, he looked exactly the same as when he had left. He took the drink with a nod of thanks and settled into a big leather chair. He took the drink down by half, wiped his mouth on his hand, and looked around. "Nice," he said. "The way you and Meyer described it, I thought it was maybe some kind of playpen. You hear what happened to Joe Delladio?"

"No."

"Head on. In the mountains on the road from Puebla down to Oaxaca. A bus with busted brakes. Wiped him out, and his wife and two of their four kids."

"Such a damned waste. Jesus!"

"I know. I didn't hear until months later. Just like with Professor Ted. Thanks for sending me that card to that box number I give you when we broke up the team. I was out of the country."

"Just you, me and Meyer left."

"To all survivors," he said, finished his drink and placidly held his glass out for a refill. "That Meyer. At first I didn't think he could hack the kind of work we were doing on the bottom of that bay. Found that goddamn gold, right?"

I put the new drink in his hand. "Right."

"The reason I came looking you up, I started wondering what happened to Professor Ted's research notes. He called it his dream book. You remember that?"

"I remember it well. The afternoon he got killed, Meyer and I went aboard the *Trepid* and broke into it and searched it all night long. Nothing. And nothing in the safety deposit vault."

"Strange."

"I know, especially since he was gearing up to go hunting again. The daughter came down from the north. She didn't have any information."

"How did he leave her?"

"In good shape. *Very* good shape. Between eight and nine hundred thousand, plus the *Trepid,* plus liquid assets to pay estate taxes and expenses."

"She around here?"

"In the South Pacific with her husband, aboard the *Trepid*, just the two of them. Fellow named Howie Brindle. They sailed out of here almost fourteen months ago."

"Just the daughter? Nobody else to leave anything to?"

"Just Linda, known as Pidge."

"Were you going along on the next hunting trip with Ted?"

"He hadn't asked me. I don't know if he was going to. He wasn't exactly your ordinary neighborhood blabbermouth."

"Know who his lawyer was?"

"Yes. I thought of that. I asked him. No, he was not keeping any books or records for Professor Theodore Lewellen. He had drawn up some trust agreements, handled some tax questions. Tom Collier. Fall, Collier, Haspline and Butts. Tom is coexecutor of the estate, along with the First Oceanside Bank and Trust."

"Collier a good man?"

"Supposed to be. Old family. Early forties. Political connections. Rich practice and big landholdings. Why?"

Frank slowly and gently scratched a newly healed scar on the back of his left hand, a patch of smooth, pink, shiny skin over two inches long, over half an inch wide.

"How'd you get that?"

He looked at it as if seeing it for the first time. "This? Some silly bastard left a wrench on the deck, below, and I stepped on the edge of it and swung my arm out for balance and hit a live-steam line. It stung pretty good."

"Frank!"

"Eh?"

"You just suddenly started wondering what happened to Ted Lewellen's research notes? No more questions, my friend. Not until you answer the ones I ought to be asking."

"A letter is sent a month ago from a Miami lawyer named Mansfield Hall, which sounds like a building on a college campus, to Seven Seas, Limited. A very careful letter. What it is saying is that Hall represents somebody who has come into the possession of some original research materials taken from original sources, indicating the possible location of sunken treasure on the ocean floor, along with geodetic survey maps, overlays, and aerial photography. This somebody wants to negotiate a deal with Seven Seas whereby they set up a joint venture to go after the items, Seven Seas to finance the first recovery attempt, take back expenses, then split the balance down the middle. This somebody wants the right to have a representative along on the recovery operation. After the first recovery, the terms are to be renegotiated."

"It *does* sound like the way Ted set things up. Very orderly, very complete."

"I thought so too. I went to see this Mansfield Hall. I don't think you could shake anything out of him because I don't think he knows very much. I'm not even sure he knows exactly who he's representing."

"How did you get hold of the letter?"

He stared at me. "What do you mean?"

"I've heard about Seven Seas. It's an offshore corporation, and it was in the news a lot last year, locating and recovering that Air France jet that went down with the gold shipment near Aruba. Based in Jamaica?"

"Grand Cayman."

"So how did you get hold—"

"Because it was sent to me, McGee. Jesus! I *am* Seven Seas. At least I own forty percent of the son of a bitch."

I looked at the stubble, the Salvation Army wardrobe. "Well, well, well. And I suppose you flew up in your very own Seven-oh-seven to see me?"

"No. We've got a piece of a Learjet, share it with two other outfits, split the costs based on percentage of use. Way back there in Mexico, I was looking to buy into Seven Seas, Limited. I'd worked for them. Mismanaged. I was looking for a big hit, and we missed it at the Bay of La Paz, but I made it the next try. Had to make it. I had an option on shares."

"Frank, I would never have believed it."

"Try hard. It'll come to you. Anyway, Mister Mansfield Hall wants me to make a counter offer and he will take it to his client and so on, and I told him forget it, I deal nose to nose or not at all. Now I'm snuffing at it from the other end. Whoever is being so careful would have no way of knowing that I ever worked with Ted Lewellen. If this somebody was looking for exactly the right outfit—skill, capitalization, equipment, and honesty —the name Seven Seas would probably come up almost anyplace he asked. It's the kind of thing we want to do. But this approach smells. Can you figure why?"

It puzzled me for a few moments, trying to figure out what he meant. And then I saw it. "You're saying that anybody with a legitimate ownership of Lewellen's research and his salvage plans would be able to raise the money, hire the experts, equip an expedition and go after the goodies."

"Right. They wouldn't have to be so secret and careful, and they wouldn't have to give away half the net."

"So somebody ripped off the dream book."

"Or he trusted the wrong person?"

"Hisp, at the bank? Tom Collier?"

"Who knows? We both know what can happen. Suppose there is a man you can trust with your life. Nothing he wouldn't do for you. But all of a sudden you're dead, and he sees an angle. Foolproof. The daughter? She's got a bundle. No need to worry. So this fellow, this true and blue friend, there he is with all Professor Ted's notes and analyses and studies. Basic research was in that journal, a book about so big. The backup research would fill a big suitcase. True-blue friend lays back and waits for heat. There is no heat at all. So finally, he makes his move, trying to set it up so there's no risk at all."

"I never heard you say so much before, all at one time."

"Ted trusted *you*, you son of a bitch!"

Never before has my jaw fallen open in surprise. Here is what happens. There are nineteen different things you can say, and you open your mouth to say them all, and you can't decide which one to say first. So you sit there like a stuffed guppy.

And then I was in midair, mouth still open. Total launch. The juvenile reaction. Honor offended and all that. He tried to tip his chair over to the side, but it didn't tip fast enough. I made a midair adjustment of arm, shoulder, and back and popped him on the side of the head as he was toppling. It made a clear white whistling pain in my hand, reminding me that one almost never hits the hard parts of people with the naked hand. One hits the soft parts with the hand, and the hard parts with a utensil.

I sailed over him and tucked my shoulder under and rolled and came up. I pounced on him, grabbed two handfuls of garments and picked him up and slammed him back against the bulkhead, and drew back to put the next one into a soft part of him.

"Whoa!" he said in a fumbling voice. His eyes weren't in good focus.

"Whoa your ass!"

"Uncle," he said. That's right. The old schoolyard word. It stopped me. It boggled me.

"*Unc*-le?" I said.

"I wanted to know. I found out. So no more hitting." His voice was clearer. He shook the mist out of his eyes. I stepped back, but I stayed ready.

"I lie a lot," I said. "But I don't steal from live friends or dead friends."

"So I know that, now." He worked his jaw, felt of his face. "That was some tag. My head is still ringing. The last time I got hit that hard, a Greek came up behind me and laid me out on the deck with a fid. You know, I had the idea I could maybe take you if it ever came to that. Even if that was a lucky shot, I don't think so." He moved around me and stood his chair back up and sat in it, with a heavy sigh.

I kneaded my knuckles and worked them into the palm of the other hand, standing the pain in order to explore for any little grinding of bone chip, grating of fracture. I held the hand out, fingers straight, and looked at it. It was puffing so fast I already had a dimple wherever there used to be a knuckle.

"Usually I keep my cool better than that, Frank. It cost me a hand. I think I steamed because I really liked Ted. I miss him. Once upon a time he saved—I forgot. You know all about that."

"Look at it from where I live, McGee. He died here. You and Meyer were close to him. Either of you could have the stuff. I knew it wouldn't be Meyer."

"Why not?"

"We played a lot of games of chess aboard that bucket.

I know how his mind works. He conceals intent by making something look like something else. He doesn't advertise the fact he's being tricky. This isn't his style."

"So it has to be mine?"

"Let's not go through the big tumbling act again. It has to be somebody else. Your hand doesn't look so great."

It took an effort to make a fist. Soon it wouldn't be possible. "I feel like such a damned juvenile, Frank. I only hit people in self-defense. Usually."

"I could stay over long enough to play some chess with Meyer in the morning, if I can get into the hospital, and if he's up to it."

"I'll get you in, and unless he had a bad night, he'll play."

Friday morning I smuggled a guest and a magnetic chess set into room 455. Blaney, the boss nurse, was all set to run Frank Hayes out of her territory. He looked like the handyman at the local drunk farm. But he turned a considerable and unexpected charm in her direction, all very courtly, gracious, considerate, and almost overdone. The Russians say it is impossible to spoil porridge with too much butter. Blaney hesitated, then shrugged, then smiled, then laughed aloud, then gave him a girlish little slap on the arm and went out, giggling.

Meyer, who had brightened considerably at the appearance of Hayes and the chess set, looked marvelingly at Frank. "Who would ever have known!" he said.

Hayes opened his big fist and looked at the diminutive chess pawn. "You get white," he said. "Shut up and open."

They got into a long closed game, dull for the onlooker. I wandered out. When I returned at noon, they were talking, and the board had been pushed aside. Meyer had offered the draw and Hayes had accepted. Meyer looked weary. He yawned and said, "The decision of the Board is that you use your contacts and see what you can find out about Mansfield Hall."

"Gentlemen, your faithful, loyal employee has just finished making a few phone calls, and begs to report on that very situation. Hall is a professional go-between. He has spent so much time sitting in a cell for contempt of court because he wouldn't answer questions, people tend to trust him. He has had ulcers so bad he has about a third of a stomach left. He is reputed to be a poker player of formidable talent. Suppose you have five thousand acres of land over in Boondox County and you want to get it quietly rezoned so that the Devastation Minerals Company can set up a phosphate mining operation there and a chemical fertilizer plant, and will pay you fifteen hundred bucks an acre for it, if you can deliver it with the new zoning. Because that comes to seven point five mil, you are willing to lay out a hundred and fifty thousand cash to buy a favorable vote from three out of the five county commissioners of Boondox County. Mansfield Hall will find a legitimate investment for you. You put in three hundred thousand and, seven months later, you give up and cash in your chips and show a long term loss of two hundred thousand. In the meantime three commissioners have become richer by fifty thousand each, in some way they are perfectly willing to explain, if they are ever asked."

"Does he do any laundry work?" Frank asked. "I mean on a straight basis. Turn it in and get it back all pretty?"

"I wouldn't know. Maybe. It's rumored he handled a big kidnap payoff. He has some kind of status with the Cuban community, for some sort of services rendered. He spends a lot of time on airplanes, domestic and foreign. Apparently he's smart, sly, well-connected, and doesn't cheat his clients."

"Where would you say he'd pick up his clients?" Hayes asked.

Meyer yawned again "From other attorneys," he said. They brought Meyer's lunch tray and rousted us. A bland diet. Food that was beige, tan and buff and looked prechewed, with the tray brightened by the dietitian's touch—a dollop of red gelatin on a very small green leaf, and a wedge of bright yellow lemon on the tea saucer.

Blaney brought it herself, saying, "Well! We should be hungry by now, shouldn't we?"

Meyer looked at it and said, "We are. We are. *You* can be the one to eat it, my dear."

"You're a lot better," she said. "Let him have a good long nap today, fellows."

It was a good long nap. Frank's gear was locked in my car. I drove him to the airport, over to the private sector and out to where his crew of two were sitting on camp chairs just inboard of the starboard wing tank of the white ship, in the noonday shade of the delicate-looking wing. Ted and Harry. Harry was a bald ex-colonel with a boyish face. Ted was much younger, a Navy type who had gotten out after 'Nam. Turn Arnold Palmer's clock back to about twenty-eight, give him overlong reddish curls and a pair of eyes of a gray even paler than my own, paler than spit. They both wore odds and ends of uniform of several services from several wars.

Some signal must have been sent which I did not recognize, because when Frank said, "This here is McGee," I got a far more than casual inspection.

After they went aboard to get on the air and order up the battery cart, Frank gave me Mansfield Hall's card, complete with penciled unlisted special number on the back.

"Tell him you're authorized to negotiate for me. Maybe you can push the door open far enough to see what's beyond it. Probably not. Give it a try. It bothers me."

"And how do I get to you if I learn anything?"

"That's on this other card. What's going to happen, I am going to take on one more project than I've got the troops to handle, and that's when you're coming aboard. I'll work you down to a nub and make you very rich."

"I'm employed. Self-employed."

"Ted and Harry gave you good marks. I worked with you once, remember? Meyer has a high opinion."

I had to laugh. "Good marks from the airplane people, huh? Oh, Jesus, Frank. Thanks a hell of a lot."

"What's so funny?"

"Having spent a certain amount of time up to my glottis in swamps, with about fifteen little ulcers per leg where the leech bites didn't heal too good, and having spent some time trying very seriously to get all six foot four inches of McGee all the way inside one steel helmet, and having listened to the airplane people flying over, high and hard and fast, on their way home to officers' clubs and steak and booze and movies and more clusters on their air medals, I am not all the way overwhelmed by getting any approval from any of them."

He grinned as wide as I had ever seen him manage, and clamped my sore hand too hard and said, "When I really need you, I'm coming after you. Count on it." That was when he let the authority show. It was heavy. While it was turned on, I could believe what he said.

And pretty soon I saw the distant little white toy come skimming down the runway and go on up and over, climbing with turbine scream through the low-altitude smutch of too many cars toward that fabled high blue yonder to level off and go arrowing across Castro-land, down to that tiny island of one hundred (100) bank$ tucked below the land mass of Cuba.

9

I PHONED Mr. Hall and used Frank's name and Seven Seas, and he said he could see me at four. I rolled from Bahia Mar out past the Port and out to the Interstate and turned left to Miami. I put Miss Agnes up to seventy, and out of respect for her prior standards of performance, I eased her up slowly.

I felt that I had violated the integrity of the old Rolls by having her rebuilt to contemporary highway standards. Ever since I had dumped her into a drainage canal to avoid hitting a fleet-footed girl in the night, I had been upgrading all the hidden parts. Now she had the big engine lifted out of a 1972 Mark IV Continental that was totaled. Rebuilding the engine with both stock and custom power assists had meant a new gear train and a new rear end. Then she had more power than the suspension and the brakes could handle. So we installed a suspension out of the biggest Dodge pickup, along with power disc brakes all the way around. Of course I had to change to a twelve-volt system, and put in two heavy-duty batteries and a heavy-duty alternator. After several weird improvisations, we rigged a power steering system that worked well enough. There was enough extra horsepower to borrow some to run a really efficient air-conditioning system.

Any true aficionado of the Rolls would have taken one look inside the hood and run off to throw up. Sometimes I want to. Funny how, in this age of miracles, I had to give up so many nice little items Miss Agnes used to have. For example, on a cold morning I used to be able to flip a little switch on the dash that activated a battery-operated oil-circulation pump and a heating device. When the oil was up to the temperature recommended by the Works, a ruby light would glow and I would turn off the pump and heater and start her up. She used to have a calibrated dial on the side of the carburetor which could be turned manually to alter the mixture to achieve maximum performance at the indicated number of meters above sea level. She used to have a handle below the dash which could be used to change the degree of softness or rigidity of the springing, so that even while moving you could adjust her to ride at maximum comfort regardless of the roadbed.

And she had a clock that wound up with a key and kept time.

Detroit has never even caught up with the 1923 Rolls, to say nothing of the ones of Miss Agnes's vintage.

But unless I had either got rid of her or upped her performance, the traffic was going to kill me. And I did not want to sacrifice all that height and leather and walnut and dignity and be trapped in semifoetal position in some squatty little pastel capsule with my tailbone eight inches from the macadam. So she cost me what a couple of those space-age torpedoes would have cost, and I still feel like apologizing to her for the total organ transplant.

I must confess to getting a certain childish pleasure

out of driving her when she is challenged. I was heading up I-75 well north of Gainesville one bright afternoon at the legal seventy, on an unusually empty hunk of highway, when three hulking youths in a yellow 'Bird appeared in the rearview moving up fast. They slowed while passing and held even, looking at old Miss Agnes, a horrid blue, corrupted by the makeshift pickup bed. They seemed to be marveling that she could push that upright windshield through the air at seventy. They were crowing with idiot laughter. They made finger gestures and sped on, back up to ninety perhaps. I gave them a couple of miles, then floored Miss Agnes. The new needle was motionless against the stop when I blew by them at one forty plus. They made a try, but kept dropping back and back until they were gone. I nearly overshot my exit. I apologized to the old lady for the extra exertion. I wonder if they ever tell the story. Who would believe them?

Taking the short run down to Miami gave me a chance to sort out what Frank Hayes had told me. Professor Ted had had a batch of future projects. Without knowing exactly how I arrived at the figure, I had the feeling he had seven or eight more lined up. He knew that he was in a dangerous line of work. It takes skill and luck to stay out of trouble on the oceans with a small boat. Underwater work can go very bad very suddenly. And people have been killing other people for the sake of gold and jewels for a long, long time. So, as a considerate father, he had taken good care of his daughter's future needs by setting up the substantial trust account at First Oceanside. Would he have not made just as careful an arrangement for the project documents? Obviously they were valuable. The total sum in trust was proof of how useful the earlier projects had been.

I remembered the time he had told me how he had researched the dream book. It seemed almost too easy. I asked why other people didn't do the same thing he had done.

He had frowned, shaken his head slowly. "It's one of the great mysteries of the human condition, Travis. Maybe we all think it is not worth doing merely because it is so obvious it must have been done already. Fantastic warehouses of knowledge rot away, untouched. The scholars seem to have no interest. The adventurers have no research skills. They've found ancient jewelry in tombs in the Middle East made of smelted platinum. It takes eighteen hundred degrees centigrade to melt it. Two thousand years ago, the Chinese made aluminum ornaments. Getting aluminum from bauxite is a sophisticated chemical-electrical procedure. In the Baghdad Museum you can see the parts of a dry battery which worked on the galvanic principle and generated electricity sixteen hundred years ago. More smelted platinum has been found in Peru, in the high country. Knowledge fades away, and some is rediscovered and some isn't. We never seem to take the trouble to really find out—until too late. For several years the public baths at Alexandria were heated by burning the old scrolls and documents carted over from the great library. Are we so arrogant we believe that there was nothing that was burned up that hasn't been rediscovered? I dug back only four hundred years or so. That's easy. Yet I found journals which had turned to solid blocks, as if all the pages had been glued together. I found old documents so fragile I could not touch them without turning them into dust, and others where the ink had faded until it was completely gone. Treasures are buried on those pages, never to be found again except by the rarest accident. It's the . . . contemporary arrogance that bothers me. The idiot idea that we are the biggest, the greatest, the most powerful people who ever walked the earth. Know something? Think this over. I could take you to the high country of Peru, to a quarry area near Sacsahuaman, and show you where a particular block of stone was quarried and dressed, and I could show you that block of stone half a mile away. It was transported there during the time of the Incas. If, on the basis of national emergency, this nation were to be required to devote all its technological skills, all its wealth, and all its people to moving that block back to the quarry, we would try and we would fail, my friend. It weighs twenty thousand tons! Forty million pounds! The only time we ever move that much weight is when we let a vessel as big as the *Monterey* or the *Mariposa* slide down the ways at the shipyard, into the harbor. We have no cranes, no engines, no levers to budge that much mass. Do you think the Incas knew something mankind has since forgotten? Bet on it. Knowledge is the most priceless and most perishable substance on earth."

And I have thought it over, many times, and it always makes the back of my neck feel chilly. I've vowed that someday I will go look at that block of solid stone in the hope that if I see it once, I will stop thinking about how to move it back to the quarry whenever I wake up in the middle of the night.

One thing was clear. The Professor had too much love and respect for knowledge ever to destroy any, even if it was only his own research and was planned for selfish gain, not for the good of mankind.

I remembered another pertinent fact. When we had discussed a possible future project before we all split up, after the pump burned out, the Professor had relied upon memory, apologizing for not being able to refer to the research notes and his backup material.

Inference: he did not want to risk losing the whole package of projects for the future if he happened to drop the *Trepid* onto the sea floor somewhere. However, we live in the age of Xerox, IBM, MMM, Kodak, with microfiche and data retrieval, and certainly Ted was a gadgeteer. The equipment aboard the *Trepid* proved that.

Okay, then he did not want the project package aboard the *Trepid* in the original or any duplicate form because he did not want anyone taking it by force or guile or default.

In setting up Pidge's comfortable future, he had to confer with Lawton Hisp and Tom Collier. He would state his desires, and they would make suggestions based on professional knowledge. I did not see how he could possibly talk about a pretax estate of over a million dollars without some explanation of where it all came from. I suddenly remembered that after Meyer had researched the estate right after the Professor died, he mentioned there had been an IRS audit of Lewellen every year for the previous four years. Meyer had talked to Hisp. The bank handled all Lewellen's personal financial affairs. So very possibly Hisp either prepared Lewellen's returns or arranged for the preparation and reviewed them.

Hypothetical question—McGee asking McGee. Is it not fair to assume, sir, that if a man is making a fine fat living in a field where one out of ten thousand makes anything at all, that man, Dr. PhD Lewellen, would give his banker, Mr. Hisp, some explanation of the reason for his success and also some indication of the continuance thereof? After all, one cannot tuck large money out of reach in a trust account without being confident there will be more money coming in.

Yes. It is a fair assumption. Boiled down to simplest form, one would have Professor Ted saying to Mr. Lawton Hisp, "I know where there's more stuff and I know how to go get it."

Hisp would believe him. The proof had been rolling in. How much would Tom Collier have been told?

A new question area for the witness on the stand.

—You and your friend searched the *Trepid* as soon as you heard Lewellen had been killed?

—Yes, sir.

—And found nothing?

—Nothing at all. We gave it a good try.

—Did anyone else conduct a search?

—Pidge. And Howie Brindle.

—Did you recall anyone else?

—Not exactly.

—That is not a responsive answer.

—I mean that I have secondhand knowledge that Mr. Hisp and somebody else from the bank came and inspected the *Trepid* and, I guess for estate purposes, inventoried everything aboard her that wasn't fastened down. It took most of a day. I don't know whether you could call that a search.

—The bank and Mr. Collier were, to the best of your knowledge, coexecutors of the estate?

—Meyer told me they were. So did Pidge.

—Now then, Mr. McGee, I wish to ask you a question which your life experience should qualify you to answer. I am asking for a subjective impression. Let us assume that there was some object, or box containing several objects, of great potential value to the sole legatee under the terms of Dr. Lewellen's last will and testament. Let us assume that this object or objects were missing at the time of death and the whereabouts not yet known to the legatee. In previous testimony we have established that the legatee and her friends made inquiry as to the whereabouts of the object or objects, and that these queries were directed to Mr. Hisp, if not to both Mr. Hisp and Mr. Collier. Assuming that Mr. Hisp and Mr. Collier were aware of the existence of such object or objects, and assuming that both men had reason to believe in the high value placed on such object or objects, and knowing that such object or objects have not surfaced to be listed in the inventory of the estate for tax purposes, do you, sir, based upon your personal observations and experience, believe that Mr. Hisp and Mr. Collier acted in a fashion consistent with the assumptions and the facts I have related to you?

—That's very interesting.

—The witness will answer the question, and then the

Court will permit the witness to expand upon his answer.

—Thank you, your Honor. No. They haven't reacted the way they should. As coexecutors, I would think they would be churning around really beating the shrubbery to find Professor Ted's research diary and his support materials. But from first- and second- and third-hand information and impressions, I got the idea they just went through the motions. They took what was in trust and what was not in trust, and went through probate procedure for what was not in trust, and used the cash reserve for taxes, and . . . settled the estate. They both had to know Pidge was very concerned about her father's dream book not turning up. No action was taken to dig up any hidden assets.

—Your Honor, may the prosecution ask the witness to speculate?

—Proceed, Counselor. If defense objects, I will make my ruling at that time.

—Mr. McGee, you have stated that the actions of Mr. Hisp and Mr. Collier were inconsistent with the assumptions and the facts in my previous question. Would you now address yourself to telling the Court what, in your observation and experience, would be a set of facts which would, as background, render the actions and attitudes of Mr. Hisp and Mr. Collier consistent?

—I object, your Honor! The witness is not qualified to—

—Counselor, inasmuch as this is a pretrial hearing based upon a motion to dismiss, I am inclined to allow more latitude in examination than would be the case were a jury in the box. Overruled. Answer the question, Mr. McGee.

—Well, I would say that if they knew where the stuff was, if they had found it, or if Ted had given it to one of them before he slid under the truck, then they would act the way they acted. It would be consistent.

—The defense may cross-examine the witness.

—Thank you. Mr. McGee, I beg your indulgence in letting me pursue the same line of questioning a bit further.

—Go right ahead.

—Is it reasonable to assume that a man of unblemished reputation, a Vice-President and Trust Officer of a bank, would conspire with a prominent local attorney to defraud a young woman out of a part of her inheritance?

—I don't know how reasona—

—Just answer the question.

—Yes.

—You think that is a reasonable assumption?

—It has happened before, all over the world, right? How many hundred times? So it *can* happen.

—And you are saying it happened again?

—No. I don't know what happened. Maybe they had some kind of deal with Ted. Maybe they're not supposed to tell Pidge about it. Maybe they don't really buy this idea of treasure maps. All I know is they didn't act like two men who know something valuable is missing. That's all I ever said.

—During your previous testimony, you stated that it was your belief that there was more than one set of these documents.

—It just seems reasonable there had to be.

—Would you tell the Court, please, why there *had* to be?

—Because my friend, Ted Lewellen, was a finikin.

—A what?

—Counselor, the witness is using an obsolete word to describe a person who is almost unnecessarily and compulsively fussy about even the most trivial details.

—Oh. Thank you, your Honor. Would the witness care to speculate about how many copies of the valuable documents exist, and where they might be?

—No. I would not care to speculate.

Mansfield Hall's office was in one of the older buildings in downtown Miami. There were a bank, brokerage house, airline offices and shopping mall on the ground floor. The eleven remaining floors seemed stacked with law firms.

He was in the middle, on the sixth floor, at the end of a corridor. It was a clever location. One could not help but associate him in more areas than geography with the suites one passed, with the handsome paneled doors and the bronze nameplates. The older buildings have the higher ceilings. They have windows which can be opened. The thick walls provide more privacy. The paneling is made out of boards, not out of woodgrain thin as a fingernail, epoxied to fiberboard.

I pushed the door open at five of four. The woman behind the secretarial desk was very close to being Mrs. Archie Bunker until she opened her mouth. A very British accent. I was expected. One moment, please. She slipped through a door, reopened it seconds later and stood aside, holding it. I went in and she closed it. Her office was very bright. His was dark and large, draperies closed, lamps turned on. Leather books and leather chairs. Gleam of silver, of oiled rosewood and polished mahogany.

He was a small, round-headed man, with thick white hair and a thick white mustache, both carefully brushed and tended. He had a very ruddy face, a bulb nose, bulging blue eyes with sandy lashes. He came around the desk to meet me, all cordiality. He was about the size of the average twelve-year-old boy, and he wore splendid tweeds, immaculate linen, a small polka-dot tie, white dots on a blue that matched his eyes.

He waved me into a deep chair and went back behind his desk, and I noticed that his black leather judge's chair was on a platform. Had he meant it to give him more presence, he would not have come around the desk. So it was for the sake of convenience.

The more common conversational hiatus breakers,

while one selects the right word, are "eh," "ah," "er," and "um." His space filler was "haw."

"Mr. McGee, I do . . . I do wish that after we talked on the phone I'd been able to . . . haw . . . intercept you before you took the trouble to come here to my office. We all seem to spend far too much of our lives dashing about on superfluous errands."

"Mr. Hayes told me to tell you he is worried about the lack of control on the expense factor. He has substantial operating capital, but not unlimited."

"It's quite . . . haw . . . academic at this point, I fear. Directly after you telephoned me, I got in touch with my principals in this matter to determine the flexibility of their stipulations so that I could relay to you the acceptable bounds of negotiation. I had previously reported my conversation with Mr. Hayes, of course. It is their . . . haw . . . feeling at this time that they wish to leave the door open with Seven Seas, but that certain other affairs require such intensive supervision it would be best to . . . haw . . . postpone the negotiations until some future date more convenient to them. They regret any inconvenience they may have caused Mr. Hayes, or yourself."

"Mr. Hayes will be very disappointed."

"Really! He didn't seem all that impressed with the proposition."

"He's a cautious man."

"The world makes us all more cautious with every passing year."

"Mr. Hall, could you tell me when they might be willing to reopen negotiations?"

"They did not say. I wouldn't hazard a guess."

"Maybe there was something in the selection of words or the tone of voice that might clue you as to whether it would be, for example, two months or two years."

"I might have been able to draw some . . . haw . . . useful inference, Mr. McGee, had I been in direct communication. But this has all been through their representative."

"Who would that be?"

"Someone they trust to remain discreet, I should imagine."

His expression was one of impassive, everlasting amiability. You get to know the breed after you've met a few of them. The professional negotiators. There is absolutely no way to irritate them, entrap them or confuse them. They cannot be bribed, bullied, frightened or cajoled. They are as unreadable as master poker players must be. They have no little nervous tics which could reveal mood. They do not smoke and they do not drink, and they seem almost independent of all plumbing facilities. They don't sweat, wilt or yawn. They merely sit across a table from you for thirty-six or forty-eight hours, looking tidy and pleasant and inquisitive, until finally you say the hell with it, and give them what they asked for in the first place.

I should have thanked him and left. But there is no law against chunking pebbles against Stone Mountain.

"On second thought, maybe Mr. Hayes will feel relieved." I waited for some response. He just sat there, amiably, waiting for me to say something he could respond to. "One aspect of this bothered him. He wondered why the person owning these documents would have to trade fifty percent of the net return for the chance of recovery. That made him wonder if there might be . . . some slight flaw in the title to the documents."

He looked appreciative. "Most . . . haw . . . delicately said, sir. The question of ownership of notes copied from documents in the public domain raises interesting legal points. So does the question of the value one could assign to such research. A treasure map purporting to describe the location of one million dollars in doubloons has not the same status as a certified check for one million dollars.

I believe that the reason for covert dealings is probably far more explicable on . . . haw . . . an emotional basis."

"I don't think I know what you mean."

"One day a man of the cloth sneaked out the back door of his church on a very holy day, changed his clothing and went to a golf course and played one round all by himself. God focused his attention on the sinner, and a young ignorant angel watched over God's shoulder. The ignorant angel watched and saw the sinner sink a three wood for an eagle two on the first hole, hit a long iron into the cup for an eagle three on the second hole, make a hole in one on the third. Following the same pattern, he finished the first nine holes in twenty strokes, and as he teed off on the tenth and hit his drive three hundred and seventy yards down the middle, the angel cried out, 'God, he is a sinner! Why are you rewarding him?' 'Rewarding him?' God rumbled. 'Think about it. Who can he tell?' "

I saw what Mansfield Hall was driving at. I grinned and nodded.

He said, "In our society treasure-hunting is a sign of . . . haw . . . immaturity and unreliability. Captain Kidd. Yo-ho-ho. Walk the plank, et cetera, et cetera. Perhaps the fellow holds public office, or is in some fiduciary position, or is a bishop or a college president, or a market analyst." He stood up, and the eight-inch platform made him look of average height as he leaned across the desk to extend his small hand. "Tell Mr. Hayes that should I ever be contacted again on this matter, I shall . . . haw . . . most probably get in touch with him."

I made very good time from his office to the elevator, to the ground floor, and to a phone booth. I got Tom Collier's office number from information. To avoid going through the coin-slot routine, I made the short-distance pay call to his office on my GT credit card. I got the switchboard and asked for Tom Collier. A girl said, "Mr. Collier's office."

I hoped I could do it without the usual practice session with the tape recorder. I said, "Forgive me, my dear, but I have . . . haw . . . recalled a matter I forgot to mention when I telephoned Mr. Collier earlier."

"Oh, Mr. Hall, I'm sorry, but Mr. Collier left about ten minutes ago, and he won't be back in the office until the second. That's next Wednesday. Is it really important?"

"No, no. Just something . . . haw . . . incidental to what we discussed earlier. Perhaps not worth . . . haw . . . bothering him at all. Thank you, my dear."

Feeling of triumph as I left the phone booth. I suppose it is childlike to give oneself a small round of applause. Especially since it was a victory within the area where I should reasonably expect to do pretty well, after spending years peeling back the layers of human guile and chicanery, an optimistic gourmet at work on the endless artichoke, ever searching for the good part underneath.

I could not have written down the reasons, one, two, three, why I grabbed at this possible way of linking Mansfield Hall to Tom Collier. A man wading the grass flats does not know why he drops the lure halfway between mangrove thicket and sandbar, but the snook comes wolfing out of the water, jaws agape to take it.

Lawyers have a little edge in personal negotiation, as they can always imply—or let the other fellow infer—they are acting in the interests of a client. When a new stipulation is presented, the attorney can gain time and psychological advantage by saying he will have to refer it back to his nonexistent client.

In this particular instance, Tom Collier did himself a little harm, perhaps, by making Mansfield Hall believe that Collier was representing someone else. That diminished Mansfield Hall's habit of caution, believing there was an intervening layer. One can assume that if Hall knew Collier was the principal, all contact would have been made much more carefully. These are the days of the bug, of the wire man, of circuitry smaller than a housefly.

I did not know where and how to reach into this funny little cup of worms, and so I decided to take it back to Meyer for consultation.

10

I didn't get back to Meyer's hospital room until eight thirty. He was sitting up in bed, glowering down at the chess set on the tray table.

"Aha! Frank Hayes won, I see."

"Shut up, just as a special favor."

I stood by the bed and studied the board. It was the beginning of the middle game. Sicilian defense.

"I went wrong right here," he said. "Eleventh move. Took the knight with the knight."

"And so after the exchange he checked you with his queen on rook five?"

"Smart-ass!"

"Should have moved your queen to queen two before you took the knight."

"I *know* that already. Look, do you want to play a game or stand around making redundant comments?"

"I want to play a slightly different game. I need to make some kind of move."

I told him the whole thing. He asked questions. I told him my reasoning. And Meyer began to tug at the loose ends.

"I had an immediate liking and respect for Lawton Hisp," he said. "He knows his job. He *knows* he knows his job. I have an idea that his trust department turns a pretty good dime for the bank. When I was up there, after Pidge told Hisp to give me any information I asked for, I was impressed by how crisp and businesslike that whole floor is, but with a flavor of people liking what they do."

"You'd rather take aim at Tom Collier?"

"For a trivial reason. I'm ashamed of this brand of illogic."

"Such as?"

"He's a very agreeable man. He's amusing. You've met him."

"Get to it."

"Remember when the *Salamah* was up for sale?"

I remembered. She was a ketch, Abaco-built, one of the biggest I've ever seen built on Abaco, and the most graceful and lovely. A doctor had owned her. Meyer remembered. It is an accident that almost happens frequently. I don't know why it doesn't happen more often. They had anchored late one afternoon in the Berry Islands and gone swimming off the ketch after putting the boarding ladder over the side. The tide and wind shifted. The doctor dived without taking a look first. The dinghy had swung around. It was tied to a stern cleat on too long a line. He dived into it and broke his skull and his back and was dead before the float plane could get to them.

"Anyway," Meyer said, "Tom Collier was handling the estate, and after the *Salamah* had been brought back here, I was walking by one day and spoke to Tom and admired it, and he asked me to come aboard and see if I wanted to buy it. I told him it was way out of my reach, but I went aboard. Beautiful. He was waiting for the boat broker, who was late for an appointment, so he was just killing time. You know those country-boy mannerisms of his, the thin crooked black cigars and the kitchen matches. He was saying he thought of buying her for himself at a fair market value, but decided he was too busy to use her as often as she ought to be used. He sighed and took out one of those cigars and looked around, then wiped his kitchen match along the varnished rail. A beautiful varnish job. The match made a scratch line and then a gray place as big as a quarter where it lit. He watched me as he lit the cigar, the match flame cupped in his hands. It was a challenge, the way he did it. He wanted me to say something. He was expressing some kind of contempt for people like you and me, Travis, who live on boats, who cherish boats. He had something to say, but I didn't give him the opening to say it. It's a damned small thing. I shouldn't dislike the entire man for one observed act, but I do."

"And now I do too."

He smiled. "So we're both strange. What's a streak on varnish? Five minutes to fix it. I went back and made sure it was gone. That was about a week later. Howie had done a pretty good job on it."

"Howie? By God, you're right! He *was* living aboard her, caretaking her until she was sold. Was he working for the broker or for Tom Collier?"

"I have no idea."

"Was that the first job he had around the marina?"

"As far as I know."

"Could he have been working as crew for the doctor?"

"I just don't know. It's possible."

We were working away on our own special form of triangulation. In another context, for another purpose, it would be called gossip. We are all concerned with the strange activities of the human animal. We are all aware of how coincidence can lead to warped assumptions. And we all keep looking for the very worst—from the couple next door to Watergate.

"He's a damned likable brute," Meyer said, echoing what I was thinking. "Comfortable. Undemanding. A listener who never butts in to tell some epic hero story of his own, who laughs in the right places, and not too loudly or long."

"Pidge wanted to know if he was trying to kill her."

"So you told me."

"I made her believe it was a little touch of paranoia."

"So you told me."

"But God *damn* it, Meyer—"

"Whoa. Settle down. If he wanted to, just how many chances do you think he's had in over fourteen months of cruising?"

"That was part of my basis for believing she was wrong."

"Well?"

"Who is Howard Brindle?"

"If that's not a rhetorical question, and if that is your starting point, I agree. But you're not going to find out tonight. The chess board is over there."

By the time Nurse Ella Marie Morse came on duty to look after him during the hours of the night, I had the game won. He had slowly worked me back into a cramped position, pressing me back against my castled king, smothering my queen side, but he had failed to see a sacrifice that gave me a very damaging knight fork and put me a piece ahead. I was trading him down to an end-game defeat, and he resigned when the nurse arrived, saying something about possibly the fever had damaged some brain cells after all.

Before she herded me out, Meyer told me he didn't expect to see me again until I had some hard information on good ol' Howie.

A big raw Saturday wind killed what was left of the strange untimely heat wave. It was the first day of the extra-long year-end weekend, meaning that offices were

closed and I could not use the logical starting place, the
detailed forms which have to be placed on file with every
little red-tape empire.

I had written down what I knew about him. It was very
skimpy. He didn't talk about himself often and never
said very much. Raised by grandparents, I think. Ohio,
Indiana, Iowa. One of those states. His grandfather retired and they moved to Bradenton, Florida. Howie was
about ten? Maybe older. Became a high-school jock.
Fullback. Straight ahead for the tough yard and a half on
third down. Partial scholarship to the University of
Florida. Out of the athletic budget. How long ago? They
shifted him to defensive tackle. Second string. Got to play
in only three out of nine games his senior year. Disciplinary problems, he'd said. I'd inferred he broke training
now and then, nothing worth spelling out. Wanted the
pro scene, but nobody picked him in the draft. The Dolphins took a long hard look at him in training camp. Not
enough hustle, apparently, according to what he said. They
let him go. Three years ago? Longer? Then a blank until
he showed up at Bahia Mar. Knows how to handle himself
around boats and the sea. Drinks beer. Doesn't smoke.
Six four, two seventy, looks sloppy but is in good shape.
Brown eyes, receding hairline, blond hair long. Voice
pitched slightly high.

I took a packet of fresh fifties out of my stash. I
studied my little collection of improvised business cards.
Title Research Associates looked good enough, and there
were six crisp clean ones left.

Her name, I learned at Bahia Mar, was Lois Harron.
Evidently she'd been able to afford to keep the house. It
was on one of those canals southwest of Pier 66, a long
low white structure with Bahamian gray trim, behind a
screen of shrubbery which would someday hide it entirely
from the asphalt road in front. There were eight vehicles
in the driveway, parked in random array on the white

river pebbles. A couple of vans, a couple of VW's, a camper body on a pickup, a couple of road-worn station wagons and a shiny Toyota. The wheels of the young. The high-performance cars are dead. A young man in Dade County has to pay twelve hundred dollars a year in insurance premiums to buy the basic legal coverage for a high-performance car, and the law says he can't get plates or inspection stickers without proof of insurance. The young used to be the meat of the market, and without their demand, Detroit can't make toys for the middle-aged role players, which is perhaps a blessing to all concerned.

I punched the bell three times before a brutally loud vacuum cleaner was turned off. Then I could hear yelps and sloshing from a pool area out back somewhere. A slender, tall woman with dark hair came to the door. She wore faded old stretch pants and a tired old T-shirt on which appeared pink ghost-writing, almost entirely gone, saying HAWAII FIVE-O. She was barefoot and she had a streak of dirt across her forehead, and she looked irritated, and she also looked very familiar to me.

She frowned and smiled, and pushed the screen door open and said, "Where, where, where? Hmmm. Bahia Mar. A year ago. What was the name of that big cruiser? *'Bama Lady?'*"

"*'Bama Gal.* The Alabama Tiger's lair."

"Sho nuff. Jesus! A year ago, I guess, but the memories are vivid. And I think a bunch of us came aboard your houseboat. Belated apologies for that invasion, friend. We were not all the way tracking. Come in, come in. Total confusion. My maid died. Isn't that hell? She didn't quit. She didn't get fired. She died. Which leaves me with mixed emotions, and I will be *damned* if I can find anybody who isn't a total dumb-dumb. What *is* your name? I can't come up with it."

"Travis McGee."

"Of *course!* I'm dreary about names. Excuse the racket. My only chick is home on Christmas vacation and I wish the dear girl wasn't quite as popular. *Look* at them out there! Wall to wall energy. It makes me tired to watch them. Get you a drink? What can I do for you, Travis?"

"I'm doing an odd job for a friend. Odd meaning maybe strange. He's doing research on the kinds of people who go around the world in small boats."

"Believe me, I am not his kind of person."

"Neither am I, Lois. But he was questioning me about the background of Howie Brindle, and I said I thought he worked for you and your husband, and he wondered if I'd ask you for your impressions of him."

She was in a good strong north light. Her face tightened just a little bit, and there were some rapid eye movements, a small pursing of the lips. "Is Howie going on some brave adventure?"

"He's somewhere in the Pacific, with wife."

"Oh, yes. That girl who inherited the *Trepid* when her father was killed. Some idiot name. Pooch?"

"Pidge."

"My dear man, the *Trepid* is hardly a small dangerous boat. It was built to cross oceans. And being with wife is not being alone, one would hope."

"I'm sorry. This isn't the epic-adventure kind of thing. It's more sociological, about the kinds of people who seek solitude when everybody else is after togetherness. A think piece."

"Can I get you that drink? No? Then sit patiently while I fix myself one."

She was back in five minutes, hair brushed, mouth freshened, smudge gone from her forehead.

She carried a colorless drink on ice. "Hatch," she said and sipped before she sat down across from me. "Sure. Howie worked for us, crewing aboard the *Salamah*."

"For how long?"

"Let me see. It was the longest vacation we ever took. It was just about the only vacation we ever took. Fred did umpty operations a day, getting the decks cleared. And he begged and bullied his best friends into taking the load while we were gone. Let me see. Howie came aboard at Spanish Wells. We'd been in the islands for two weeks, because I remember it took two weeks for me to realize Fred wasn't getting much vacation trying to run the boat by himself. I'm an idiot about those things. So that means Howie was aboard for just about six weeks. And then he brought her back by himself, of course, after Fred—after the accident."

"He was in Spanish Wells looking for work?"

"No. Not the way that sounds. There was a couple from Charleston in a cruiser, and Howie was working for them. Actually, the woman approached us about hiring him. She said he was an absolute jewel. There wasn't anything he wouldn't do, and he respected your privacy and all. But her husband was having angina too bad to keep on cruising, and they were going to fly back home as soon as he felt up to it, and that left Howie at loose ends. It was an answer to prayer. We interviewed Howie and we both liked him a lot. So he moved into the crew cabin forward that same day, and Fred started showing him all that he should know about the *Salamah*. He really worked out fine. We stopped having all those narrow escapes we were having when Fred was running it alone. And he scrubbed and helped with the cooking and all. If you mean competence, I think Howie could probably sail around the world in an old bathtub. He seems to know when the wind is going to change before the wind knows. He's so huge you're conscious of how his weight tilts the boat. But he's so light on his feet he doesn't seem . . . ponderous."

"So he was there when your husband had his accident?"

She raised the glass to her lips so deliberately I wondered if she was trying to buy time, and why. She took a deep swallow and said, "Whatever would that have to do with anything at all, Travis?"

"I'm just guessing, but I'd say that there'd be some relationship between how these deepwater people react to emergencies and their desire to get away from the world."

"He reacts beautifully."

"What happened? I mean where was he when it happened?"

"You have no idea how many times I told this, over two years ago, how many times a new official popped up and had to hear it all over again."

"I'm sorry. Forget it."

"It doesn't matter as much now as it did then. It so happened that Howie and I were both below. The three of us had been swimming. We were anchored just outside Little Harbor. It was a very calm sea. It was about three thirty in the afternoon. Both Howie and I heard this strange thumping sound. He ran up and as soon as he saw what had happened, he yelled to me. Fred was on his face in the dinghy with his legs trailing in the water. The dinghy had shipped some water. Somehow we got him up onto the deck and got shade over him. Howie got on the emergency frequency right away and pretty soon there was a doctor on the way in a seaplane, but Fred stopped breathing before the plane landed even. There was an investigation and all that. And I flew back in the same chartered plane with Tom Collier and with the body. Tom has been an absolute doll about everything. I don't know what I would have done without him."

"So you think that Howie Brindle would be a good person to sail around the world?"

"I guess so."

"Some reservations?"

"Not really. It's just that I thought people like that were great readers, and kept journals and did a lot of heavy thinking. Howie is just sort of a physical person. I don't think he really has much going on up here. You know? He's terribly pleasant, and he figures out the little problems, the best way to do things, but if you said to him, 'Howie, do you think there is a hereafter?' he would look sort of startled. I can tell you almost exactly what he would say. He'd say, 'Some people believe there is and some people believe there isn't. I guess there's no way to find out for sure.' "

"Do you feel you really got to know him?"

"You know as well as I do that six weeks aboard anything the size of the *Salamah* is no way to remain strangers. After Howie brought her back to Lauderdale, Tom asked me if I had any objection to Howie living aboard her and caretaking. I said none at all. I went down and removed the personal stuff, and Howie helped me load it all in the station wagon. Funny. I was so positive I wanted to sell her until the day she was sold. And then I was sorry."

The young were shrieking and yelping. She took her last sip of drink, looking at me across the rim of the empty glass. The ice chinked as she put the glass down. A handsome woman with the eyes of a gambler. I've got aces back to back, and I dare you to bet into them. Good smile lines.

She said, "I'd like to come see your houseboat some day when things aren't so drunk. I remember an absolutely gigantic shower stall, or did I dream it? *Much* too big for a boat."

"It's there. It's real." She was waiting for the definite invitation. No thanks, widow lady. With that figure and mouth, you can get all the safe, healthy fellows you want. I stood up. "Thanks for letting me bother you with these weird questions."

"It's okay. I needed a break. I hate cleaning the place. If I can't find somebody soon, I'm going to have to sell it before it works me to death."

"It's the right time of year to advertise in Boston or Chicago."

"You just may have something there. After school opens, I could fly up and interview applicants and bring the best one back. See you around the marina, Travis."

I went back to Bahia Mar to fill in a very troubling

blank in Brindle's history. Meyer had stimulated my memory to the point where I knew Howie had been aboard the *Salamah* until she was sold. But she was sold before Professor Ted was killed. So he would not have met Pidge until she came down from school when Ted died, and to meet her and to be available to give her a helping hand, he had to be living somewhere else in the marina complex.

The cold wet wind had swept the area fairly clean of both residents and tourists. The parking meters at the beach area stood like a small lonely forest of Martian flowers. Some young folk in wet suits were trying to find breakers to ride. They weren't breaking often. They were sliding in round and gray and slow, as if quieted by oil. The black suits are the last step in unisex. Out there with their boards they looked as neuter as black seals.

I checked out several neighborhoods before I came up with anything. Any big marina has neighborhoods. The charterboats, the rag bums, the fat cruiser crowd, the horsepower freaks, the round-the-worlders, the storekeepers, the staff.

Fat Jack Hoover was replacing a compressor aboard the *Miss Kitty,* the ornate top-heavy old single-screw mahogany yacht he captains for a crazy old lady from Duluth. She comes down once or twice a year for a week to ten days each time, bringing along a maid, a cook, three poodles and four friends. When she comes down, she wants to cruise up and down the Waterway, very slowly. She doesn't want any rocking and lurching, or any more noise than necessary. Fat Jack sends all the billing to a bank in Duluth. They pay with hardly ever a question.

He wiped his greasy paws on a ball of waste and sat on the crate the new compressor had been shipped in. "Now who would know the most about it would be Rine Houk."

"That sells yachts?"

"The very one. From the shape that Harron ketch was in while he was showing her, he come to believe

Howie was reliable, which is a rare thing especially lately, especially anywhere. Like with a house, it is a good thing to have somebody living on it when you are selling it, so the air isn't stale, the bugs stay hid, the bird shit gets wiped off the overhead. So what he does is make a deal, Howie moves onto that big son of a bitch of a thing out of Corpus Christi, that QM crash boat that was custom-made into a yacht, big old high-octane Packards in her, you couldn't blow fuel out a fire hose as fast as she'd suck. Ninety foot? A friggin' fiasco, that thing, what was the name on it? Weird. Oh. *Scroomall*. Big sacrifice sale at forty thou, but the way I looked at it, Howie agreeing, you'd have to pull the Packards and put in diesels, change the tanks, gearing, trim. Nineteen and forty-four it was built, and all as solid as you could expect with the owner trying to hammer it into pieces on any little ripple whenever he run it, so you would end up with seventy-five to eighty in it, conservative guess, and what do you have? Another freak PT conversion is what you have, roll you sick on a wet lawn. The owner got it this far with a new wife on her, just a kid she was, and she said enough, she wouldn't even go back onto the son of a bitch to get a toothbrush, so he put it up right then. Fahrhowser his name was, round bald fella with a voice to rattle the dish cupboards. There was work to do on it, so Howie got more pay, Rine Houk getting approval from Fahrhowser.

"I couldn't see any rich man getting stupid enough or drunk enough to buy that *Scroomall*. One day there was a girl on deck, one of those spindly saggy kind, long blond hair hanging, a face that if she was dead it would have a livelier expression on it, sorry old clothes like a ragbag. Turns out, talking to Howie, she's the daughter of this Fahrhowser, took off from school, she's broke and wants to stay aboard only don't tell the old man. He doesn't know what he should do. She must have moved in, because it was anyway a week later I saw them on the beach and didn't know it was the same girl for sure, because in a swim outfit you could see what was hid under those raggy clothes, and it was pretty nice. From how they were horsing around together it was clear to any fool she'd moved in all the way. What was her damn name? Susan. That's it. Not so long after that my crazy old lady come down from Duluth and I had to run up and down that damn Waterway for a week and a half. I disremember seeing Howie for a time, and then I seen him one day on the *Trepid,* helping out Pidge Lewellen. I stopped and asked him if somebody bought that *Scroomall* crock and he said not yet, he was still living aboard, and it hadn't even nearly been sold, as far as he could tell. I would guess that he stayed aboard that Texas boat until the wedding. Sometime later, one day that crock was gone, and you'd have to ask Rine Houk about what happened. And whyn't you go below and drag us up a pair of beers, McGee? It's a cold day for beer, but talking makes me sweaty."

For about fifteen seconds I didn't know I was talking to Rine Houk. It had been a year and more. The man I knew had a long head, bald on top, a cropped stubble of salt and pepper around the edges, glasses with big black frames.

When he called me by name I peered at him again. "Jesus Christ, Rine!" I said before I could stop myself.

He shook his head and sat down behind his desk at his big boatyard. "I know. I know. You should try wearing this goddamn thing in weather like we were having lately. Trav, it's like wearing a fur hat with ear flappers. The sweat comes apouring out from under it and runs down the inside of these wire glasses like you wouldn't believe. If I see myself far off in a store window and I squint up my eyes, I can almost believe that's a young fellow I'm seeing. Selling is a young man's game, Trav, and don't you forget it."

"Bullshit, Rine. How about Colonel Sanders and his greasy chicken?"

"I'm not exactly selling box lunches."

"Don't get huffy with me just because I don't like your hairpiece. We've never been great friends, Rine. But I like you. You are an honest man in a business where they are rare. I want to know a couple of things. Why that red-brown color like a setter dog?"

"That's the color my hair was when I had any."

"Do you sell boats from fifty feet away, or talking up close?"

"I sell them right across this desk."

"Have you got a young girl friend?"

"Me!"

"Are you looking for one?"

"Am I looking for a coronary?"

"Rine, somebody gave you a bad steer. Are you selling more yachts lately?"

"Business is generally rotten."

"Listen. I did not think of you as being young or old. I thought of you as being Rine Houk, the boat broker. I never especially thought of your face. But now I see your face underneath and between all that shiny hair, and your face looks so damn withered and old, I don't know whether to laugh or cry. You look silly, Rine. You look like you had bad judgment. You look desperate. I wouldn't buy a leaky skiff from anybody who looks the way you do right now."

"Get out of this office," he said, but he wouldn't look right at me.

"Rine," I said gently.

He took a deep breath and let it out. He blinked rapidly, and I saw the tears squeeze out of his eyes. He jumped up and went around the corner of his desk, bumping into it, and went into the bathroom off his office and pulled the door shut. I felt rotten. People make such strange evaluations of self. Why upset them? It's none of my business. I waited. And waited. And waited.

He came out, sans wig. He was back in the big glasses.

He didn't look at me. He sat on his heels in front of the executive icebox with the genuine cherrywood paneling. "Black Jack do you?" he asked.

"Fine. No mix. Just rocks."

He made the two drinks the same and made them heavy. He brought them to the desk. The intercom said, "Mr. Houk?"

"Yes, Mark."

"There's a Mister Mertz here who's interested in the Matthews fifty-two."

"So sell it to him."

"But you said—"

"Forget what I said. It's a beautiful thing for that money. Sell it to him."

He picked up his drink and gave it a little lift in my direction, then drank it down. He ran his hand over his bald head. "Had the old glasses in the cupboard in there."

"Handy to have a spare."

He hit the desk. "You don't know how *hard* it was, dammit, to all of a sudden one day start wearing that hair."

"I can imagine."

"No. You can't imagine. Jesus. All that wasted effort."

"Are you giving it up?"

"You told me what I already knew. Now I'm just another bald old fart. Feels good already. Thanks, Trav. Can I sell you . . . some kind of a leaky skiff?" He grinned and then blew his nose.

I asked him about the *Scroomall,* shocking him for a moment with the misapprehension I might be interested in it. He remembered the boat, but he had to look at his files to remember what had happened to it. The owner had finally sent two men over from Corpus Christi to take the boat back to Texas to try to sell it there. The men had to turn back twice before they got it running properly.

"And Howie Brindle worked out well?"

"I wish I still had him. I wish I had one round dozen

Howie Brindles. He didn't break his back looking for things to do, but when you told him, they got done. And if he'd put his mind to it, he could have sold boats."

"Was it Tom Collier who recommended him?"

"It could have been. Or Mrs. Harron, or both of them."

"Never any problems with him?"

Rine tilted his head. "What are you being paid to do?"

"Funny question."

"I guess so. Fahrhowser had to have money to back his bad judgment in buying that old crash boat. He could still be looking for his daughter."

"Susan? The one who stayed on the *Scroomall* with Howie?"

"Not *with* Howie. Not that way. He actually loaned her some money to get home on. He told the guys who came looking for her, and he told me the same thing, he made a deal with her. He'd let her come aboard and get rested up provided she'd go home, no arguments. He said he was seriously thinking about calling her people anyway, but decided not to. I guess she never made it back to Texas. And if she hasn't by now, she never will."

"Maybe she's home. I wouldn't know."

"Oh. Then why are you asking all about Howie?"

"I'm conducting a survey. Fahrhowser's first name is?"

"Jefferson."

I thanked him. As I got into my car I looked through the show window into his office and saw Rine Houk standing rubbing his head and looking at himself in a wall mirror. He brought himself to attention. He still looked damned old, either way.

I got back to the *Flush* at three thirty, and after I had made a big sandwich and eaten half of it, I looked at the map in the front of the phone book and dialed information for Area 512, and asked for Corpus Christi information, the home number of Jefferson Fahrhowser, F as in February, A as in April, H as in Hudson River, R as in Railroad—Fahrhowser.

I direct-dialed it and got a woman with a drunk voice. She had a lot of slurring range, most of it baritone. I wanted to talk to Jeff and she said I had to mean Jeff senior because Jeff junior was in Cuba or some other goddamn commie hideout, and if I just happened to mean Daddy Jeff, then I was shit out of luck because about six months ago, give or take a week, his heart blew up like a baked potato you forgot to stick a fork into before you put it in the oven, son of a bitch was dead before he hit the floor, and besides that, I was slowing up a great pool party and tequila contest, which I could come over and join if I needed some laughs. I said I was in Florida and it would take too long, and she said this had the look of one of those parties that would go right on through the end of this year and into the next one, and she said she was Bonnie Fahrhowser, the grieving widow lady.

I said that I was looking for a line on Susan, the wandering daughter, and where could I get in touch. She said she wished she could get back all the money Daddy Jeff had spent in that jackass search for that dreary girl. "And you wanna know the worst, Florida boy, the very bitter goddamn end? There is one big slug of dough all locked up in an escrow account, and we've petitioned the probate court and so on, but she can't be declared dead for years and years and years. Jesus! Any fool could tell you that dim little slut was an OD years ago, buried someplace by the taxpayers. I got to get back in the game. It's Zen water polo. You play it with an imaginary ball. You can still make the party, friend. The best parts haven't even started to get warmed up yet."

As I walked around finishing my sandwich, I tried to guess what Meyer would tell me. Not to walk while you eat. It makes crumbs and you step on them.

I opened the shallow drawer under the phone desk and pawed through the junk in there. It is where I too often empty my pockets. I quickly found the envelope Pidge had forced upon me. "Take it away," she said. "I don't want to throw them away, and I don't want them around where I can look at them and get strange again. Keep them, darling, and we can look at them again when we're old and gray."

Twelve square prints, twelve negatives in strips of three. I sat where the light was strong and good, and studied the first nine prints, one at a time. I knew that waterfront area of St. Croix. And it was a nice trimaran from Houston. Howie was in two of them. Smiling. Huge. Happy. And then the last three. The snapshots my Lou Ellen had taken of the imaginary stowaway, Miss Joy Harris. Empty forward deck of the *Trepid*. Empty hatch cover. No one standing at the rail.

I noticed that the color values weren't quite as good in the last three. Probably due to the direction of the light. Automatic cameras were never meant for taking pictures in the light. Overexposure bleaches the emulsion out, fades the color values.

Then I realized it wasn't really overexposure. It was more of a kind of yellow-green cast over the whole print.

Suddenly I was aware of the bump, bump, bump of my heart, and of coldness in the pit of my belly. My hands shook as I tried to put the prints back into the envelope. I dropped half of them, and after I finally got things organized, I headed for the phone.

11

I KNEW Gabe Marchman would be home, simply because he never goes anywhere. He had the sense to buy some so-called ranchland west of Lauderdale years ago and keep five acres of it, and put his house smack in the middle of the five acres. He was a combat photographer, one of the great ones, until a booby trap smashed his legs into a poor grade of hamburger and put him on crutches for life. He and his Chinese-Hawaiian wife, Doris, have seven kids, six horses, uncounted dogs, cats, geese, ducks, all living in a noisy and peaceable kingdom. He has a photolab almost as big as the main house. He does experimental work, and he does problem assignments for large fees. He is the most sour-acting happy man I know.

Doris came out of the house as I got out of the car. She said, "He's very angry with you, and you really have to stay for barbecue, Travis. He loves to talk to you. Talk and talk and solve all the problems of the world."

"I should stay because he's angry?"

"Because like I heard him say to you on the telephone, you never come around unless you have a problem."

"It's strange, you know? I really relish coming here. I like to be with you two. What happens?"

She has that lovely matte Chinese complexion, without flaw, and looks more like a sister than a mother to her eldest daughter, age thirteen. "What happens? We all waste our days doing dreary things, Trav, instead of the things we want to do. You will stay and eat with us? Wonderful! Let's see how Gabe is doing."

We walked around the big house to the back garden. Gabe was chugging the length of the new pool, getting almost all the impetus from his powerful arms. He paused and held up three fingers.

"Three more laps only," Doris said. "It's best he finishes the whole forty at one time."

"Is it helping?"

"Oh, yes. For the first time, this year, he's been almost without pain. Poor lamb. He so hates exercise."

Soon he clambered out, pulled himself up, shouldered himself into his terry robe, and leaned against the step railing to dry his face and hair. Then he came swinging nimbly over to us on his aluminum crutches.

He stared hard at me as he sat down at the glass-topped terrace table. "Well, what do you know!" he said.

"That's a weird greeting."

"There was an edge to your voice on the phone. I wondered if it showed in person. It does. So, whatever your problem, it's more personal than professional."

"Darling!" Doris said sharply.

"It's okay," I said. "It's okay if Gabe Marchman reads me. He's read a lot of faces in a lot of bad situations."

"It happens in the eyes," he said. "And something about the tilt of the head and the shape of the mouth. Mostly in the eyes, though."

"Somebody very important to me could be in a very bad situation. I don't know. It depends on what you tell me. I almost don't want to ask you."

"Do we go into the lab?"

"Maybe you won't have to. Here. A roll of twelve exposures, Kodacolor, shot on an inexpensive Instamatic. Tell me anything you want to tell me about them."

He slipped them out of the envelope and dealt them out on the plate glass like a game of solitaire. I watched him separate the three of the empty forward deck of the *Trepid* and put them in a row of their own.

Next he turned the nine prints face down. In a few moments I saw what he was doing. It irritated me that I had not figured out something so simple. The paper had a pattern on the back, the word "Kodak" over and over, imprinted in diagonal rows. He worked by trial and error until finally he had the nine prints all in a row, with the trademark matching at every edge. Next he tried to find even one of the three greenish ones which would fit at either end of the strip of nine. None would fit. He found that two of the greenish ones matched. But the third would not fit on either end of the short strip of two. Only then did he examine the negatives. He turned all the prints face up, in the same order. He matched them up with the negatives, which were in strips of three. He gave the most intensive examination to the strip which related to the three prints of the empty foredeck.

He leaned back in the white iron chair, shrugged and said, "All I can tell you is that the prints come from at least two separate rolls and possibly three. If I had to bet, I would say two rolls. This shift toward the greens and yellows indicates that the film, before exposure, either in the film package or in the camera, was subjected to too much heat. Probably when in the camera. That's how it usually happens. The other nine are from a roll that didn't get too hot prior to exposure. I am guessing two rolls because the degree of shift seems to be identical, on these two taken in sequence and on this one. This one is a stranger. At first glance it seems to be a print from this end negative on this strip of three, but if you look at the top of the negative and the top of the print, you see that the print covers one support of the rail that the negative doesn't. I would say that whoever developed and printed these runs a small operation. He's a little slow or a little stingy about changing his chemicals. And you can see that the prints were clipped apart by hand, probably on a small cutting board. Here is one where someone made a false start, backed off, and got it centered better between the two prints. That's all they tell me. And I can see that it isn't what you want to hear."

"No. It isn't what I want to hear."

He looked at the front of the envelope, hand-stamped with the name of the establishment. He read it aloud. "Pierre Joliecouer, Rue de la Trinité. Fort-de-France. Martinique. Photographic services and supplies. What haunts you, McGee?"

"You might as well be a hauntee too. A man and a woman are cruising the islands, alone on a motor sailer. At a port the man smuggles a transient girl aboard. I don't know how he hoped to keep her a secret. Maybe he didn't give a damn. The stowaway comes up through the forward hatch to sneak some sunshine. The wife sees her and makes a record of it. Three pictures. The stowaway sees her taking the third and last one. She ducks below. She tells the man. Meanwhile the wife takes the film out of the camera and hides it in a safe place aboard. When the wife is asleep the man filches her camera and drops a cartridge of film in it and takes a full roll, twelve shots, of the empty forward deck from several probable angles. At Fort-de-France he manages to follow her—or maybe there are not too many places where you can get color film developed—and takes his roll to the same place. I would guess he uses money to persuade the proprietor to rush the processing of the two rolls. Maybe he says he wants to play a harmless joke on his wife. He returns to the shop and sorts out the prints and negatives. He removes the pictures of the stowaway and substitutes pictures which show roughly the same area, but empty, of course. He makes one mistake, as you pointed out, in matching negatives to prints. He leaves the prints there for his wife to pick up."

"I don't feel haunted yet," Gabe said.

"You see, he had already told his wife that she had imagined the girl. They had a scene about the stowaway. He said no girl had ever been aboard at all."

"Oh, dear," said Doris in a small voice.

"And he even dropped a raft into the sea and paddled away and let his wife search every inch of the boat, and there was no girl, and they had not been anywhere near land since she had taken the pictures of the girl."

"Now I feel haunted," Gabe said. "That is very nasty."

"I am a very sound and logical and all-wise person," I told them. "So when the wife called to me for help I flew out to Hawaii and looked at these pictures and convinced her that she had been hallucinating."

"I would say that you should get back to her in a hurry," Doris told me.

"That is a very sound idea. Except that right now she is somewhere south southwest of Hawaii in that very same motor sailer with that very same wonderful guy."

Doris's hand was on my arm at once. A good gesture of comfort. "Oh, my dear," she said. "How really foul. He has to be quite mad."

"Where are they headed?" Gabe asked.

"Pago Pago, with an ETA of Thursday, January tenth. Twelve days from now. She's going to break up with him. Or has broken up, whatever you want to call it. She's helping him take the boat down there because he has a buyer for it."

"And she is very important to you?" Doris asked.

I tried a smile which probably looked like the best efforts of a skull. "She's very rich and she can cook. She's too young for me. She says we're for keeps. I've been fighting the idea every way in the book."

"Wait a minute," Gabe said. "They took the boat all the way from Martinique to Hawaii? Just the two of them?"

"Yes."

"Why is she in any more danger now than she was then?"

"She was in danger then," I said. I told them about the two other incidents. "I've been trying to figure it out," I said. "Let's say, just for the hell of it, that Howie Brindle is a total flip, and he knew when he was marrying her that he might kill her. What if they took off from Lauderdale together and three days later he arrives in Nassau saying she fell overboard? It would be one big loud dirty news story. The authorities and the news people would start unraveling his background."

"Howie Brindle!" Doris said. "What a marvelously ordinary name that is."

"And he never met a man who didn't like him. Dammit, he is a big cheerful likable guy."

"What about his background?" Gabe asked.

"I haven't really begun to dig, and I've come up with two possible kills, not counting the stowaway."

"For money?" he asked.

"I don't think there has to be very much reason. Mostly it would be a case of opportunity, plus some kind of minor annoyance. He's quick and powerful and sly. I don't think he's clever. I'd say a clever man would have gotten this set of pictures back from his wife after they'd had the desired effect on her."

"To make her think she was losing her mind?"

"To make her tell a few friends she thought she was losing her mind. The way she told me. And he can tell people how worried he is about her. Maybe this is the first time he ever tried to plan something out. By the time something fatal happens to her, he is going to be able to point back to all the months they had together, nearly a year and a half of cruising the oceans, before she did herself in. And there are friends to step forward and say that she has been getting very, very strange. Maybe always before, he killed strangers. And there wasn't any real gain. But this time it is the best part of a million dollars. So he has to be careful. I have the feeling that he doesn't really feel anything very much. He cries easily. He might be one of the most plausible liars in the world."

Doris said, "Can't you get them by radio or something? Won't ships see them? Or airplanes?"

Gabe said, "You are a very nice girl, honey. Let me tell you how big that ocean is. Several wars ago a lot of airplanes, a lot of ships, a lot of people on islands and on radio watch tried for weeks to locate a whole *fleet* of warships. Oh, and a lot of submarines were hunting too. It was located finally by accident. An old tin goose was way off course, going from here to there, and happened to see it. And a fleet, honey, is a very distinctive-looking thing. It covers several square miles of ocean. One motor sailer is something else. There are hundreds of little inter-island craft out there, under sail. But you can fly across ten times without ever spotting one. If you can track down a radio contact, and if the vessel gave its location and you know where it is going, it is possible to find it, if you are standing by with a long-range search plane."

"There'd be no reason for the *Trepid* to give a position unless they were in trouble," I said.

Silence at the round glass table. Gabe squinted at the bright hazy sky. The old instincts of the newsman were at work. "Coming into port alone would be bad," he said. "If a man says his wife fell or jumped overboard, my first guess is she was pushed, no matter how many years they've been sailing across the oceans. So you check and you find they're married less than two years, that it's all her money. And any idiot would realize he would have to have a body aboard, or it will be a long time and a lot of heavy legal expense in order to collect."

I wondered if the lawyers' union put the same big bite on an estate under those circumstances as they do in the case of a contested will. If the litigant wins a piece of the estate, the standard practice almost everywhere is for the lawyer to take 45 percent of the amount awarded, regardless of how strong or how flimsy the claim, regardless of how much or how little work is involved in pursuing it. And what agency regulates and enforces these legal fees? The Bar Association.

There is one thing they don't do. They don't publish their rate schedules in advance. They let it all come as a surprise. A big surprise.

When I recover something that the victim never expected to see again, I take half. That is made clear in advance. And who regulates my rate? The victim. He can try other methods. Sometimes we can negotiate the percentage, especially when it is a very simple salvage job. It would be easier to sit behind a desk and shake my head solemnly and sadly and say, "Buddy, I surely wish I could cut the fee, but I have to abide by the rules and regulations of my association."

And by the same rules they take 4 or 5 or 6 percent of a gross estate even when there are absolutely no problems at all. Absolutely no chance of paying an hourly rate. Know why? "It wouldn't be fair to those heirs of other estates where a lot more work is involved. Your dead daddy left you a gross of one hundred thousand, fella? My six percent comes off the top. Six grand. Local bar-association schedule. Hmmm. Then there's an estimated thirty-two percent additional taxes and expenses, so you will stand to inherit . . . sixty-two thousand dollars! I know it will only take about two hours of my time and about a half a dozen forms for my secretary to complete and process. But you are paying to have it done *right*, fella."

When there are things you don't want to think about, your brain slips down the easiest back alley, whistling and kicking cans. It is a sickening wrench to bring it marching back out of the alley to stand at attention and pay heed. I suppose that when it stays in the alley and won't come out, the world says you have gone mad. At Annapolis they have developed a brain-wave detection device to keep the cadets focused on the books. When the alpha wave gets the shape of daydreaming, you get beeped out of your reverie.

I forced myself back to the here and the now and bullied my reluctant imagination into guessing what Howie Brindle would probably do to my girl. His wife, yes. But my girl. I could name the day, hour, and minute when she stopped being a wife.

"Witnesses are always nice," I said.

"I don't understand," Doris said.

"Somebody who really believes," Gabe confirmed. "They really think they saw what somebody wants them to see, hear what somebody wants them to hear. Suggestibility. But they are alone. Mr. and Mrs. Brindle, in the middle of the sea."

"Because I convinced myself and convinced her that Howie is a nice dumb guy and she was hallucinating. He now knows this is the last chance he gets. And the only thing in the world I can do is be at Pago Pago when he gets there."

"She'll be aboard," Gabe said. "Too much stink, too much investigation if she isn't."

"But I don't even know if he can think that clearly. I don't even know if he's that smart."

"If he is, maybe you should be all geared up to have him picked up for something else. One of those possible kills you talked about. Or this girl." He tapped the envelope of pictures.

I went digging back through memory. I had made some notes and, though I doubted I could find them, the making of notes is a good crutch. "Two girls traveling together, trying to hitch a ride from St. Croix to Plymouth on the island of Montserrat. Joy Harris and Cecile? Cecilie? Celia. Yes, Celia Animal. Wolf? Bear?"

"Katz?" Gabe asked.

"You're a lot of help. Fox! Celia Fox, who has a sister married to a lawyer in Plymouth. Maybe I could do it by phone on the day after New Year's, if Meyer can remember the name of the lawyer we met down there, and if Celia and her sister were both a Miss Fox, because I would think the guy would have to be English, probably colonial-born, and being married to an American girl would be unusual enough to be identification. But look, where does that leave us? Suppose I find the young Mrs. Barrister and get her on that weird island radiotelephone deal, and convince her she should give me Celia Fox's address, if she had one, in the States, and assume I get hold of Celia and she says yes, Joy Harris left St. Croix on the *Trepid* and no one has seen or heard from her since. Suppose I get in touch with the grieving and worried parents of Joy Harris and they have not heard from the girl for a year. So what? The girls were bumming around the islands. What would be the jurisdiction? I would bet very large odds that very soon after Joy Harris told Howie about Pidge taking snapshots of her taking a sunbath on the bow, Howie worked out his freaky little deception, snapped Joy's spine, and flipped her into the sea along with her backpack, hiking boots, spare jeans and guitar."

Doris winced and made a gagging sound. "That's a little too vivid," she said.

"Sorry. There's another thing I should have figured out. She said that when the generator was on, she imagined she could hear Howie and Joy talking and laughing. It would be no big problem to wire up a tape player with an endless loop, in sequence with the generator so that it played whenever the generator ran. Howie is a member of the tape generation. They all fool around with components and editing and splicing. Hearing voices and laughter mingled in with a sound—that of an engine or water roaring into a tub or a noisy compressor—is one of the most common hallucinations."

A whole bright birdlike flock of little Marchman girls and friends came whirling and chirping into the garden area, asked permission to use the pool, and went darting off to change.

Doris asked me if I would stay for barbecue, and I said it was very nice to be asked, but my stomach felt as if somebody had slammed it shut. And I was not going to be very good company to have around. When she began to insist, Gabe interrupted and told me I had a rain check.

He walked me out to the car. He leaned against the high fender of Miss Agnes and said, "And what you want to do is take all the bits and pieces back and spread them out in front of Meyer and see what he says you should do."

"And hope that it's what I've already decided."

"Bring him out here with you when this is all over."

"Sure, Gabe, I'll do that. Thanks."

"And . . . bring that girl along too. Like to meet her."

As I drove away I wondered if Gabe could be mellowing. Where was the sour, savage, bitter man I had learned to know and to like? Then I realized that never before had I gone to him with something that affected me personally, deeply. So Gabe had the warmth and the strength when you had need for it. Otherwise, keep your guard up.

His advice as to how to spend the waiting time was good. Get geared up to be ready to nail Howie for something else. And make some air reservations.

12

MEYER was sitting up in a chair in his room having his evening meal when I arrived. I sat on the bed and told him that he looked a lot less like a reject from a wax museum.

"I took a shower," he said. "I am eating a steak, as you can plainly see. A very skimpy little sawdusty steak, but a steak nonetheless. This will be the last night I shall be attended by Ella Marie. You can pick me up and take me home Tuesday noon. That is New Year's Day, I believe. If the prospect displeases, I can make other arrangements."

"You are better. And up to your old standards of unpleasantness."

"Let me know when I exceed them, please. Then I can back off a little. If you are wondering what this is, they started with green blotting paper, ran it through a shredder, soaked the pulp in bacon grease, and then pressed it into little molds so that it came out looking exactly like overcooked string beans. They have other esoteric—" He stopped and put his fork down. "I'm sorry. I was so busy showing off, I didn't really take a good look at you. What's happened, Travis?"

I got through the explanation about the pictures and my other discoveries. He took giant steps in logic which made detailed explanations of significance unnecessary.

He said, "Sorry to be so slow to see that something had you by the throat, my friend. Illness is an ego trip, especially after you begin to feel a little better. You turn inward. How do I feel right now compared to five minutes ago, an hour ago, yesterday? Is this pain in my hip connected with the infection? Is it something new? Why can't they come when I ring? All intensely personal. Petulant. To each one of us, the self is the most enchanting object in all creation. Sickness intensifies the preoccupation with self. And, of course, the true bore, the classic bore, is the person who is as totally preoccupied with himself all the time as the rest of us are when we are unwell. The woman who spends twenty minutes telling you of her last four experiments with hair styling, for example.'"

"I like that Spanish definition of yours better."

"Gian Gravina? 'A bore is a person who deprives you of solitude without providing you with company.' "

They came and got his tray. He got up cautiously, waved away the helping hand, and waddled slowly to the high bed. He operated the side buttons to give himself the perfect angle of repose, the right degree of support under the knees. And then he sighed. The sigh of tiredness and great accomplishment.

"Gabe said that—"

He stopped me with a hand slowly raised. His eyes were closed. "Let us think. Let us erase all past impressions and conceptions of Howard Brindle and then paint him back into our stage set without going too far the other way, creating fangs, hair on the palms and the fetid odor of the great carnivore."

I tried to think. Linear logic was beyond me. My mind kept bouncing off the stone barriers of anxiety and running in circles. He was breathing deeply and steadily, and I wondered if he had fallen asleep.

"Marianne Barkley backed me into a corner right after the doctor's death and bent my ear into strange shapes with her dossier on Fred and Lois Harron," he said.

Sometimes there's no way of sidestepping her. She is a large lady who dresses in gypsy fashion and runs a small successful shop in the complex called Serendipity-doo. She sells yarn, needlepoint kits, creative pots, literature of the occult and Japanese prints. She works up detailed horoscopes, breeds Siamese cats, instructs in decoupage, gets around on a Honda and writes a weekly society gossip column for a throwaway called the *Lauderdale Bystander*. She knows everybody, has a certain fringe position in the old-settler social order and has outlived three husbands, all rumored to have been talked to death.

Meyer went on. "Twenty minutes of conversation boils down to pure soap opera. Dr. Harron had started to have some real trouble with the bottle. The doctor union was very close to closing the operating-room door. Booze had put the marriage in jeopardy for the usual reasons. His impotence making her wander afield, a few drunken beatings. Marianne suspected that a psychiatrist friend had recommended the long vacation aboard the *Salamah*. The whole point of her assault on me was to tell me how lucky Lois Harron was. Some mutual friends had tied up fairly near them in Spanish Wells and reported that Fred was getting so totally smashed all day every day, the Harrons had to hire a fellow to operate the ketch. Death by swimming accident left Lois pretty well fixed, she pointed out. The long slow death from booze would have meant professional disgrace and bad memories and no money left at all."

"It sounds more likely than the account Mrs. Harron gave me. But where are you going with it?"

"I'm linking it up with a conversation I had about that time. I can't remember who I was talking to. But they had an aura of reliability. Maybe somebody official. Something about a blood alcohol test in Nassau, and a mild astonishment that a man carrying that much load could stand up long enough to dive."

"Oh," I said. "But I don't think Lois Harron is a very good liar. She said that she and Howie were below and heard the crunch when he dived into the dinghy."

He opened his eyes. "Let's say they anchored off Little Harbor for a swim. All three of them swam. Fred Harron drank and swam and passed out on deck, loaded. And then Lois and Howie went below and took off their wet suits and had sex. Afterward, let's say that Lois drowsed off. Howie heard the dinghy swing in the tide and wind change and bump against the hull. He certainly knew the marriage situation. Maybe he wanted to do her a little favor. He could give such a great start it would wake her up and he could pretend to be agitated and say, 'What was that? What was that? Didn't you hear it? A big thumping noise. Maybe we pulled the hook.' He could yank his swim trunks on, hurry topside, take a quick look around at the empty sea, scoop the surgeon up and launch him headfirst into the dinghy, bawling to Lois to hurry up just as the doctor landed."

I got up and looked out his window into the early darkness. "A little favor for a lady, eh? Like killing a hornet, or parking her car in a narrow space, or helping her over a fence. Meyer, you never used to be able to think so badly of people."

"I used to lead a sheltered life. Does it fit, emotionally? Does the concept have internal logic?"

"Enough to give me the crawls. No proof possible. Ever."

"You take a turn. Try Susan from Texas."

"Okay. Erratic, neurotic, alienated. And hostile. So she located her father's boat somehow. Maybe she was still in contact with a friend in her hometown who would know. She moves aboard, pleads with Howie not to tell her folks. They become intimate. He likes living aboard boats. She is an added convenience. He doesn't have to go out and find a girl if he wants one. Maybe he never wants one badly enough to go to any great lengths to find one. But if one is right there, within reach, he'll reach when he feels any mild urge. Okay, so she thinks she'd got the leverage on two counts, letting her stay aboard and laying her. Hostility is the clue, maybe. A little lady lib mixed in. Do just what I want you to do, or I'll blow the whistle on you, Howard. And maybe she would anyway, because she was erratic. End of a convenient way of life. Big problem of where to live and what to do. So he turned her head a little further around than it is supposed to go, wired her into a weighted tarp, put her and her stuff into the launch by the dark of the moon, and probably deep-sixed her up one of the canals. How many of those freaky, wandering, bombed little girls disappear every year without a trace? Thousands? I don't know. But I think it adds up to a lot of them."

"Very nice," Meyer said. "It fits the same pattern. A casual response to a minor problem. Why do we like Howie Brindle?"

"Rhetorical question?"

"Not exactly. There is something childlike about him. A kind of placidity, a willingness to be moved about by events. You sense that he does not want to be an aggressor, to take anything you have from you by force. He is cheerful, without being at all witty. He loves to play games. He likes to be helpful. He watches a lot of daytime television. He has a short attention span. He won't dream up chores, but he'll do faithfully what you tell him to do, if you're explicit. His serious conversation, a rare phenomenon, seems to come from daytime television drama.

He loves chocolate bars and beer. He doesn't want trouble of any kind, and he'll lie beautifully to get out of any kind of trouble. He has absolutely no interest in the world at large. Retarded? Hardly. I think he may have a better intelligence than he is willing to display. But something is wrong with him. For lack of a better word, call him a sociopath. They are very likable, plausible people. They make superb imposters, until they lose interest in the game of the moment. They form few lasting attachments. As a rule, they are liars, petty thieves, sometimes brawlers, but seldom are they killers. I can explain why they are so dangerous, the ones willing to kill. Because they are absolutely immune to polygraph tests. The polygraph measures fear, guilt, shame, anxiety. They don't experience these emotions. They can fake them by imitating the way the rest of us act under stress. But it's only an imitation. When the only thing in the world that concerns you is not getting caught, you would kill for very small reasons. In fact, murder that is the result of irritation plus casual impulse plus an elementary slyness is the most difficult to solve."

I went to the foot of the bed. "We've seen some of those, Meyer. Remember?"

"Not if I can help it."

"We like him because he's just a mischievous little kid."

"That's the ultimate simplification. Mommy gives all her time to new baby sister and won't make peanut butter sandwiches when you come home from school, so put the pillow over baby sister's little face and push down on it and listen to the clock going tick."

"But what the hell *good* is all this doing Pidge?"

"She doesn't fit the pattern of his other . . . solutions."

"No. This seems more complicated. Seems! It is. It's as if . . . he hasn't been able to figure out the best way to go—to kill her or drive her crazy."

"Remember his first and only rule. Don't get caught."

"So?"

"So if the ramifications of killing her made him cautious and indecisive a year ago, nothing has really changed so much. And you are in the equation now. He knows you talked to her about the things she couldn't comprehend and convinced her she had been hallucinating. I think that might be the best favor you could have done her."

"I don't understand."

"I'm thinking out loud. And not making much sense. Sorry. I think that if she were to confront him on this trip to American Samoa with his having tricked her into thinking she was losing her mind, she might not last the whole voyage."

"But you think she will?"

"My God, don't take my hunch for reality. She could be face down right now, off a lovely atoll, drifting down and down into that incredible turquoise blue, with Howie squatting and watching her sink, his only lament a vague disappointment at having to give up something of about the same pleasure quotient as a chocolate bar."

"Why are you—"

"Whoa! The veins in your neck are standing out. I had to steer you away from childish optimism. Remember, there is a very cold and strange entity that hides inside Howie Brindle. It is the imposter. He is the stage effect. It has refined the role until good ol' Howie knows all the tricks of quick acceptance, of generating fondness, of making people glad to help him out. The thing inside pulls the strings and pushes the little levers, and Howie does all your chores for you. Cheerfully."

"What the hell should I *do*?"

"First, stop yelling. Second, on your way out, tell them I am ready to go to sleep. Third, you could backtrack Howie a little bit further. Fourth. Hmmm. Fourth. Oh. Tom Collier comes into this thing too often to be shmmm . . . suggle. . . . "

"Meyer?"

"Garf," he said softly, the "f" lasting on and on. His eyes were closed. I stared up through the ceiling, hands spread wide, and spun and left him there.

13

SUNDAY morning was crisp and bright, but so windless the smog was going to build up quickly. Coop flew me over to the Sarasota-Bradenton Airport in his little red-and-white BD-4. It is a very happy and responsive four-place, high-wing ship. It is comfortable, reasonably quiet, and cruises at a hundred and seventy miles an hour on its hundred and eighty horses.

Coop is always ecstatic at the chance to fly me anywhere in the state. I buy the gas and pay the landing fees. He can't charge for the flight or his services because he built his airplane from a kit. The FAA classifies it as an Experimental Amateur Built airplane. Coop paid $7200 for the kit. He is one of five or six hundred people who fly planes made from the same kit. He put in twenty hours a week for forty weeks, and the FAA, who had been looking over his shoulder as he built it, watched him climb into it and fly it, and gave it an airworthiness certificate. There is nothing about it he doesn't maintain perfectly, and nothing about it he can't fix.

I always forget his square name until I see it behind the glassine on the instrument panel. Pelham Whittaker. He is known as Coop because he looks astonishingly like Gary Cooper until he either talks or stands up. He has a very fast high-pitched voice. And he is about five foot five. He teaches in the adult-education program in the high school at night, so he can fly his BD-4 in the daytime. His wife teaches in junior high in the daytime, so she won't have to go flying with him.

He is a very careful, fussy pilot. They are the best kind. It was such a nice morning he took it right across the peninsula and emerged a little north of Fort Myers. Once over the Gulf, he took it down to a thousand feet and stayed a half mile off the beaches as we went up the coast. Even looking toward the morning brightness, I had a good view of the coast. I hadn't seen it from that altitude for several years. Boca Grande looked much the same. And so did Manasota Key. But the small city of Venice, and Siesta Key, two keys north of Venice, were shocking. Pale and remarkably ugly high-rises were jammed against the small strip of sand beach, shoulder to shoulder. Blooms of effluent were murking the blue waters. Tiny churchgoing automobiles were stacked up at the lift bridges, winking in the sun, and making a whiskey haze that spoiled the quality of the light.

After he had his instructions from the tower and had turned inland to start his pattern, I could see, in the haze to the north, the tall stacks of the mighty Borden phosphate and fertilizer plant in Bradenton, spewing lethal fluorine and sulphuric-acid components into the vacation sky. In the immediate area it is known bitterly as the place where Elsie the Cow coughed herself to death. I have read where it had been given yet another two years to correct its massive and dangerous pollution. Big Borden must have directors somewhere. Maybe, like the Penn

Central directors, they are going to sit on their respective docile asses until the roof falls in. There are but two choices. Either they know they condone poisoning and don't give a damn, or they don't know they condone poisoning and don't give a damn. Anybody can walk into any brokerage office and be told where to look to find a complete list of the names of the directors and where they live. Drop the fellows a line, huh?

Coop put it down and rolled it over to the apron in the private aircraft sector. I knew he would stay in the area, answering questions about his kit plane, and talking flying—with hand gestures—with all the other Sunday flyers. When I neared the terminal and looked back, I could see that he had already acquired an audience of two, and would tell all about Jim Bede and his magic airplane kits.

A lanky miss behind the Hertz counter leased me a pink Torino which stank of stale cigar, even with the windows down and the speed up. I hesitated, then found my way out to Route 41 and turned north to Bradenton. I had checked a phone book in the airport to be certain it wasn't going to be too easy. No Brindle. I didn't even know if it was his paternal grandfather who'd brought him to Florida. Fast traffic was zapping by me on the north-bound side of the divided highway, whooshing through a tacky wilderness of franchised food, car dealerships, boat dealerships, trailer dealerships, motels, auction houses, real estate agencies, factory clothing outlets, furniture ware-houses, rent-anything emporiums, used cars, used trailers, used campers, used boats. Had I not seen a boat for sale every few hundred yards, I would never have known I was within five hundred miles of salt water. That's what's going to flatten the old wallets, guys, that missing feeling of being near the sea. It has done gone.

A Sunday that is the next to the last day of the year is a poor time to run a trace back through ten years, even in an area that hasn't grown an inch. But I was impatient, and I hadn't been able to get in touch with Tom Collier. And Coop wasn't doing anything.

I fumbled my way out of the fast traffic and down to the heart of town, and from there, with some directions, found the City Police. I parked the pink cigar a block away and went into the station. The two men on the front didn't come panting over to see what I wanted. It is the way with cops to make you wait a little while because a great deal can be read from the way a person waits. And it is a nice opportunity to look the visitor over. They were looking while they talked. Okay, so I am large, leathery, big-boned, with some visible signs of violent impact in years past. The shirt, fellas, is L. L. Bean, lightweight wool. The pants are Sears best quality double-knit stretch. This here cardigan I am carrying over my shoulder is Guatemalan, knitted by durable little brown people up in the Chichicastenango clouds. The shoes are After Hours, pony hide I think. The watch is by Pulsar.

And I wait amiably, see? Sort of lounging here, with half smile. So I could be the guy who comes and climbs the pole and fixes the phone. Or the driver of a big rig looking for a safe place to leave it because he can't deliver it today. Or I could be fuzz on vacation, stopping in to patronize the local brotherhood. Or I could be a dude from Palm Beach stopping by to report the theft of an original Dufy from the salon of his motor yacht. An eccentric dude without styled hair, capped teeth or tinted contacts.

All I know as I wait so disarmingly is that I have done a lot of things wrong here and there, but with what there is left of this Howie Brindle fiasco, I am not going to make bad moves.

"Help you, sir?"

"I don't know. If I could get a look at a back file of city directories."

"Trying to find someone?"

I quickly suppressed the terrible compulsion to tell

him that I wanted to see if I could still tear them in half. "He moved here when he was about twelve, I think. That would be thirteen or fourteen years ago. I guess he left when he went to the University of Florida, which would be about seven years back, give or take. Howard Brindle."

"You say he left? Then he's not here."

"That is right. That is absolutely right, Officer. I want to see if he has relatives still living in Bradenton."

"What have you got in mind?" The questions are always automatic. The more you ask, the more you know. And you might get an answer you don't like. I gave him one of the six clean cards. "Title Research Associates," he read aloud. "McGee. Fort Lauderdale."

"It's just a little research to clear a title," I said.

He pushed the card back across the counter and I picked it up, tucked it away. "You come around on a business day, you can find old city directories at the Tax Office, and maybe the Chamber, or even the library."

"I had to come over here anyway, and I guess I was trying to save myself two trips. You know how it is."

"Sure. I don't know how I could help you."

"It might be that somebody in the Department would know Brindle. He played football for the high school here. Offensive backfield. Big fellow. Light-colored hair. Went to Gainesville on a football scholarship."

My man looked blank, but the other one put a file folder down and ambled over, saying, "Sure. I remember him. A great big son of a bitch, more pro size than high school. Short yardage situations, they'd bring him in to get the distance or be a decoy. Quick as could be getting through that line, but once he got into the backfield, they could catch him pretty good. He couldn't go for the long gainers. He never did much at Gainesville, and I expected him to show up in the pros, but he never did. What ever happened to him?"

"He married a little money, I understand."

"That's the way to go! Say, dint you play some pro? I

heard Dave here say McGee. First name?"

"Travis."

"Oh, sure. Tight end. Kind of way back. Like you were up there two years, and you got racked up bad. Give me a couple of minutes and I can come up with the Detroit guy that clobbered you."

I stared at him. "Nobody can remember *me*, much less who messed up my legs. You've got some kind of hobby there. It was a rookie middle linebacker named DiCosola."

He put his hand out. "Ben Durma. I memorize all that stuff. My wife thinks I'm nuts. But I win a lot of beers. Too bad you couldn't stay in long enough to last into the good money like they get nowadays. You're a good size for a tight end. Well, about Brindle's folks, I wouldn't know. But I got an idea. Let me check the duty roster."

He came back and said, "I asked the dispatcher to bring Shay back in. He was playing for the high school the same time Brindle was. Stan Shay. He was too small for a scholarship."

"I don't want to upset anything. I could wait around."

"No problem. It's very, very slow out there. Tonight it will start building and tomorrow night will be a disaster area. We're running light so we can beef up the shifts for the trouble time. In the last hour and a half, one stolen bike, one guy chasing his old lady naked around the yard with a ball bat."

Shay was one of those elegant cops. Handsome and dark and trim, the kind who has blue jowls no matter how close the shave, wears tightly tailored uniforms, sports a very careful hair style, walks like a lazy tomcat, and looks as if the eyelashes are false. But they are real, and the toughness is real, and you do not want to say anything which could possibly be interpreted as a challenge to his virility or authority. The desk had business when he came in They aimed him over at me where I sat on a bench, but Durma called him back to give him a better fill-in. I was standing when he arrived. We shook hands and he said he had to be next to his cruiser because he was on call. We went out to the parking area and he sat behind the wheel, door open, turned sideways so he could hook his heels on the step plate. I leaned against the side of the car.

"We were on the same squad. He was a good kid. He never crapped out on what had to be done, but he never exactly pulled more than his share either. He liked to get by. You know. I had to work my tail off to stay even, to make up for not having the beef, and I used to tell him that if he worked like I worked, he could own the world. He could have been big. I really mean it. You want to know about his folks, Ben says. I went there a couple times when there was something he wanted to pick up and we were on our way somewhere else, so it was a couple of minutes. It was an old trailer park called the Bayway Trailer Haven, and they were way back in toward the middle—you could get lost in there—in a blue house trailer with a screen porch on one side and the built-on room which was Howie's room on the other side. The only people he had, they were his grandfather and grandmother. Their name was Brindle. They seemed to be jawing at him all the time he was there, the two or three times I was along, but he didn't seem to hear anything they were saying to him, or even be able to see them standing there. They could still be there, for all I know."

I wanted to ask if Howie got into any trouble while he was in high school, but I had the feeling Stan Shay would jump on any deviation from pattern. So I moved at it sideways. "I guess you're right. He could have made it big. But when there isn't enough motivation, natural ability isn't enough. From what I hear, he's gotten pretty close to trouble a few times. Since he got out of college."

"Trouble?"

"I don't know any of the details. I just got the impression he might have a bad temper. And if a man that big loses his temper. . . . "

"No. Not Howie. I can guaran-damn-tee you can't make ol' Howie mad. There was an old country boy named Meeker, moved over here from Arcadia, a good running guard, took it on himself to rile Howie. Called him Fats, asked him when he was going to buy a bra, snapped red marks on his ass with a wet towel, put his good shoes in the shower. That was third year. Howie just beamed and chuckled. Some of Meeker's tricks were mean. There was no use asking Meeker to ease off because it just made him go after Howie more. But Howie never minded it one little bit."

"Where did Meeker go away to school?"

"He would have had a lot of offers, but he never made it. First of June, that third year, we had a class party over on the beach at Anna Maria Island, bonfires and beer and all that. Meeker got pretty loud and pretty drunk, and so did a lot of other people. If he'd driven out there, probably he'd have been missed sooner. But he rode with somebody, so they thought he'd rode home with somebody else. There was so much noise and music, nobody could have heard anybody yelling out there in the dark. About everybody went swimming at least one time, but Meeker went ahead and drowned, and nobody knew it for sure until two days later a fisherman wading next to Tin Can Island spotted his body coming in on the tide, rolling over and over across the bar."

I tried it. A hearty laugh.

He snapped his head up. "That's some kind of joke to you?"

"No offense. I was just thinking. After all that towel-snapping, maybe Brindle went swimming at the same time as Meeker."

I saw his eyes change. His eyes went back into uniform. He was accepting it as a possibility. The cop years had given him the cynical awareness of what people are willing and capable of doing to one another. The first time a young officer of the law finds a starving three-year-old in chains, curled up on a cement floor amid its own fecal matter and dotted with the festering burns made by cigarets wielded by its loving daddy, who only "wanted her to mind," that cop becomes a better cop because he is more aware of the dimensions of his profession.

"The whole squad was honorary pallbearers," he said. "And Howie cried. I remember that. He cried quietly the whole way through."

"Didn't that strike you as strange?"

"I thought it was because he was just a nice guy."

Just as I saw a beginning suspicion of my motives, he got an emergency call to go help with traffic control. A gas truck had flipped over at the intersection of DeSoto Road and Route 41. He was under way as quickly as it can be done.

I parked the car under the shade of ancient live oaks and walked back into the trailer park. The park had been there a long time. Shade trees and tropical plantings had grown up around them. The Sunday birds sang. So many "Florida" additions had been affixed to these old aluminum boxes that it was hard to visualize any of them as having once rolled along the open road. The dewheeled village seemed to be trying to nestle itself further into the turf, forgetting the old bad dreams of tires, traffic and tolls. I saw a dedicated game of bocce, some chess boards, some people merely sitting, moving their chairs to follow the warm December sun. From radios and television sets, turned politely low, I heard the Sunday intonations as I walked past. " . . . and so I say unto you, brethren. . . . " " . . . the everlasting glory and the infinite mercy and the chance of everlasting life. . . . "

They looked with curiosity at the new face going by, suspicious and unsmiling unless I smiled. Then the smile was answered. When I asked, they told me that T. K. Lumley knew the history of the park. He kept records. Go ask T.K. Straight ahead, turn right at the big banyan that the road goes around, a hundred feet on your right. An old square trailer painted gold color.

T. K. Lumley was cricket-size, all of him except a W. C. Fields nose—a red potato with pores like moon craters. He was in a wheelchair painted in the same gold fleck as his trailer.

"Set," he said. "Can't get up because I broke my goddamn hip last July. First the quacks said I'd die of it, then they said I'd never get out of bed, and now they say I'll never walk again. Maybe what they do is try to make you so goddamn mad, you get better just to spite them. Greedy bastards charge a left tit to look at you, then figure they can put it in the bill to the estate. You wanted to know about the Brindles? Shit, I don't even have to go look them up. They moved into number one-oh-eight way back about . . . fourteen years ago. Molly and Rick and that fat kid named Howie."

"One-oh-eight?"

"Number of the site. You buy the mobile home that's on it and take over the land lease. Used to be people named Fitterbee had one-oh-eight, then he got so crazy their kids moved them into a nursing home, her too, so she could help care for him. Then she died there and he got over the crazy spell and got married again, but you don't give a damn about that. We don't get so many kids in the park. People here had their litters long back. That fat kid was okay. Obliging. Ask him to stop doing something, he wouldn't give you a lot of mouth. And he didn't have a bunch of outside kids coming in here racing around. He didn't mind being alone. Rick and Molly didn't have any extra change to spare, so the fat kid was handy to run errands for two bits or a dime. One thing he did got on my nerves a little bit. If he'd run an errand over to the grocery store, if he had enough money, he liked to buy himself one of those cans that squirts out whip cream or icing or chocolate for the top of a cake, and he'd go walking past, happy as a fat clam, squirting sweet goo straight into his mouth. It's hard for grandparents to bring up a kid, but Howie was just about the only kin they had left in this half of the country. There was a married daughter in Oregon with family, but nobody left back in Ohio. Terrible thing happened. Rick and Molly couldn't talk about it without choking all up over it. Howie was the middle one of three kids of Rick and Molly's son and his wife, and they had a little cabin on a lake where they went summers. There was a roach problem, and apparently young Mrs. Brindle forgot over the winter what container she'd put the poison in, because she used it in cooking, and the only reason the fat kid didn't die in the night too was because she'd fixed something he didn't like much and he ate only a little. Maybe that was why the fat kid wasn't like other kids, the way he could fool around all alone and be perfectly happy. There were some here said they missed little odds and ends of things, change and postage stamps and candy, but the truth of it, the people around here are always missing things, with or without Howie Brindle around. They just forget where they put them last. I'm taking one hell of a time getting around to when Rick and Molly Brindle left. It was . . . four years and four days ago. I can remember because it was the day after Christmas. Night of the twenty-sixth, twelve minutes past two in the morning, there was the goddamnedest WHOOMP you ever heard, and then *clang, bang, tankle, ding* as big pieces and little pieces of that old trailer came falling back down into the park, landing on other trailers and cars and all. It nudged three trailers off their blocks close by. It killed old Bernie Woodruff. He hopped out of bed and started running up and down the road, whooping, and finally just fell on his face. Heart attack. And it sure killed Rick and Molly. They never knew what hit them. The way it was reconstructed, they got new bottle gas delivered the day after Christmas, and there was a cracked fitting in the copper tubing right where it come through the trailer wall. The pressure of the new tank opened that fitting a little, a slow leak. Propane is heavier than air. So in the night it filled the trailer up like a faucet turned on slow, filling a bathtub. When it was full up to this high, it got up to the little pilot light on the counter-top gas range, and that's all she wrote. Wasn't one piece of side wall standing. We had a big switch to electric around here. Real big. If you squint through the bushes, you can see a big white job with blue trim past those cabbage palms. That's number one-oh-eight, and from coming to going, they lived there just about ten years, a little over."

"Lucky for Howie he wasn't home."

"He was home up until noon on the twenty-sixth, and then the friends he was expecting came and picked him up and they all went off back up to Gainesville, because that year they had some kind of bowl game going on New Year's Day, and there was final practice. Howie never got to play. Maybe he could have, but that boy was just too stunned. It took the heart right out of him. It was pitiful the way he walked around here like walking in his sleep. Everybody tried to do for him, but there wasn't much of anything to do except bury what was left. Never have seen him since. He never came back here at all, and nobody would blame him for that. That boy is as alone in the world as anybody can get."

T. K. Lumley backed his golden chair up and ran it forward again at an angle, chasing the sunshine.

He grimaced and said, "We got all the kinds of dying around here anybody can ever hope to use. We got the cancer, coronaries, strokes, pneumonia, the emphysema. Gobbles us up, one by one, and the new ones move in getting ready for their turn. A good woman in this park could use up all her days cooking up a covered dish and toting to wherever somebody died. So when somebody goes violent, the way Rick and Molly went, it's a strange feeling. Death in the midst of death. Like when C. Jason Barndollar fell off the pier and drownded. Or when Lucy McBee was setting at a window table in the Sears restaurant and some old tourist stepped on the gas pedal instead of the brake and leapt his Dodge through the window and killed her right there, eating shortcake. I keep a log of the coming and going. A history. But I don't know who in hell will ever care one way or the other. Every day people give less of a damn about the day before. Nobody wants to even listen to anything. You are a real good listener, young fellow, and I want to tell you I appreciate it. And it's keeping me from what I have to do and hate even thinking about, which is I got to roll around the side there, where my neighbor fixed me up a bar where I can hang on and stand up and take baby steps. It hurts like the fires of hell, but it's the only way on God's earth I'm going to get to stroll into the office of that doctor and tell him how goddamn little he knows about how much it takes to kill T. K. Lumley."

I went back to the airport and turned in the pink car, found Coop, and took him upstairs in the terminal to buy him some lunch.

"I showed them the stuff on the BD-5 that just come out," he said. "A lot of them are going to send out to Kansas for the poop. Forty-one hundred and fifty-five parts for twenty-six hundred bucks, including the forty-horse engine. Single-place, thirteen feet long, twenty-one-foot wingspan, cruise at a hundred and eighty-seven, weighs three hundred and twenty pounds, a thousand-mile range. Are you listening?"

"I guess not. Sorry."

"Did you get some bad news?"

"We can skip Gainesville. All I would find out there would be more of the same. And I've hit my gag limit."

"If I built me a BD-5, I wouldn't have any room to take anybody anywhere."

"What?"

"Oh, forget it. I didn't say anything."

"I'm sorry."

"Once we get off the ground, you'll start to feel better. Up in the air, everything looks better."

14

LATE that afternoon, Meyer sat brooding in the chair placed at an angle to the window. I sat in the straight chair on the other side of the bed, waiting for Meyer to digest the lumps of information I had brought him.

"I would guess," he said, finally, "that your Officer Stanley Shay was off at some other college or off in the service when Howard was orphaned for the second time."

"Or he would have mentioned what happened to the grandparents. Right. I went through that equation."

"Had we but the two disasters, the poisoning and the explosion, and knew nothing else about Howie Brindle except the impression he made upon us before they got married, we would label him a person luck frowned upon, and marvel at the adjustment he has made."

"And wonder why he never mentioned the disasters?"

"Too painful to mention. Or maybe even a kind of traumatic semiamnesia. We'd make excuses for him. Even right now, we have no proof of anything. Only a chain of incidents so long and so consistent that our life experience tells us he is an amiable maniac. Both of the incidents involving family fit what we discussed before, Travis. An almost casual impulse. Irritation plus opportunity plus slyness, plus a total absence of human warmth and feeling. Maybe his parents had put him on a diet because he was too fat. Maybe his siblings had everything they wanted to eat. So put the powder from one container into the other container, and eat just a little bit. God knows how the grandparents managed to irritate him. I would guess that he didn't know, or didn't even really care very much whether the act of loosening or cracking a fitting on the gas line would be lethal. They could smell it and have to go to a lot of trouble and worry to get it fixed. It could start a fire which they might flee from. I would guess that he has often booby-trapped the environment and left, not knowing what the results, if any, would be. The act of laying the trap would give him the satisfaction he needed. A parallel would be writing bad words with spray paint on the wall of a business which you believe overcharged you. Letting air out of tires."

"This has to be going somewhere."

"Of course. It just points up how different the current situation is. Let me put it in terms of an equation. H is for Howie. V is for victim. O is for opportunity. M is for motive, even though it is only a very casual and unimportant motive. D is for death. And so, time and again, we have $H + O + M = V + D$. Number the victims. V sub 1, V sub 2, V sub 3, up to God only knows what score. Maybe Linda Lewellen Brindle is V sub 20. Follow? Good. Now let us examine what is happening to the equation. It is stalled, short of completion. Is there any change in the values of our symbols? Howie remains the same, I would say. Opportunity has a far higher value than ever before with anyone. Certainly, as regards motive, she has given him cause to be very irritated with her, many times. As regards the D for death, we have two occasions where he acted it out but stopped short, causing her to fall overboard but then rescuing her, and shooting a rifle at her head but intentionally missing her. Can we say that were she to disappear at sea, the subsequent notoriety would unmask him as a killer? It might, of course, but I don't think his mind would work that way. So we have to put a new factor on the left side of the equation, something or someone which has changed his pattern insofar as Pidge is concerned. Call that factor X. And I believe the right side of the equation has become less precise and less simple. There is a solution other than D, possibly. L for lunacy? Such an end result requires far more complex planning, making us even more sure of the X factor on the left."

"Go shake up Tom Collier, which is what you started to tell me when you fell asleep last night."

"Did I?"

"You could have said it again, instead of all this formula and equation stuff. Instead of giving your brain to science, I think I'll have it dipped in ferro-cement and use it for a doorstop."

"If you underestimate Tom Collier, I'll be the one trying to decide what to do with your head."

"So give me an approach."

"I don't think you can trick him. I don't know if you can scare him. He is a tough-minded man. I would assume that the trust officer, the man I liked, Lawton Hisp, might have some knowledge. You might do better going at Hisp first."

On Sunday night I phoned the Hisp house and got a girl with a strong Scottish accent who said they were out for the evening and would not be back until late. There was a lot of child-noise in the background. On the morning of the last day of the year, I borrowed Arn Yates's red Toyota wagon and went to take a look at 10 Tangelo Way, home of the Lawton Hisp family. I did not want to take anything as memorable and remarkable as Miss Agnes into the neighborhood.

The house was a little more than I had anticipated, a daringly architected structure, like seven or eight huge boxes of various dimensions, with redwood siding applied diagonally, stacked one box and two boxes tall, as by an indifferent giant child. There were slit windows, horizontal and vertical, and there were railings around terraces on top of the boxes, several outside stairways of heavy timber, planting areas of rough gray stone at ground level. The area at the sides of the house and beyond it were enclosed by a shadow fence of horizontal cypress boards with a vehicle gate at the end of the driveway. It was the sort of house which murmurs a base price of two hundred thousand, and once you get a look at the inside, you can start upping the estimate.

It was not take-home pay from the First Oceanside Bank and Trust Company.

I drifted slowly through the elegant neighborhood and made a selection of a round woman in a purple jump suit, yellow picture hat and red garden gloves, kneeling and digging in a flower bed beside the step and got out and went toward her with my best smile.

"Mrs. Dockerty?" I said, mostly because the little metal sign stuck into the lawn said "The Dockertys."

She sat back on her heels, expression dubious. "Yay-yuss?"

"My name is McGee. I'm not selling anything."

"That's a lovely coincidence, because I'm not buying anything."

"I'm doing an informal survey in regard to a possible ordinance regarding approval of architectural plans for new residences in established neighborhoods."

"Do you work for the City?"

"The reason I'm making inquiry in this neighborhood is to get honest reactions to the architecture of the Hisp residence. Were you living here when it was built?"

She sprang up, concealing the effort it cost her to be nimble. She looked startled and slightly disconcerted to find that I still towered over her. "Oh, yes, we were here. They moved here . . . five years ago. You want an honest reaction? I'll give you an honest reaction. We all thought it was some sort of horrible joke. We tried to find some way to stop it. It looked like some kind of warehouses. It's enormous. We thought it would hurt property values around here. But . . . I guess we've gotten used to it. And they are a very nice family. It really doesn't look at all bad to me now. And I haven't heard people complaining about it in a long time. It even won some awards in magazines."

"Do you think neighborhoods should be protected against a new residence which is out of keeping with the others already there?"

"I don't really know. It's kind of a landmark now. Maybe we're almost proud of it or something."

"People who go in for strange architecture often have quite unusual life styles."

She looked puzzled, and then said. "Oh, you mean like artists and writers and pot parties and so on. Not in this case. Mr. Hisp is a banker. They are . . . a little different, but I guess that's because Mrs. Hisp, Charity, has money in her own right, and she has full-time help. And she is a great one for reading and concerts and so on, and going to New York to the galleries. They have four wonderful children. I'm sorry ours are too old for them. I guess the youngest is six and the oldest thirteen or fourteen. I would say that we see them socially . . . maybe twice a year."

"Thank you very much for your cooperation, Mrs. Dockerty."

"Do you want to talk to my husband too?"

"Does he feel the way you do?"

"Yes, but he wouldn't admit it. He'd tell you he still hates the house and there should be a law against it. But he doesn't believe that, really. He likes to object to things.

I guess that if you have money you can afford to be different. Maybe that's the best part of having it."

"From the looks of the house, Mrs. Hisp has it."

"Oh yes. Her maiden name was Fall. You know the law firm, of course. Fall, Collier, Haspline and Butts. The senior partner was her grandfather, and I understand that once upon a time he owned four whole miles of ocean beach frontage. Imagine. Four miles!"

"Pretty nice little piece of land. Well, thank you."

As I backed out, she got back to her digging. I drove two miles to a shopping center and called the Hisp residence and got the Scots girl again. No, Mr. Hisp was out. Mrs. Hisp? Just a moment.

She had a young voice and she was panting audibly. "Hello?"

"Hi. I wanted to find out when Lawton would be home. Have you been running?"

"We've been trampolining. Who is this?"

"My name is McGee. Travis McGee."

"Is this some sort of business thing? Today *is* a holiday, you know, and I just hate to have him use his holidays to. . . ."

"It is a business matter, and it is a very serious business matter, and it is the kind that neither he nor I would care to discuss at the bank."

"There isn't anything he can't discuss at the bank! What are you trying to say?"

"Mrs. Hisp, I can imagine that there were some matters which came up that old Jonathan Fall in years past preferred not to discuss in his office, and I do not imagine your grandmother knew much about those matters, do you?"

"Who *are* you? Do I know you?"

"I can't recall ever meeting you."

"You make it sound as if my husband was involved in . . . "

"Is he due back soon?"

"He just went to buy . . . on an errand. He'll be back any minute."

"I'll come right out. I think I owe Hisp the courtesy of listening to what he has to say before I go to the U.S. Attorney."

I could have made it in five minutes. But forty minutes gave them more stewing time, more time for discussion. Lawton Hisp answered the door himself. He was an inch or so over six feet tall. Narrow head, a big beak of a nose, a thick and glossy and neatly tended squirrel-color mustache. I put him at about thirty-five years old, minimum. Hair darker than the mustache, but just as thick and glossy. Long chin and a long neck, prominent Adam's apple, sloping shoulders. He wore big glasses with a faint amber tint. He wore shorts, sandals and a yellow sport shirt open at the neck. The shape of his head and the long neck gave him a look of frailty. But the bare legs were sturdy, brown and muscular. The chest was deep, and the arms looked sinewy and useful.

Even before I gave him my name I saw that he was right on the edge of losing control. He said, "You have ten seconds to tell me why I ought to let you come into my home."

"Ten seconds? So I'll do it with names. Professor Ted Lewellen. Tom Collier. Howie and Pidge Brindle. Take your time. I'll come in and talk or I'll go away. It's your choice."

"We manage a trust account for Mrs. Brindle."

"Else I wouldn't be here, Lawton baby."

He looked pained. "Do you purport to represent Mrs. Brindle?"

"No."

"Because I cannot discuss any aspect of any trust agreement without direct authori. . . you said no?"

"I said no."

"I don't understand. What do you want?"

"I want to talk to you about hanky-panky."

"You have to be out of your mind, McGee. The estate and the trust were handled exactly as the decedent wished, and there are no problems at all."

"So maybe there is some hanky-panky you might not know about. And if you don't know about it, somebody might want to find out if you were negligent not knowing about it. In other words, hanky-panky can rub off on the bystanders."

He smoothed each side of the mustache with the ball of his thumb. He looked over my shoulder into remote distances. "Come in, Mr. McGee," he said.

It was very nice inside those big boxes. They had balconies with doors opening off them. He led me into a tall box and down into an oval conversation pit entirely carpeted in gray shag. The cocktail table that filled the middle of the pit was the biggest oval hunk of slate I have ever seen. There was the sound of children at play, very muted, and some music coming from everywhere, softly.

She came quickly into the room and said, " I am going to sit in on this. You must have *some* reason for letting him into our home."

She was a slender, sallow, pretty woman, dark hair pulled tightly back and locked in place. White slacks, black turtleneck, no makeup except pale lipstick. No jewels. A general air of neurotic sensitivity.

"Mr. McGee, I would like to—"

"My God, Lawton, you don't have to do an introduction. He knows who I am, and he told me his name is Travis McGee. This is not a social situation. It's an intrusion."

"How do you do, Mrs. Hisp," I said.

"You're too tolerant with boors, dear," she told her husband. She sat on the other side of the pit, a dozen feet away. Hisp and I sat a few feet apart, half turned to face each other along the curve of the steep padded step.

"I have to know relationships," Hisp said.

"I was friendly with Ted Lewellen. I went on one of his excursions with him. You remember Meyer, who came to see you with authority from Pidge to find out from you the status of her father's affairs?"

"Yes. I do remember him. A most acute interrogator."

"He is my best friend. I know Pidge well. I saw her in Hawaii in early December."

"You did! I sent funds to her there. We'd been holding them in an interest-bearing account because she'd been out of touch. She didn't want the entire accumulation. Just a few—"

"Who are these people you're talking about?" Charity asked.

Lawton Hisp's neck seemed to grow longer. "My dear, you are welcome to sit in on this discussion, but in the interest of saving time, I believe you can wait until Mr. McGee is gone. Then I will answer any questions you may have."

He kept staring at her until she nodded agreement. He turned back to me. "So you are acting as a friend. You will have to explain to me exactly what you mean by hanky-panky."

"Ted Lewellen conducted original research to unearth documents regarding the location of sunken ships. As a result of the several salvage projects he undertook, he was able to leave a handsome motor sailer and almost a million dollars' net estate to his daughter. His daughter knew, and I knew, and Meyer knew, and another mutual friend knew that Ted had eight or nine more projects. He was getting geared up to head out on one when he was killed in the rain in traffic."

A lot of rigidity seemed to go out of Lawton Hisp. "Oh, *that* again. I can assure you that a most careful search was made by Mr. Collier and by me. We couldn't find any trace of his research records."

"Did you decide they didn't exist?"

"How do you mean that?"

"You must have had long conferences with Dr. Lewellen when he was setting up the trust for his daughter."

"Of course!"

"He would have had to tell you where the money came from and where future money would come from."

"I knew what line of work he was in, of course."

"Could he tap Pidge's trust fund if he went broke?"

"No. There was no way he could touch it."

"Wouldn't a banker think that sunken treasure is an iffy way of life?"

"It seemed very intriguing."

"Here is the question that the U.S. Attorney can ask the Federal Grand Jury, Mr. Hisp. The reasoning seems clear to me. He will say, 'You have heard testimony to the effect that Mr. Hisp was advised by three different people on three separate occasions that Lewellen's research records were missing and that they were of great value, and very probably unique. Does it not seem odd to you that Mr. Hisp, aside from one routine search of the vessel *Trepid,* made no effort to find these records, nor did he report their loss to the authorities?' "

He frowned. "Almost anything can be made to look suspicious and ugly. It depends on how you phrase it."

"Then *you* phrase it for me."

"All I can say is that the estate has been and is being handled according to the specific instructions of the decedent."

"So Professor Ted left instructions about the dream book?"

"If I am ever going to be questioned about this, which I doubt, it is going to be by proper authority, Mr. McGee."

"You will be, friend. You will be."

He stood up. Dismissal time. "I guess we will just have to wait until it happens, won't we?"

"It's going to be triggered by Tom Collier. He tried

to peddle the dream book to the wrong person. For a half interest."

He tilted toward me like an unsteady stork. Something happened to his face, and his mustache looked as if it had been borrowed and pasted on. "Wouldn't!" he said in a gargly voice. "We agreed. . . . "

"You two agreed to some hanky-panky."

"No!"

"Then you better tell me, or I'm going to blow you out of the water."

"You better tell both of us," Charity said.

He sat down. "Shut up, dear," he said.

"We're both listening," I said.

He took off his glasses and pinched the bridge of his big nose. "I have to explain to you some elemental facts of life as regards tax regulations. Tom Collier, Lewellen and I had several conferences on how best to handle the research information for estate purposes. There were seven more projects. He said each one represented a very good chance of recovery. He said they would represent from ten to fourteen years of salvage work, and would probably yield between two and five million dollars on a conservative basis, or eight to fifteen if his luck was good. Now then, had all the material for those projects been included in the estate, it would have been necessary to value them for estate purposes. There are no precedents. He died at just the wrong moment. Collier and I were trying to work out some sort of contingency sale arrangement, so that we would have a specific value, and a cash flow in that same amount. Suppose the research project papers had been listed and suppose the IRS had valued them at four million dollars and we had negotiated them down to two million. Can you see what the estate taxes would have done? They would have cleaned out the cash we needed on hand in order to leave the daughter what he wanted to leave her. And there was always the chance that the last seven projects would have been seven failures. There was no guarantee that they would ever pay off."

"Where was this stuff when Ted died?"

"Tom had the originals. He still has them. I have Xerox copies of all the pages and photocopies of all the charts and maps and overlays. As I said, we were trying to work it out when Ted was killed."

"His will left everything to Pidge."

"Yes."

"So she is the rightful owner."

"I certainly have never had any intention of depriving—"

"Then how come, if you knew of the existence of those records, you didn't, as coexecutor, put them in the inventory, dammit!"

"I *told* you! It could have bled all the liquid assets out of the estate to pay taxes on something that might turn out to have no value at all."

"And your concern for the daughter of your trust customer was so great that you decided to risk concealing specific assets from the IRS, that you signed false statements when you certified as to the completeness of your accounting?"

"Well, it seemed . . ." He recrossed his legs. "When you put it that way . . . " He stood up and looked around as if he had forgotten whose house he was in. "The way it seemed to us . . . "

"What in God's name were you two clowns going to do with Ted's future projects?"

"Well . . . Tom said that it would perhaps be best to wait and see how well the marriage thing worked out for Pidge. He said she had a certain amount of . . . instability. And maybe, if the marriage broke up, it would be good therapy for her to . . . to sort of reconstruct her father's plans, and then maybe on that basis, Tom could get a little investment group together to back an expedition."

"To reconstruct from memory?"

"There could be important things that might be left out

of the research materials, Tom said. We'd have no way of knowing. We weren't competent to judge."

"And you were going to be asked aboard that little investment group, right?"

"There was . . . that implication."

"You two are the perfect friends for a girl who has just lost her father. She needed friends like you."

He stepped up out of the pit. "Damn you!" he yelled. "You just don't know. You don't know how . . . how a man can get boxed."

"And how did you get boxed, Brother Hisp?"

"I was going to list those records. I insisted on it. It's a felony to conceal assets on any pretext. He told me I shouldn't make any hasty decisions. And . . . he *is* a director of the bank. He said we had to have a talk. We talked in his office, after the secretaries had gone home. He had a file of documents about six years old. Not a thick file. About fifteen transactions that originated in my department. It was back when new issues of convertible debentures were coming out and selling in the aftermarket at big premiums. At first the documents looked okay to me. Then I figured out what had happened. Gary Lindner had been ordering new issues from a brokerage house on a pay-on-delivery basis. Delivery was a month to six weeks after the issue came out. That way he was able to order a sale of the debentures and get the money before they ever arrived and he had to pay for them. A floor man was in collusion with Gary. He was holding the payment in a special cash account, and when the debentures would arrive, Gary would grab them and deliver them to the brokerage house for proper transfer to the new buyer, and they would be paid for out of the cash account. Then Gary would apparently pull all copies out of bank records. Mr. Collier's file was made up of photocopies of the brokerage-house records of each transaction, and my okay and initials were on the bottom right corner of every order."

"How could you be so damned stupid?" Charity yelled.

"Stupid? We were ordering those same issues for our trust accounts based on our investment advisory services, taking as many as we could get. Gary Lindner was negotiating a lot of purchases. I had to initial the orders. Most of them were legitimate. I can't be expected to remember all the TA numbers in the bank. These were fake."

"How much was involved?" I asked.

"Not an awful lot. Maybe about a thousand dollars a transaction, or a little more. Fifteen to seventeen thousand over a period of a year." He stopped pacing back and forth behind me and came and sat down once again, sighing and slumping.

"Where's Lindner working now? Still with you?"

"No. He got out of banking. He works for GeriCare International. It's something about hospitals, rest homes, insurance programs, and a line of special medications and diet foods."

"Did you get in touch with him about all this?"

"There didn't seem to be much point in it."

"What point was Tom Collier making?"

"He explained that it was possible that the National Association of Security Dealers might get around to auditing the local brokerage-office records regarding that period when there were a lot of abuses of the new-issue situation, and if that happened there wasn't much he could do for me. He said they would relay all findings to the FDIC, which in turn would notify the U.S. Attorney's office that there was reason to believe that I had been involved in a violation of the criminal code, and they would ask the FBI to investigate and report, and very probably they would indict."

"Do they indict people for stupidity?" Charity asked.

"Just tell me how I explain that I did not know anything was going on, that I didn't realize Gary was using the bank's buying clout to sweeten his own income?"

"How did Collier pressure you?" I asked.

"He said that he believed that there was a way, if he moved slowly and carefully, to get the original orders out of the dead files at the brokerage office and have someone who owed him a favor make photocopies of the originals with my initials masked, and put the copies into the file and destroy the originals. He said that for the good of the bank, and to save me and my family from the kind of publicity an indictment would bring, regardless of my decision on whether or not to let the Feds clean out all the liquid assets in the Lewellen girl's inheritance, he would go ahead and try to erase all traces of my involvement in the debenture swindle."

"Involvement?" Charity said.

"I should have checked every one."

"Do they get that picky?" she asked.

I nodded at her. "Yes. They get very, very picky. Collier was giving your husband a good reading."

Lawton Hisp said in a tired voice, "So I told him that he was asking me to perform a fraudulent act in leaving any tangible asset off the estate inventory. He said that as coexecutor and as the attorney of record, he would of course certify my inventory as being full and complete to the best of his knowledge. There were no threats, really. But in the end I left it off."

"And now that bastard owns you!" Charity said.

"Please, dear."

She jumped up. "Oh, boy. Mister Rectitude himself. The soul of honor and duty. I *never* could stand that Tom Collier. Jesus, I don't even mind you turning tricky as much as I mind you being so damn *dumb!* Don't you see that Collier can cut you and that girl out of any part of this, and you can't do a thing? Don't you even see that this McGee person can say jump, and you'll have to ask him how high? Wow. You talked the good game of piety until you got into your first jam, and then you ducked your head and scuttled into a hole. I—I—I thought you were r-real!"

"Shut your damned mouth!" he roared.

I got up and walked out. I did not go on tiptoe. I could have been leaving on fire, hammering a gong and shooting off cherry bombs without slowing the argument a bit.

I backed out onto the street and paused for a moment and looked at that house again. It looked exactly the same, but it had fallen down. Those big boxes were emptier than ever before. There was no good way he could mend it. She knew and he knew and I knew that he should have gone directly from his talk with Collier to the authorities and explained what he was being asked to do and why. He shouldn't even have paused to pick up a personal lawyer to sit in. Integrity is not a conditional word. It doesn't blow in the wind or change with the weather. It is your inner image of yourself, and if you look in there and see a man who won't cheat, then you know he never will. Integrity is not a search for the rewards for integrity. Maybe all you ever get for it is the largest kick in the ass the world can provide. It is not supposed to be a productive asset. Crime pays a lot better. I can bend my own rules way, way over, but there is a place where I finally stop bending them. I can recognize the feeling. I've been there a lot of times.

From now on, Lawton Hisp was not going to have a very nice life. They might never come after him, but it just wasn't going to be very joyous from now on.

Happy New Year, Mister Hisp.

15

I COULDN'T get a line on Tom Collier. His office did not answer. I finally found somebody who knew his unlisted home phone. I tried that and got a woman with a booze-blurred voice.

"Now what'n hell would he be doing here?"

"Mrs. Collier?"

"Uh-uh. Mizzzzz. We have got a legal separation, thank you so much. Say, you want a nice holiday drink?"

"I've got to find Tom."

"Baby, if you are a client, forget it. He's too busy with his new image. Forty-two years old and I guess what hit him was some kind of change of life. You know? Oh, we had these plans. We remembered names and smiled at everybody. Senator Collier? Governor Collier? Why not? Onward and upward, hand in hand. Why'm I telling you my troubles? Well, two reasons. I have a logical mind. I look for the reasons. One, you've got a nice sympathetic voice. Two, I am slightly smashed. Three, it's the end of another goddamn year. Four, it is very empty around here. Did I say two reasons? Make it four. Or ten. I can keep going. Sure you don't want a drink? I am known far and wide as a pretty good-looking broad in my own right."

"I know. From pictures in the newspapers. But first I have to talk to Tom."

"Hah! There is an obligation duly stated in there somewhere. First. The implication is there will be secondly. The address is fifty-one Dolphin Lane. Are you a spindly little old man with a nice voice, McGraw?"

"McGee. I'm a precocious twelve-year-old, Nancy."

"Y'even know my name! What you do to find Tom, you look for Mister Swinger. You look for a two-hundred-dollar hairpiece, and clothes for a twenty-five-year-old musician, and diet and exercise and vitamins and hormones and suntan, and his private little brownie pack of girls."

"Okay. Where should I look first?"

"Let me see. He'd either be having a party at the dock aboard the *Strawberry Tort* . . ."

"That's his? I've seen it. Somewhere up the line, isn't it?"

"At the Atlantic Club in Pompano Beach, at the club marina. Or he'll be at his so-called horse ranch—about halfway to Andytown on the right, there's a bridge across the New River Canal, private, and the sign hasn't any name on it. It's two horseshoes sort of entwined. He's got big plans out there, some kind of executive club with conference rooms, airstrip, apartments and, of course, girls. Where the hell do all the girls come from, McGraw? Somewhere they are stamping them out of plastic, some gigantic production line, programmed to roll over onto their little backs for all the Tom Colliers in the world. Look, give him a message for me. Tell him Nancy is doing just fine. Absolutely, totally fine."

I phoned the Atlantic Club and got the dockmaster. I said I didn't know if Mr. Collier wanted the ripplicator delivered to the boat or the ranch. He told me it was probably the ranch, because the boat had been hauled to get some bottom work done.

I went out State Road 84 and started looking before I got to the estimated halfway point. It was another two miles to the horseshoe sign, big golden shoes on a big black shield. The bridge was a new timber bridge, very narrow, and the road beyond was freshly graded gravel. Before it turned sharply past a screen of wetlands brush, there was a sign which no one could fail to see.

PRIVATE PRIVATE PRIVATE
No trespassing. No hiking. No hunting.
No camping. No soliciting. No deliveries.
No visiting of any kind except by
special & specific invitation.
VIOLATORS
will be subject to immediate
citizen's arrest & prosecution.

It made you feel warm and welcome. I went rolling along, thinking of the various things I could tell the guard I expected to find. It was a long way back in. Birds burst up out of cover. I think I went at least a mile and a half, winding to stay on high ground where less gravel fill was needed to build the road. And then I emerged from the scrub-country brush and palmetto thickets and oak hammocks, and there was a white fence on my right. Four horses stared over the fence at me, snorted and wheeled, and went pounding down their side of the fence line. It was apparently a familiar game. Race the funny car and beat the funny man. In the distance I could see a confusing cluster of buildings.

I let the horses win by just enough to let them know they had to work at it. Beyond their fence corner was an asphalt landing strip with a wind sock, a small hangar, six brightly colored little airplanes tied down to the ring bolts, and another one coming in, teetering on the wind. Beyond the hangar the road curved and I saw thirty or so vehicles. About half of them were four-wheel drive. And half the remainder were sports cars.

It was half after four, and I could hear the sounds of party time. I parked Miss Agnes between a Toyota Land Cruiser and an ancient jeep with a big winch on the front, mud-caked up to its ears. I followed the sounds of party. The music was very loud, and it wasn't anything anybody was ever going to be able to whistle. The party was taking place in and around an indoor-outdoor swimming pool. Bright canvas was laced to framework made of pipe to take the sting out of the December breezes. And there were some big electric heating units turned on, glowing toward the pool from atop poles ten feet tall. Eighty to a hundred guests, maybe. There were some earnest young men in ranch gear taking care of the two little bars, and the long table where hot food was apparently in continuous supply.

A six-foot lady, startlingly endowed, pushed a drink into my hands and said, "You better like it, buster. I spend valuable time getting it made *zactly* the way he likes them, and I turn around and the son of a bitch has disappeared. Don't just stand there! Drink it, you silly clutz!"

Before I could tell her it was a splendidly dry martini, she had prowled away, snapping her head from side to side, looking for the gin gourmet. I moved further into the fringes of party-land and looked around. It was happening in my side yard, so I could pick out some faces. Two or three of the hustlers with the highest going rate on the beach, in season. A baroness who sang here and there, badly. A couple of girls from the water-ski school. The others looked like college girls, beach bunnies, store clerks and secretaries. The men, outnumbered about two to one, were harder to identify. There was that certain burnished, heads-up arrogance which spoke of gold credit cards, and the authority to move people around, and the pleasures of the predatory life. They were men who would keep their lawyers busy and their doctors concerned.

I finally spotted Tom Collier, Genial Host. He was in a lime-yellow jump suit with two entwined horseshoes, in black, on the breast pocket. He was coming out of the house, guffawing at something a little blond gem was whispering to him as she clung to his arm with both hands. As he listened, he made a slow sweep of his party, and the appraisal swept past me and hesitated and swept back and came to close focus. I nodded and smiled. He smiled and waved.

It had not been easy to recognize him. He had taken on the coloration of the group. He could have been selling generators in São Paulo for Swiss francs he was going to fly to Hong Kong to buy a shipment of motorbikes made in Taiwan. Or he could have been putting together a syndication deal on a dozen old television serials. Or greasing a bill through the state legislature which would improve the profits for his clients. Or supplying the tail at his own party.

I am never quite certain exactly when I make a decision about how to open people up wide as a Baptist Bible. Different strokes for different folks, they used to say. It is a combination of hunch and instinct. Here was a very smart, tough, ballsy fellow right at the peak of his power and glory. He had shed the dull old ways, and he was living big and living rich. He was tasting it all, and so far he loved it.

I was going to have to run a bluff, and a very good one, because this man had seen them all. He had the ruddy, fleshy face of the sensualist, and the air of the search for gratification that has become the reason for living. In this sense, he had a lot to lose. No more low bows and special tables. No more big hello from celebrities. No more invitations to come in on cute little deals and payoffs. And that, perhaps, is the vulnerability of the corrupt, the terrible fear of losing the fruits of corruption. To put it another way—to be asked to leave the party.

But I knew he was the X in Meyer's strange formula, the added factor on the left which had changed the outcome on the right—or delayed it.

I flipped through a half-dozen ways of cutting him out of his happy holiday pack, made a choice, and moved on an interception course. When I caught his eye I made that useful Latin-American sign which asks for a few moments of your time, a thumb and first finger held a half inch apart. He unwound the little blond beauty from his arm, patted her on the rear, and sent her off toward the food. He moved aside, pulling me over with a head gesture.

"I've seen you, but where?" he said.

"Here and there. Not often. Not to talk to. The name is McGee."

He did a good job at covering any impact. I could not be sure I had seen any. But it was obvious that Mansfield Hall would have used my name when he had . . . haw . . . phoned Collier about my pending visit. And because he had some association of the name McGee with Professor Ted and his daughter, he had immediately turned off any negotiation with Seven Seas. The genuinely sly man will not rationalize any coincidence. Instead, he'll slam doors.

"McGee? McGee. Is it supposed to ring a bell?"

"Not really. I've got something out in the car. Frank Hayes told me to show it to you."

"Frank Hayes?"

"I didn't know you were having a party. I tried the Atlantic Club first. Some tall girl handed me this drink because she couldn't find the man she made it for."

"On the last day of the year I'll buy anybody a drink, McGee. Go get whatever it is this man I don't know thinks I ought to see."

"You've got to be kidding!"

"Kidding? I don't know any Frank Hayes."

"I mean about bringing it in. I lifted it into the pickup

by myself, but I couldn't carry it more than ten feet without taking a rest. It was three hundred feet deep. I don't see how they got it up into a boat without busting it. Look, all I want is that when Frank Hayes asks me, did Collier see it, I can say yes, he saw it. That's my only part in this."

There is something about a pickup truck which disavows guile, which gives a commonplace, workmanlike flavor to any transaction. Night had come quickly. He looked off toward the tops of pine trees, black against the last gray of the sky. The pool lights were on. His nostrils widened, as if he hoped to smell gold adrift on the night breeze.

"Okay. Let's go take a look. What is it anyway?"

"Tell you the truth, I'll be damned if I know. You'd have to ask Frank."

"How do I ask him if I don't know him?"

"I'd guess he'll get hold of you."

We went through the night to where all the cars were parked.

"Some pickup," he said. I was a half step behind him as he reached it. He peered into the bed. In what light was left, all he could see was the big tool chest that was spot-welded against the front end of the bed. I moved to where the light was perfect for me, and I took my right fist back, right shoulder turned away from him, both heels rooted to the ground, the fist six inches from my ear, and aimed at the sky.

Yes, Virginia, there is a button. As in right on the button. If you have a dimple in your chin, the button is an inch and a half east or west of said dimple, along the jaw shelf, lower jaw. That particular area seems to give the maximum jolt to the brainpan. You *can* knock someone out by hitting him right between the eyes, but the blow requires much more force. The most effective stroke is slightly downward, tending to knock the jaw open at the instant of impact, thus saving the problem of a collapsed knuckle. When striking someone, strike at an imaginary target well beyond the point of probable impact. Then you will not draw the punch at the last microsecond, muffling the blow.

My hand was still sore from hitting Frank Hayes on the side of the head, but the swelling was gone. Collier was aware of where I was standing, and I knew he would turn his head and direct a question at me. As I saw the first movement of his head, I started the punch at grass level. It came up through the muscles of thigh and behind, up the back, and reached the hand last of all. It resembles the old game of snap-the-whip, played by the foolhardy young on roller skates or ice skates. The fist is the last person at the end of the whip. The fist exploded down onto the turning jaw, knuckles nicely aligned along the shelf of bone. It blew his mouth open. He said, "Uhhh!" and dropped facedown so close to me his forehead hit the toe of my left shoe, and it felt as if I had dropped a bowling ball on it.

Two cars were coming to the party. The headlights swept across me. They parked where they would not pass close to me on their way to the fun and games. They did some whooping and door-chunking. When they were gone I listened to party sounds. There was another sound much too close, and I had a moment of alarm before I identified it. It was coming from an all-white Continental not more than fifteen feet from me. It was angled away from me, which put me back off the stern port quarter, in its blind spot. It was a measured *phlumph,* of enough weight and purpose to rock the white success symbol on its mushy springing. Once identified, I realized that there were two blind spots operating to hide me. A woman made a cooing sound, which rose to a question at the end and was answered in rumbling, effortful grunting. The *phlumph* cycle accelerated, and I squatted and slid my arms all the way under Tom Collier, kept my back straight as I stood up, and used the momentum to hoist him up over the high side of the pickup bed, giving him a half roll as he fell onto the metal floor.

I had seen a side road where the horse fence started, so I drove down there and went a hundred feet along the road and stopped, with my lights off. I climbed into the back. Collier was still slack. I fingered his jaw; nothing felt broken. I unlocked the tool chest and found a pencil flash in the top tray and used it to locate my roll of one-inch filament tape, on the handy dispenser. Better than a five-hundred-pound breaking strength. I shoved his short sleeves out of the way and took a turn around his left arm just below the elbow, then pulled his two arms together, the insides of the forearms pressing against each other. I took the tape around the two arms just below the elbows four times and nipped it off with the dispenser trigger. I took three turns around his ankles and nipped it off.

When you think back, you can remember how many melodramas you have watched where the captive worked his hands loose from the ropes, or went hippity-hop to where they keep the kitchen knives, or broke a bottle or a light bulb and sawed on the broken glass, or even found some way to burn himself free.

Too bad. All obsolete. Try the filament tape. Trust a friend. Or truss one. No way to get teeth or fingers anywhere near it, or get the hands anywhere near the ankles. No way to stand up, or keep your balance if you do. No knots to learn. And I had him secure thirty seconds after I found my tape. I threw a tarp over him and shoved him forward where the wind wouldn't catch the tarp. Then I went looking for a place. I had the feeling I had seen a canal-bank road heading left and right just as I came off his bridge onto the ranch side.

It was there. I took it slow. We'd had a dry December. I headed east, parallel to the highway, over there on the other side of the canal. After I had begun to wonder if I would ever find a place to turn around, I came to a hurricane-wire fence with a padlocked vehicle gate in it and enough room to turn around. The ground was firm along the fence line. I walked it first, and then drove back away from the highway and the canal for two hundred yards or so.

I dropped the tailgate and reached in and pulled him out to where I could get hold of him and lift him. There were little resistances in his body that told me he was doing the shrewd thing and playing possum. I sat him up, put a shoulder into the middle of him, and hoisted him over the shoulder, my right arm around his meaty thighs, his head and arms dangling down my back.

Using the pencil flashlight, I walked into the edge of the brush and found a mounded area of coarse grass, sand, shell and limestone, probably a place where some small current in the sea had pushed up a window of sea bottom when mankind was only an unborn threat to the distant future.

I carried him with as much of an effect of effortlessness as I could manage. Standing straight, I unclasped my arm from around his thighs and rolled him off my shoulder. I felt him tense up as he went off. He hit without a sound other than the thick thud of impact. That is another way to tell. When a person is unconscious, a jolt like that will rasp the air through the slack throat with an easily audible noise.

I left him in the dark and went back to the toolbox and got the short-handled spade and also a couple of Coolite sticks. I like to keep them on board the *Flush* and in the car. You peel the wrappers off, and bend until they make a little snapping sound, and then shake them to mix the chemicals. They provide a good strong light for three hours, with no trace of heat. It is a white light with a slight greenish cast to it.

He was on his right side with his back toward palmettos. I activated the Coolite sticks and tossed them onto the ground about ten feet apart. I stood between them

and stepped the spade down into the coarse stuff, levered
a load loose, heaved it to the side. It was easier than I
expected. Once I was through the top crust, the con-
sistency was predictable, and I was able to get into a good
digging rhythm. When I worked my way around to where
I could look at him without appearing to, I could see little
catchlights against the wetness of his eyes and knew he
was watching me.

I made it six feet long and about three feet wide. My
hands began to tingle in a few spots, warning of where
the blisters would puff up if I kept going much longer.
By then I was almost down to my hip pockets. I had begun to get a sucking sound when I pried the bottom loose.
I put the light on the bottom and saw the water beginning
to seep in. I sat on the edge and stood the spade up in my
dirt pile and rubbed my hands together and rested for a
little while. Then I went over to him and rolled him far
enough so I could check the pockets in that jump suit. I
found a wallet. I took it over to a Coolite and squatted on
my heels as I checked it. Nice wallet. Some kind of fine-
grained lizard hide with a grey cast to it. Gold corners.
Gold initials, lower case, t.j.c.

American Express Gold Card, Diners, Cat Cay membership, Bunnyworld, the Riviera in Vegas, Atlantic Club,
Air Travel Card, Abercrombie & Fitch, Shell, Texaco,
Exxon and BP. Three fifties, four twenties, a pair of tens
and a pair of ones. I prodded around in the money section
and found another flap and pulled it up and found two
five-hundreds and a one-hundred. Thirteen hundred and
fifty-two dollars for digging a hole. I put his driver's license
and his cards back into the pretty wallet. They were his
identity. They were Tom Collier.

So the symbol was inevitable. I shoved the money
into my pocket and I half turned and flipped the wallet
into the grave. It hit with a small splat.

"McGee," he said. Nice tone control. Nice modulation.
Good for a speech on the floor, or at the jury rail.

"Sah!" Hard and sharp, the enlisted man's protective response.

"I am a very good lawyer. You're going to need one."

"Not if I think everything out."

"You're not thinking. Do you intend to drop me into that hole? If you do, you're not thinking clearly. I'm worth one hell of a lot more to you than you took out of the wallet."

I sat on the edge of the hole again, feet dangling inside. "You're cool about it. I like that. Just take my word, Collier. You have to go into the hole. I won't put you in live. I'm not some kind of kink. I'll give you a good one across the nape of the neck with the edge of this spade before I put you into the hole."

"Why do I have to go in?"

"They have to be looking for you. They'll figure a man like you would be all set to run at any time. Tricky. If you're around, they'll look for somebody else. And they could get lucky and come up with me."

"Are you sure you have the right person? I'm the acting senior partner in a very reputable law firm. 'Tricky' is a strange word."

"I'll have to tip them off. It's too much to put into one phone call. Maybe three calls will be best. Three different phone booths, miles apart. Tomorrow. I'll be able to say I read it in the morning paper."

"Read what? About me being missing?"

"They won't know you're missing until they come looking for you. Look, it went wrong. I screwed up the detail. It was a good chance and I worked hard on it, but I know when it's time to cover the tracks and run. It has to be you because you're the logical one."

"Logical one for what?"

"The one that killed Lawton and Charity Hisp this afternoon."

"What!"

"We were having such a nice talk, me and Lawton.

From time to time I had to encourage him. He'd get over hurting from the last time and get brave again. And, damn it, we were right down to the final item, just how and where he was going to give me his copy of Ted Lewellen's seven projects, with the maps and overlays."

"Lewellen?"

"Oh, come *on*! Do you think I'm that stupid? There's no point in going on with this." I reached and plucked the spade out of the dirt pile.

"No, no! That was just a reflex. I'm sorry, Okay. Professor Lewellen. I'm coexecutor of the estate. What about Mr. Hisp?"

I laid the spade across my thighs. "It was just one of those damn-fool things that happen. Bad luck. You know that long skinny neck of his. He took a chance and tried to duck around me and I swung to stop him and the edge of my wrist hit him right on the throat and crushed something in there. He started making a funny, gagging, gargling sound and he started digging his fingernails into his neck. His face began to get red. He fell down and rolled around and his eyes bugged out. Then he hammered his heels on the rug and died. No doubt about how dead he was. She and I knew it the minute it happened. I nearly lost her. Ran like a deer. I caught her by the nape of the neck in one of those little garden places. Great day for necks. I held her head under the water in one of those reflecting pools. After she stopped buckling, when I let go of her, she stayed right there, facedown on the stones with her head under. She saw me hit Hisp. I knew that if I was going to have any chance at all, she had to be number two."

"Were you driving that idiotic blue Rolls truck?"

"No. I borrowed a car."

"Their children were out?"

"Every one."

"Look. Having my arms like this is beginning to make

my shoulders cramp so bad, I can't think. How about cutting my arms loose?"

"Not one chance, lawyer. Forget it."

"Well . . . what time did this happen?"

"Two o'clock. I know you've got the original. I know that stuff was in your hands because at the time Ted died, you were trying to work out some way it could be handled in his estate if he died. Okay. Frank Hayes and I were with Ted a few years ago in Mexico, looking for something in the Bay of La Paz. We crapped out. Our big pump quit and the weather began to turn, and before we could get back there, a hurricane changed the bottom so much we'd have to start all over again."

"And this Frank Hayes is the Hayes of Seven Seas, based at Grand Cayman?"

"Right. We were both lined up to go with Ted on the one he was getting ready to leave on when he was killed. It was going to be rich and easy. He brought me the letter from Mansfield Hall and we agreed it sounded like whoever he represented had hold of Ted's research. And I knew it belonged to the daughter and that she didn't have it, and nobody had seen it since he died."

A couple of tree toads tried their pitch pipes and the whole chorus gradually joined in. Some moths had been attracted to the Coolites. They could land on them without frying, and their wing shapes made big moving shadows.

I knew his mind was spinning, running back and forth and up and down the cage, looking for a way out. "Mansfield Hall," he said. The tone was not questioning. It was bitter.

"No," I said. "He didn't name you. I figured if somebody was trying to make a deal through Hall to set up a treasure hunt, it had to be Hisp. I got to you through Hisp. In my phone tip I tell the law that you and Hisp defrauded Ted Lewellen's daughter. I tell them it was your idea. I tell them you owned Hisp on account of

knowing how he and a man named Gary Lindner specu-
lated in bonds in the bank's name six or seven years ago. I
tell them you are a director of the bank and you were
trying to turn the estate assets into money by secretly
making a deal with Seven Seas. I tell them that you and
Hisp were fighting about who was going to get what.
They'll really look for you, Collier. They may look a lot
of places, but they won't look in this hole. Sorry, friend.
It's the only way I'm going to get home free. Find something wrong with it."

"Just one thing wrong. Jesus, this hurts! It keeps me
from thinking clearly. Can't you . . . "

"No. What's the one thing wrong?"

"Assume it works. You walk away empty."

"I'll be in the clear. I'll settle for that."

"Killing the Hisps is going to be very big, McGee.
When they can't find me, it's going to be more and more
important to pin down exactly where I was when last
seen. And who I was with. I can make you a better offer.
I'll swear I asked you to the ranch early. You arrived
about one o'clock. I'll turn over all the Lewellen papers to
you."

"And then blow the whistle on me. Who would they
believe? Thomas J. Collier, or me? No thanks."

"But you don't know how much ammunition you have,
man! You know that I betrayed my trust as coexecutor of
the estate. You know I learned of illegal bond dealings
and didn't report it. You could completely ruin me. They'd
pick me apart. Blow the whistle on you? You could even
make a pretty good case that I was the one who sent you
to beat some sense into Lawton Hisp."

I thought it over. There is the precise point in the poker
game when you have to give the impression of carefully
computing the odds. Most people with a bust hand bet
too quickly and smile too much. You hesitate a long time
before you make your heavy bet into that strong hand
across the table.

I got up and tossed the spade aside and went over and picked him up off the ground.

"What are you . . ."

I carried him to the hole.

"Hey! Oh, my God!"

I bent over and swung him over the hole and let go. He landed on his back in three inches of seepage.

"McGee!" he roared, from the darkness.

I chunked the shovel into the dirt pile, picked up a full load, dropped it where I figured the middle of him had to be.

"Wait!" he roared. "Wait!" and then he began yelling. He was trying to make words, but he couldn't get his mouth closed far enough to make them. He was breaking.

I went over and got one of the Coolites and dropped it into the hole next to his head. I sat on my heels and looked down at him. He stopped roaring.

"I don't see why I should have to explain all this to you, Collier. You're just too damned tricky. There's no way I could trust you to do what you say. I'd worry all the time. I'd wonder if you don't own somebody on the cops who'd come to pick me up for questioning and blow my brains out of the far side of my head for resisting arrest. You're too important. You sell people this big successful image called Tom Collier. I almost forgot to give you the message from Nancy. She says to tell you she's doing just fine without you."

"Listen! Please listen! I'll write everything down. Things they can prove. Please get me out of here! Oh, Jesus! You've got to be crazy. I can write down . . . terrible things I've done. You're right. Nobody should ever trust me at all."

"Ted Lewellen trusted you. Pidge trusted you. How did you expect to get away with making a deal on Lewellen's research and maps? Big strikes get publicity. She'd remember the name of the sunken vessel, wouldn't she? Publicity would smoke you out. Then she'd have some questions."

"Get me out of here!"

"No way."

"Wait! What did you want to know? About the daughter? She'll be locked up. Nobody will be paying any attention."

"Locked up for what?"

"Emotional problems. There's a history of instability. The deal is I can get appointed guardian. Her husband gets the income from the trust."

"You made a deal with Howie Brindle?"

"Help me. Please."

"Want to see how many shovels it takes to cover your head?"

"What do you *want?*"

"Howie wouldn't make a deal with you. Even in a hole in the ground, in the last five minutes of your life, you keep on lying. Howie is a wonderful guy. Ask anybody who knows him."

"Brindle is a bug! Listen, he *worked* for me. Any lawyer with experience in criminal defense knows that kind of a bug. Five minutes after I started chatting with him about the death of Fred Harron, I knew he'd killed Fred. Maybe he did Lois a favor. That's beside the point."

"Howie wouldn't hurt a fly."

"Dammit, man, he admitted he killed Fred. He sat in my office and blubbered and moaned and howled and wrung his hands and swore that he hadn't meant to hurt the doctor, that he was just horsing around, and he'd never hurt anybody before in his whole life. He was good. You could almost believe him. But if he's true to form, there's a whole full-strength platoon of bodies stretching back into Brindle's past. He wasn't going to admit a thing, not even after I'd trapped him three or four times. Then he began to realize I was going to push for an indictment if he kept lying, and might make a deal if he would admit it. So he admitted it, and it didn't make him very happy when I played the tape back to him. Not right then, because I think he'd have taken the tape and left me on the office floor. Later, when I could tell him that he was listening to a copy of the original tape. Nobody had ever owned him before. It was very hard for him to get used to knowing that he had to do whatever I told him. I told him to stay in the area and keep in touch. I had a different project in mind for him, but then Ted Lewellen got killed in an accident and it shaped up into a better project. I told him to marry her."

"You thought he could?"

"The water is getting deeper."

"So drown a little."

"My heart is beating too fast. It really is."

"It'll get a long long long rest."

"You're a bug like Brindle. You're rotten! You know that? You've got a cold heart. Yes, I told him to marry her and he married her. He hung around. He ran her errands, did her chores. He was always there. She was alone. He seems like a nice boy. I told him the cruise was a good idea. Why not? They had the boat and the money. I told him to use any way in the world to make her think she was losing her mind. When people start to think that way, it can happen. They get irrational. They act funny. And once they're on the inside, you can usually manage to keep them there."

"You'd say he's a murderer. Why didn't you tell him to kill her?"

"She's worth too much. So there'd be too much publicity, especially about where the money came from. And there might be too many pictures of Brindle in a wire-service pickup, and somebody might show up with some stories out of the past. I warned him that if he killed her, I was going to cook him good, with an apple in his mouth. McGee, I could write the whole thing out for you."

"Do you think he's killed her?"

"I don't know. People like Brindle, they get impatient. They get bored. If he could figure out a way where nobody would question it was an accident, he'd do it. Or suicide while of unsound mind. They've conned people ever since they could walk. They think people are uniformly stupid. They think we're all as empty on the inside as they are. It's a risk. Either way, I thought she couldn't raise any questions. Dead or crazy, she's out of the picture. McGee, it's worth taking risks for. It could be millions. You won't get another chance like this. You'll live small all your life."

"I guess I will," I said quietly. "I guess I expect to."

There he was down in his hole, with water up to his ears. Ted had probably trusted and respected him. Please help me with my problems, Mr. Collier. Help me take care of my girl in case I happen to slide under a truck.

Collier took care of her. He had a jolly sociopath standing by, waiting for an odd job, and then this new opportunity came along. Take care of Ted's girl. *My* girl. Give her to good old Howie Brindle.

The white cold light filled the hole, and the moths were down there, fluttering around Tom Collier. He made a strange sound and I looked closer and saw that he was crying. His underlip was protruding and vibrating. Poor Tom. Playtime is ending. All the sweet tastes are fading away. Someone else will have to chomp the good steaks, snuff the bouquet of the wines, count the crisp bills, spread the warm ivory thighs, buy the favors, laugh at the jokes, buy the trinkets.

I held the spade handle so tightly my hands ached with the strain. It was my impulse to start spading that dirt into the hole as fast as I could, working from the feet toward the head, fill it in and stamp it down and spread the shell over the raw place. The weeping noises were almost as small as the sounds of the tree toads.

I stretched out and leaned into the hole and sliced the few layers of filament tape that held his arms snugged together. I picked the Coolite stick out of the water, retrieved the other one, and used their light as I walked back to the car. So intense had been the desire to kill him

and so narrow the escape, I walked like a gawky mario-
nette with an amateur working the strings. I could not
remember which arm was supposed to swing out first when
walking. It was like those supreme attacks of insomnia
that are so bad you cannot remember where you put
your hands and arms when you sleep. I couldn't even
find the lights on Miss Agnes. As I backed out, my
coordination came back, and then I began to shiver with
reaction. I turned around by the locked wire gate and
hurried back along the canal bank, turned over his bridge
and hit the highway toward home.

When the shivering went away, I began to take some
relish in thinking of the jolly host returning to his party.
I'm back, girls! Here I am in my sodden jump suit. My
hairpiece is full of mud. My wallet is empty and I've got
these shoulder cramps and this sore jaw. And I've been
crying a lot.

I knew what he would probably do, after he found
his way home and got cleaned up. He would shut himself
in a room and phone Hisp's home. And when Lawton
Hisp answered, Tom Collier would wish him, after a long
pause, a very happy New Year. And then Tom would
hang up and sit there and think about it. He would think
of all the things he would like to do to me. In the end he
would realize why there was not one damned thing he
could do.

There were two hours left in the old year. I did not
want to spend them with anybody. Not even Meyer.

At Bahia Mar, I threaded my way past some parties I
wanted to escape, and when I was aboard *The Busted
Flush*, I was chary about turning on too many lights. There
were some residual shivers from time to time. I quelled
them with a chill flagon of Plymouth gin. It cheered me
enough to warrant my digging out a personal steak and
preparing it for broiling when I was ready. I leafed through
the cassette stacks and put Mr. Julian Bream on, wanting
something expert, mannered and complicated.

I showered and changed to an old blue robe, rebuilt my drink and sat and picked tenderly at the new blister on the heel of my left hand. Meyer says that somewhere between aphorisms and sophistry there is, or should be, a form of expression called sophorisms. These express the mood of emotional sophomorism. If the wish is the deed, then I killed him. If I hadn't killed him, somebody else would have. If Howie hasn't killed her yet, he isn't really trying.

I got up and got the big atlas and opened it on my lap and pulled the lamp closer. I found the big double-page spread of the Pacific and slowly ran the edge of my thumbnail down the shades of blue which showed the great depths, the rare shallows.

They were out there, a microspeck moving down the flat blue, as invisible to the naked eye as a microbe on an agar dish. Now they would be coming up on the Line Islands. A five- or six-hour difference. The sun had wheezed its hot, tired way westward, and the girl to be known henceforth as Lou Ellen was under its late-afternoon glare, lifting and falling to those big bland rollers, with six or seven hours before her New Year's Eve.

I studied the good names out there printed on the blue dye, Christmas Island Ridge, Tokelau Trough, Pacific Basin, and tried to think about those names, tried to wonder how they had measured the shocking depths out there. The mind is a child that keeps turning back, reaching for the WET PAINT sign. I kept seeing, superimposed upon the blue, Meyer's image of her, with the slightly negative buoyancy of the newly drowned, going down and down, through the lambent layers of undersea light, through the blues, greens, turquoise.

Tom Collier was right. Bugs like Howie have this terrible, incurable optimism. If nobody sees you do it, nobody can prove you did it. And people have always believed you. Howie is a *nice* little boy. He's so helpful and willing and happy. Fat people are jolly people.

Next step, McGee. If, through some miracle of timing and coincidence, you should achieve radio contact, what would you say? Hello, there! By what law of the high seas can you send Captain Hornblower aboard his frigate to wrest the legal wife from her legal husband? How do you get yourself air-dropped onto the deck, assuming the *Trepid* could be located at all?

The next step is wait. Wait here, or fly out and wait there. But wait, no matter what. It would be ironic indeed if the one Howie flipped out of the tree would be McGee. I sweetened the drink, changed the music, put the steak in. I had a slight and somber buzz from the astringent gin. Whee. Whoopee. Happy New Something.

16

MY jet flight from Honolulu arrived at Pago Pago International Airport at three in the afternoon on Saturday the fifth of January. The airport is at Tafuna, about seven miles from town. The airstrips are on crushed coral rock, extended out into the sea. It is the only way one is going to find any flat land on those islands.

We were supposed to come in a little earlier, but it was the rainy season and a black, heavy tropical storm was moving across the big island, covering most of its fifty or so square miles. There are tricky winds in those storms, so we strolled around in a big circle on high, waiting for it to move away from the field.

We came down into a scrubbed, shiny, dripping world, full of a smell of flowers, rain freshness and jet fuel. I had learned that there is an *n* in the name when it is pronounced, that the first vowel sound had about the same value as the *o* in mom, and the *g* was halfway between hard and soft. Hence Pahng-o Pahng-o. When you say things correctly, you become an instant world traveler. Because of the rains, it was off season, and about eight of us got off. I had only carry-on, an unusual event at Tafuna, apparently, when the visitor is not reserved back out.

It is known as American Samoa. The U. S. dollar is accepted. The taxi driver accepted an impressive number of them to drive me into town to the Intercontinental Hotel. I had heard that the place was hot. It had seemed very hot to me when I came off the bird. But that had been the coolness after the rain. The driver said he would take me everywhere during my wonderful stay on the incredibly beautiful island of Tutuila. In his shiny elderly Plymouth with its square wheels and its ineffectual little fan buzzing directly into his sweat-shiny face, he would take me up and down all these perpendicular green mountains for a very nice price.

As we came around a corner of the coast road, I saw Pago Pago Harbor. I had seen it from the air, but height flattens things out. I'd been told it was the most beautiful harbor in the world. It *is* the most beautiful harbor in the world. Once, uncounted centuries ago, it was the fiery, bubbling pit of a volcano. The crater ate at its own walls, consuming itself, growing larger, until finally a whole side of it fell into the sea, and the sea came smashing into the red, boiling crater. That must have been a day. That must have been something to see and hear. We don't know how long it took the sea to win. Now, inside the steep green hills, it is tranquil in victory.

He turned into the hotel drive. The first half-ounce of raindrops from the next cloud began to splat as I paid him. It was a very handsome hotel—low buildings, rounded thatched roofs, in the turtle-*fale* island style. But the thatch, of course, was covered ferroconcrete, and there were a hundred and one rooms, all air-conditioned, and a lower level with free-form pool, umbrellas over the tables, an outside bar and a view across the harbor of Mount Pioa, the Rainmaker. The Rainmaker was on the job. The day deepened from bright sunlight to deep dusk as the rain thundered down.

It does not take very long to make your appraisal as you walk across a lobby. A gift shop on the left full of bright overpriced instant artifacts. Little scraps of this and that on the floor. Bleared windows. A man in a uniform yawning and scratching his behind. Some overflowing ashtrays.

Three girls were in busy conversation behind the counter, with giggles that made them bend double and stagger around. One of them kept glancing at me. I waited placidly until she came over to the desk. The girls were three shades of brown. She was the shade in the middle, chocolate fudgicle.

"You want something, ah?" No inflection. No expression.

"A room."

"You got a reservation?"

"No."

"You haven't got a reservation."

"No, I haven't got a reservation."

"And you want a room."

"I want a room. A nice room. Big. With a view. I want a nice big bed in the room. I want somebody to come on the run with ice and booze once I am in my nice room. I want it for maybe five days, six days, maybe more. I will eat my meals here. If you have no serious objection, give me something to sign. You have lots of empty rooms. Here is a five-hundred-dollar bill which I happened to come across the other day. Give me a receipt for it, please. It is an advance on the room and the service."

"You're pretty funny. You knock me out," she said unsmiling.

"I can see that." I filled out the registration card, while she scowled at the key rack. I knew the first one she gave me would be the worst in the house. I expected to come back for another key, and did. I didn't expect another bad room, but I got one, and finally on the third try, she decided she'd gotten even. The room was very nice. It was even reasonably clean.

The whole hotel has a disease called The Only Game in Town. If you don't like it, too bad. It has a secondary infection called No Ownership. In other words, management has a contract without a piece of the action.

But hotels, no matter how slovenly, are staffed by humans, and with a little care and some useful observation, you can usually manage to find a bartender who will not slop half your drink on the back of your hand, a waiter who will tell you what the kitchen does best, a maid who will change both sheets. We are all at the mercy of the hostility of the service industry. And I had begun to sense that most of these gentle, brown, warm, charming, simple children of nature, as it said in the brochures, would in fact enjoy splitting, cleaning, and deep-frying every Yankee they could reach. They tell me that in free Samoa, this feeling is even more apparent.

In the relative cool of the evening, I walked slowly from the hotel past the docks to the village green and found some stores beyond it, up a dirt road. I found something called the Pacific Trading Company. Samoans selling clothes from Japan, India and Taiwan to Samoans. I found two thin white shirts of Indian cotton which fitted well enough, two pairs of walking shorts in a cool weave, a pair of madras swim pants, a pair of crude leather sandals and a straw hat from Uruguay with a big brim and a high crown, nicely woven. Every price ended in 99¢. No tax. I put the hat on. A small boy wanted to carry my bundle. I had to give him a dime to let me carry it. He understood the logic behind our arrangement and said that every day I bought anything, he would be glad to make the same deal again.

I got back to the hotel in the last of the beautiful golden light. I ordered a rum drink in the air-conditioned bar on the upper level and finally picked out a useful type. The bartender did not have to ask him what he wanted and seemed very quick to serve it. The customer was a tall, hunched man with dusty black hair, a nicely tailored bush jacket of bleached lightweight denim, an air of weary authority.

After an initial hesitancy, he was glad to chat. His name was Revere. Wendell Revere, some sort of under-secretary of the Department of the Interior, who had been sent over to do a survey on education which was supposed to last a month and had lasted three. I found out that the Department of Interior administers American Samoa, and the Secretary appoints the Governor.

I explained that I had flown down to meet friends who were coming down by small boat from Hawaii. This astonished him. He said it was one hell of a long trek. He said that, no offense meant, it seemed that of late more and more damned fools were roaming the oceans in small boats, apparently to get their names in the papers and their faces on television.

I said that my friends, the Brindles, were actually de-livering the boat to a man who had seen it in Hawaii and said he would buy it if they could deliver it. A man named Dawson. A recent arrival. He was in the land-development business.

Revere scowled at me. "A recent arrival? How can that be? No one can come in here, not to work and com-pete. In our infinite paternalistic wisdom, we decided that it should be Samoa-for-Samoans. Of course, there have been some exceptions made, like the Japanese fisher-men."

"I beg your pardon?"

"You saw the cannery across the harbor, didn't you? That warehouse-looking thing on the waterfront with those damned rust-bucket fishing vessels rusting and rotting away at the docks in front of it. Tuna fish. Management decided that Samoans were too lazy and undependable to use as a work force, so they pulled the strings to permit the importation of fishermen from Japan, a great horde of squat, dim little subhuman robots who are managing to kill all the porpoise in the Pacific along with their damned tuna fish."

"Mr. Revere," the barman said in a warning tone.

"I know, Henry. I talk too much. Talking too much is what gets me assignments like this one. I was a marine on Guadalcanal a long time ago, many wars ago, Mr. McGee, and I am afraid I have not yet learned to love and treasure my little yellow neighbors. Two more please, Henry. I'll try to behave, after I tell Mr. McGee about one of the sights. Tomorrow, sir, take that cable car and keep a careful eye on the harbor in front of the canneries. You will see clouds of nauseous guck flowing directly into the harbor. Here they are permitted eighty times the pollution permissible stateside. The harbor is the sewer of the tuna business here. But if you can get inside them, which is unlikely, then you can really test the strength of your gag reflex as you——"

"Mr. Revere!"

"You're right, Henry. I must behave. I should not become exercised at one of the facts of life, that industry resists controls which cost money, and a setup like this, an unincorporated territory with a toothless constitution, makes for very low operating costs. And that is the obligation to the shareholders, right? Management's prime responsibility. How did this start? Oh, a man named . . . "

"Dawson. In land development."

"He would be Samoan, sir," Henry said. "One of the ASDC scholarships. They go to the University of Hawaii usually."

Revere saw my look of puzzlement. "ASDC," he said,

"means American Samoan Development Corporation. All Samoan. They own this hotel and they have some big tourist plans. You can come here and stay, provided you can prove a continuing income, post bond, and so on. I think the ASDC wants to get some of the red tape cut so they can open up some beach land for well-to-do retired people. There are some here now, of course."

"How would I find this Mr. Dawson?" I asked.

"Please, Henry?" Revere asked. Henry nodded and went off backstage somewhere.

Revere had talked himself out. After Henry came back and told me that Luther Dawson would be along in about ten minutes, Revere excused himself and left. Henry polished a glass and said shyly, "Everything is not as bad as he says."

"I know."

"He is a good man. He thinks it should be better here. It should be. I guess it should be better everywhere than it is."

"That is a very wise observation."

"And sometimes it is a little better than it is other times."

I looked around the bar area. "This seems to be a very quiet Saturday night, Henry."

"Oh yes, sir. Very very restful. Many people go away this time of year."

"Where is the action?"

"It is very nice to ride the tramway across the harbor, sir. It goes from Solo Hill every seven minutes all the way up to the top of Mount Alava, which is sixteen hundred and ten feet high."

"Thank you, Henry."

"On top of Mount Alava, sir, you will find the educational television station KVZK, which is famed for broadcasting into every schoolroom in American Samoa. You can walk through and see all the programs which are going out to the schoolchildren."

"You are very kind, Henry."

"Also, many people buy *laufala* mats to take home. They are the very best in the world because they are dried in the sun in a secret way which retains the natural oils. Also . . . "

"You are telling me that if I get restless, I should go out and buy a mat."

"Or perhaps some tortoise-shell jewelry. Very nice here."

Luther Dawson arrived before Henry could further inflame me with his inventory of mad delights. He was a sturdy, handsome and agreeable young man. The Samoans are attractive people. I offered a drink and he said that he would appreciate a Coca-Cola, please. He and Henry exchanged some brief phrases in an incomprehensible island lilt, and I took Luther over to a table. Luther wore one of those shirts which, about five thousand years ago, looked very jazzy on Harry Truman in Key West. On Luther it looked apt, even conservative.

He was baffled, in a humble way, that anyone would want to seek him out. And there was some concealed suspicion there too. The four years at the University of Hawaii had given him speech patterns which were strangely at odds with the sternness and impassivity of his expression.

"Oh, sure. Of course. Howie and Pidge. Right! That is some kind of boat there, believe it."

"I know the *Trepid*. I lived on her for a while when Pidge's father was alive."

"It has absolutely everything. You could hack it anywhere in the world on that."

"You're really making one hell of a buy. At a hundred and thirty thousand, you're stealing that boat, Mr. Dawson."

I looked, but there was nothing to read. Dark eyes

looked out of a beautifully carved head. "It seemed fair, Mr. McGee."

"I flew here from Honolulu to ask you what you'll take for your option to buy the *Trepid*. I represent a very interested party."

"Then they *are* on their way?"

"Why not? It was a firm deal, I heard. They'll be here by the tenth, according to their estimate. Is there any chance you might change your mind about buying her?" I raised my voice. "Can you come up with the hundred and thirty thousand?"

He glanced over toward the bar. "Maybe they won't want to sell when they get here."

"I don't understand."

He explained his situation. If they moved the decimal point two places to the left, he still couldn't buy the *Trepid*. He had met Howie on the docks. They'd had some long talks. Howie was really a beautiful person. He told Luther his problems. Howie felt that one more long sea voyage together would mend the marriage, and then they could go on around the world as they planned. But she wanted to fold up the trip and the marriage, sell the *Trepid* right there in Hawaii, and fly home. If Luther would just agree to buy it if they'd deliver it to Pago Pago, that would be a big help. Luther had told Howie that Pidge wouldn't believe he could buy that much boat, and Howie said that if he just told Pidge he was in land development in Samoa, she'd believe it. Howie said it was a little white lie. Howie said he would be doing Pidge a fantastic favor because she was a very nervous and neurotic person and her behavior was very erratic and frightening lately, and she was at her best after long days at sea. Howie said he was very worried about her.

Luther said, "Maybe it didn't work, and you can buy the vessel. I got the idea that if she still wanted to split, she'd fly home from here and he'd take it on alone to

Suva, Auckland, Sydney and so on, picking up crew for short hops. He said maybe he'd write a book. But if he changed his mind about that, the *Trepid* could be for sale here. This might be the best place in this part of the Pacific, because there'd be import duties other places, maybe. I was just doing the guy a favor. You know how it is. I mean a person should get a last chance to fix up the marriage. Right?"

"Absolutely. Thanks for leveling with me."

"No stress, Mr. McGee."

"So I'll hang around and see them when they get in."

"If they made up and they want to go on, they might head for someplace else. Apia. Suva maybe, if they've got the range and supplies. I mean it might be easier for Howie to do that than explain to her that he talked me into a setup."

"Possible," I said, with a smile that hurt my teeth. "What would be the situation for setting up radio contact with them?"

"Go toward the *malae* from here and you'll come to the Communications Office. It's open every morning, eight to eleven thirty. We've got direct teletype to Honolulu and San Francisco. Did you know that? They've got a big radio setup, broadcast the weather and all that. They'd know."

After my solitary dinner, where the only entertainment was a retired admiral and his lady on the other side of the dining room, on tour, I went yawning to bed. They were both deaf. He kept roaring at her that the hotel was right on the site of the good old Goat Island Club, and she kept shrieking at him that she didn't have to be told the same damned thing fifty times running.

Heavy rain awakened me in the night, and for a half a breath I did not know where I was. Where is a product of who. And identity seems raveled by jet lag. To the

tune of "Who Is Sylvia?" we sing "Who Is McGeevia?"
I was on the wrong side of the world, and my heart was
a stone.

17

ALL creatures seem to seek comfort in routine. The cows bawl at first light for the milker. In Ireland the cows are milked at ten, a more reasonable hour, and begin their bawling then, if the ceremony is delayed. The cat comes to the kitchen at five, sits to wash, knowing it is time for supper. (Take a note: Check with Chookie and see how fares the cat name of Raoul I turned over to her after somebody strangled the lady who owned him.)

We put on the same shoe first every time and take off the same one first every time, and feel obscurely uneasy when we vary our dumb little pattern. We start the shave at the same place every time, put on a hat at the angle that feels right because it feels like all the other times.

Patterns hold us in place, give us identity. And patterns are a kind of freedom, because if all the little motions of life vary each time, they require thought. When the memories are imprinted in the fibers of the nerves and muscles, the shoes are on, the face shaved, the belt latched, with no conscious awareness of how it happened.

There was so little to do, my days became the same very quickly. An early breakfast of tropical fruit and bad coffee. A slow uphill stroll in the relative cool of morning to the station, from which the cable car took off for the summit. This was far up the slope of Solo Hill, because when you want to go from here to there by cable car, you have to get high enough to allow for the deep sag of the cables.

Service started at eight in the morning. Two dollars and a half for the round trip. The Samoan fare taker bore a slight resemblance to Satchmo, was exceedingly jolly, and, if you didn't give him the exact fare, never failed to go through his little act. Great flustered consternation. He could not make change. Oh, dear. Then his face would light up. Ah! I will have it for you when you return! I saw him work it on the tourists. When the cable car would return, he would hop about and point and cry, "The taxis are leaving!"

It was a harmless little larceny. He tried it on me every time. Every time I said I would wait right there for change, because I was walking down the hill. Each time he told me I shouldn't walk in the heat. I should take a taxi. Each time I said I enjoyed walking. Then he would slap his pockets, show sudden pleased astonishment and produce my fifty cents, and say, "I had it all the time!"

Each morning I would take my ride in the little cable car. There was just the one car, rectangular with rounded corners, about nine feet long, five feet wide and seven feet high. It was painted dark maroon with two gold horizontal stripes. It dangled from the cable by a device that looked like a miniature oil-drilling derrick about eight feet high. This was fastened to a long housing with internal wheels and a brake system which clamped it securely to the cable. Underneath were two big skids made of heavy bent pipe on which it rested in the cable house on Solo Hill and on the arrival pad atop Mount Alava. Going up, there were three windows on the port side, two windows and a central door on the starboard, said door locked from the outside on takeoff, and opened by the attendant at the top. There were two windows in each end. All the windows could be opened by pulling the top half down. They were double-hung, with a fixed lower pane.

Some mornings I rode alone. The capacity of the car was eleven persons, and I never saw it full, though I was assured that in season there was sometimes a wait of over a half hour for the ride. I rode with ships' officers, with German tourists in hiking boots, some young Japanese girls, fresh and delicate and lovely as spring garden flowers, some gigantic Indiana schoolteachers in flowered pants suits, honeymoon couples from Nevada, Montreal and places unmentioned, Samoans from the other islands, an Italian travel agent, two vulcanologists from Yugoslavia.

Some people would take a look at the cable, take a look at the distant destination, blanch, and back away, shaking their heads, smiling in the nervous apology of sudden terror. The aerial cable car is, after all, the safest mechanical form of transportation ever devised by man. Uncounted hundreds of millions of passenger miles are logged without incident. When the rare incident occurs, the setting is so dramatic, the whole world knows it the same day.

Most of the women made little squeals and yelps of delighted alarm. Most of the men would have done the same, but for tradition. Had some sadist replaced the floor with a thick plate of Plexiglas, there would have been a lot more volume to the screaming. The car rode downhill on the cable from Solo Hill to a low point about a hundred and fifty feet over the dock area, where the freighters and the big passenger ships (in season) tied up. And from there it climbed nearly fifteen hundred feet, passing directly over the canneries, so high above them the long buildings with the tin roofs looked like freight cars jammed onto parallel sidings, seven or eight rows side by side. You could see the corroding vessels docked in front of the cannery, some of them barely afloat, some resting on the bottom. You could see a big rusty water tank behind the cannery. From high above, when the conditions were right, out beyond the slots where the incoming Jap vessels were unloaded, you could see the unfolding clouds of glop staining the harbor, browning the blue.

Then up and up the slope, the car hanging level, greenery close below. That fantastic greenery of total tropics, with a thousand lush hungry varieties jammed in so close no scrap of bare ground was visible. Giant ferns, flowering vines, plants with huge green leaves, choking, reaching, clasping each other and climbing over each other, strangling and quarreling, elbowing and complaining.

About fifty feet below the platform, the cable car would always stop while they changed the clutch, or something. It would swing gently and the passengers would stare at each other wide-eyed and ask questions nobody could answer. They would sigh and smile and hug each other when it continued.

Once at the top, I would walk to the right, through the big television studio, where a dozen monitor screens showed a dozen programs being beamed into classrooms, and walk on up a small slope past the big red legs of the base of the television tower, past the big star I could see by night, fashioned of light bulbs hung on high, and up a walk with a railing on each side made of two-and-a-half-inch steel pipe, out to the little round pavilion at the end, open, with a thatched roof.

It was always cooler on top of the mountain. There I would take out the ten-power monocular I had purchased at the store near the Pacific Trading Company. It was a Japanese item. The proprietor and I had a long discussion about the narrow field of vision, about a small dent in the barrel, a flaking away of the blue lens coating, and a patch of fungus visible on the inside of the large lens, and compromised on a price of eleven dollars. Including imitation leather case.

I would stand beyond the pavilion and brace myself and slowly sweep the horizon in all the likely and unlikely directions. I had a chart of Tutuila and knew that if their navigation was sound, they would come down on a course that would keep them east of the island, well off Cape Matatula. Once south of the small, close-in island of Aunu'u, they could come due west, staying well in, skirting the harsh shore with its flat black shelves of ancient lava rock, the mist of sea spray from the waves breaking on rock. Off Laulii the harbor entrance would open up for them and they would turn north northwest, past that ridiculous little round tall cake of eroded land with palms on top of it, and come into the quiet of the protected harbor.

The power of ten pulled the distant dots close, and usually they were the Japanese tuna boats coming or leaving, high bow with a boom, low amidships, and red rafts stacked up on top of the high and ugly aft. I could see weather moving across the sea. And from the pavilion, without the monocular, I could read the knife edge of the rim of the old crater, an irregular curve out toward the harbor entrance.

Sometimes I walked over to look down into the harbor and use the lens to check the little flotilla of lovely schooners and sloops and yawls at anchor along the shoreline beyond the commercial docks, wondering if the *Trepid* could have sneaked in by first light. And then I would remember I had taken my look from the cable car on the way up. Across the way, there were private homes climbing the slope, invisible in all the greenery, except for their pale roofs in a shallow pyramidal angle, like Chinese hats. In contrast, the roofs of the hotel buildings were bulging and rounded, somehow like beehives, set on the promontory just to the left of the two sets of commercial docks. The cables dipped down toward the harbor and finally were too far away to be seen, and thus seemed to disappear into nothingness. The tourists did not like to look at that optical illusion. It made them feel dizzy.

When I had satisfied myself that the sea was empty, I would take the next trip back down. I would look at the wind textures on the harbor surface, like crinkled foil from the cable height. Once I saw something on the dock I could not identify. Tiny gray-white things in a neat line, dozens of them. On my way back into the town, I went over to take a close look. They were used golf carts from the Crestridge Golf Club in Scranton, Pennsylvania. I decided not to ask why they had been consigned to Pago Pago. It seemed one of those things it is best not to know. The rear ends of the power establishment of Scranton had been cradled in these whining contrivances for the five years' estimated life allowable for depreciation purposes and the men had ground up hill, down dale, uttering glad cries of triumph, loud groans of consternation, shouting wagers back and forth. It is difficult not to anthropomorphize the elderly battered golf cart swung suddenly up out of the black hold and lowered to the dock in the hot sunshine. Where am I? What am I doing here? The more human reaction would be, What did I do wrong?

I went from Solo Hill to the Communications Office. Yes, sir, we have had the call for the *Trepid* on all the traffic lists. No, sir, no response. We'll keep trying. If there's any word at all, we'll get in touch with you at the hotel.

Then the slow walk back to the hotel, if it wasn't raining. I would pause at a small boatyard and see how much they had done since the last stop. Never very much. There was a small cruiser, a workboat with a broad beam, heavy construction, that I liked. It was named *Au A Manú*. I never asked what it meant. I was afraid it would turn out to mean Windward or Kitty Kat or Buster's Folly or Me Too.

Change to swim trunks and go down to the pool area

and sit with a book at a table under an umbrella and have two very good rum drinks. They were good because I was finally able to convince the house that I wanted no sugar at all in them.

Swim hard for thirty minutes. Go up and change. Take the book to the dining room. A light lunch. Back to the room. Siesta time from two thirty to four. Afternoon swim. Then a walk to the park and the waterfront, if it wasn't raining or about to rain, back to the upper-level bar for one of Henry's drinks. A late dinner, in no hurry. More of the book. Early to bed.

When my head cleared, when the jet lag was gone, I was repositioned on the underside of the earth, and everything around me became ever more real and ever more unremarkable.

On Saturday, the twelfth day of the new year, as the first trip of the cable car moved out over the bay, I looked down in my habitual, methodical search of the harbor and saw the *Trepid* tied up to a floating platform around the corner of the larger commercial dock. I had been looking for her so long, I had to look at her three times before I could believe that I was seeing her. The slight side-to-side movement of the cable car plus the movement along the cable made it difficult to hold the ten-power lens on her deck. Sails all neatly furled and lashed. Fenders in place. No one on the deck. And I was heading away from it.

It was an interminable trip up and back. I waited by the cable car. The only other people aboard had been a Japanese couple, with a basket of lunch. The attendant topside felt he had to keep the car for his full allotted time, and he kept holding up fingers to tell me how many minutes were left. I stood leaning on the hurricane fencing which enclosed the huge pulley wheels for the great length and weight of braided wire cable. One turn constantly. There was some sort of clutch arrangement to disengage the other one. At last he called to me and I went down and got in, and he sent me down through the air, down to the final knowing. And suddenly it seemed that it was happening too quickly. I needed more time up there at the top, thinking about it.

I started in sunlight. The last third of the descent was through heavy rains, and winds that tugged at the car. Five minutes after I got out of the car, the rain stopped, but by then I was soaked through and I was halfway down Solo Hill, taking long strides in my sodden spongy sandals.

There was a man sitting on a keg on the floating platform. He was beefy and authoritative. He had a blue cloth cap and a Spiro T. Agnew wristwatch. No sir, the boat was private property and nobody was to go aboard except official persons. It had come all the way from Hawaii. Where the rail is smashed, there and there, a bad storm did that. The launch was washed away. The windows of the pilothouse are smashed. There is bad weather out there on the sea, and this is a small boat.

"How many people were aboard?"

"I think he did not turn to. I think with a sea anchor she would have been fine. No damage."

"Was there a woman aboard?"

"The lines are good for a sea boat. What? Yes, the woman is ill. He helped her off. They went in a taxi to the clinic after the inspector looked at their papers."

He told me where to find the clinic. They were doing a good morning business in pregnant women. There were two sturdy young Samoan women in white. They looked like identical twins, but one was a nurse and the other was the doctor. Dr. Alice Alasega.

Dr. Alasega could not spare a minute for anyone who was not either unwell or with child. I waited forty minutes before she could see me in her small office.

"You were asking about Mrs. Brindle?"

"Yes. What is wrong with her?"

"What's your relationship to her?"

"A friend."

"Then shouldn't you ask her husband?"

I hesitated. "I am going to ask Howie about it, of course. But I want to make sure that . . . he isn't kidding himself."

"I don't understand."

"Do you think Linda Brindle should continue this kind of deep-sea cruising? The *Trepid* really took a beating on this run. I mean, is she well enough, in your opinion?"

She studied me, while I tried to look earnest and reliable and concerned. At last she said, "I am not a psychiatrist. I don't know what to say. She seems to me to be in an acute depressive state. She's listless and unresponsive. Blood pressure low. Reflexes minimal. She made a determined effort to do away with herself a week ago today. Cut her wrist before her husband caught her. He did a good job of dressing it. It's healing nicely. She doesn't really remember very much about it. But she seems to believe she'd be better off dead. She said she would rather be dead than crazy. I put her on a psychic energizer, an amphetamine compound recommended for persistent depression. I told him I want to see her again on Monday. They seem to have all the money they need. I said it would be better for her to stay at the hotel than aboard their yacht."

"Some married couples are bad for each other."

"I know. In this case, I don't think so. He is obviously very much in love with his wife and very concerned about her. And she is very dependent on him, very subservient to him. I told them to relax and try to forget their problem and try to enjoy our beautiful island. It is a very romantic place."

"That's what the brochures all say, Doctor."

"You don't find it so?"

"I find it an unforgettable travel experience, Doctor.

It is unspoiled and unhurried. And picturesque."

There was an unexpected crinkle around her eyes. "How about the intoxicating scent of white ginger on a moon-drenched tropical evening?"

"Mmmm. Yes. And rain-fed waterfalls cascading over glistening rocks after a tropical shower."

"The incredibly blue Pacific?"

"One should never leave that out."

"Never, Mr. McGee. On Monday I'll find out more about the conditions aboard the boat, how demanding it is on her, and how she adjusts to it."

"Thank you, Doctor."

The sun was bright and hot and the streets were steaming as the taxi brought me back from the clinic. I happened to look down toward the hotel pool area and saw big Howie in red swim pants, with a white towel over his shoulder, heading quickly along one of the walkways toward the pool. He was burned a deep red-brown, and his long hair, cropped off straight across the back of his neck, was bleached almost white.

I caught up to him just as he was hooking his toes over the edge of the pool. He turned, squinting in the brightness, and his face lit up. "Hey! Trav! I'll be damned! What the hell are you doing way the hell and gone out here!" He pumped my hand, banged me on the shoulder. "Son of a gun! Gees, I'm glad to see a friendly face."

"You look very healthy, Howie."

"I've been outdoors a lot. That's a long haul down here. We did a lot of it under sail. Good winds. Too much wind for a while. How come you're here?"

"Pidge wrote me from Honolulu."

"No kidding! You came way out here just to meet us?"

"Among other things."

"Hey, how about ordering me a beer while I get in a swim?"

He dived in. The outdoor bar was just setting up. I went over and picked up two Fiji beers and took them to a table that caught the breeze. I watched him make some laps, splashing and blowing, using a clumsy choppy stroke that moved him at a better speed than I would have expected.

When do you open it up? And how? Soon he came padding to the table, drying his face and hair on the white towel. His brown eyes were merry and friendly. He sat down and took a deep pull at the beer, tasted it, tried again. "Not too bad."

"How is Pidge?"

He frowned. "Not so good. She started to come around pretty well back in Hawaii. After you talked to her. You know, she seemed a lot better after you talked to her, Trav. It got to be more like old times. There was just one flippy idea left, and that was her idea we should split. Sell the *Trepid* right there and split. That doesn't make any sense at all. I love that little lady. I really do. If you know we were bringing the *Trepid* down here, I guess she must have told you I had a buyer for it."

"I came down to make a better offer. A hundred and thirty is too small."

"Hell, Travis, I wouldn't let Pidge sell the *Trepid* for small money like that! I was just fumbling around finding some way to keep her near me until she gets over this bit about splitting. I found a Samoan fellow who backed me up in a little white lie."

"I've talked to Luther."

"You have! Then you know all about my little trick."

"You said she's not so good?"

"I had her to two doctors in Honolulu, and this morning I took her right from dockside to a lady doctor at a clinic. A week ago Pidge cut her left wrist pretty good. Blood all over. Scared hell out of me. The doctor said it's healing fine. The thing is, she has severe depression. She's very . . . I can't remember the word. Like nothing means anything to her."

"Lethargic?"

"Right! I think what we'll do, we'll stay right here while I get the *Trepid* repaired from the storm, and we'll stir around and see the sights and get Pidge back to being herself again."

"I'd like to talk to her."

"Sure! She'll want to see you. She's resting right now. We're in one of those huts. Number eight. Grass roof. Nice layout here, isn't it?"

"Very quiet this time of year."

"That suits us fine."

"I'll make a deal with Pidge on buying the *Trepid*."

"We don't want to sell her!"

"Well, suppose Pidge does want to sell. It's her boat to do with what she wants. Once repairs are made, I'd like to go over to the Society Islands and the Marquesas, then maybe Easter Island, and run from there to Santiago and up the coast, back through the Canal, up through the Straits of Yucatan and home."

He tried to laugh. "Hey. You're confusing me. She isn't for sale, McGee. No way."

"Here's what I'd like you to do, Howie. I've got an open airplane ticket back to Lauderdale. I can turn that over to you. Then Pidge can help me sail the *Trepid* home."

"That's a pretty dumb kind of joke there. It really is. I could get sore about something like that. You're talking about my wife."

"And that offends your sensibilities, Howie? That inflames your sense of righteousness and rectitude?"

"Well . . . why wouldn't it?"

"No more games, Howie. No more pretend. I got interested in you. I checked you out."

"Checked *me* out? For what?"

"Shut up, Howie. You are right at the end of the line."

"Line?"

"Shut up. I don't have to go into how and when and why. I couldn't get very far into why because only you would know why. But there are some names I know. Meeker. Rick and Molly Brindle. Dr. Fred Harron. Susan Fahrhowser. Joy Harris. There are a lot of names I don't know, but it doesn't matter, because any one will do. Fred Harron will do. You put that killing on tape, for Tom Collier. Why don't you just fly home on my ticket and talk to Tom?"

He kept the baffled look almost all the way. It slipped just once, and gave me a quick glimpse of what he was. I can remember exactly when I felt that same way before. I was eleven years old. My uncle sent me down to the lake shore for a bucket of water at dawn. My sneakers didn't make a sound on the packed dirt of the trail. The wind was blowing off the lake. The old sow bear was black and huge, drinking at the shore with a pair of cubs. She reared silently, facing me, blotting out all of the sky except the little bit around the edges. She did not move. She looked at me. I could smell her. My bones had turned to stalks of ice, and my heart was empty as smoke. Then she wheeled and dropped, grunted at the cubs, herding them ahead of her, along the shore and up into the alders.

I couldn't tell anyone how it was. They would think it was just a bear. It could kill you, but it was just a bear. It was more than a bear. It was something out of the blackness. It was night. It was evil. It colored that whole year of my life with a taste of despair.

The blackness was there in Howie Brindle, and then it was gone. "What the *hell* are you talking about, Trav? I mean. This is the *weirdest* conversation I ever heard anywhere. Tape? Killing? You've spent too much time out in the sun."

He looked up and past and smiled and said, "Hi, honey!"

As I turned my head, he hit me. I don't know how or

what with. A quiet time of morning. A few people around, and doubtless he knew that nobody was looking our way. The sky spun over and around me, and there was a ringing crack of my skull against the stone, a dim and distant roughness against my cheek. Then there were gabblings, excited chatter, with the voices sounding as if they were down in deep barrels. I was jostled, tugged, shifted, then lifted into the air. "Just show me the way to his room," a huge voice said. It was a blurred voice with double images, like a badly tuned television set. I was jolted rhythmically as somebody walked with me. Stairs. A rap against the anklebone, which meant a doorway. All my wiring was ripped loose somehow, left in a listless dangle.

"Touch of the sun," the huge voice said. "See, he's coming out of it. A little rest is all he needs."

I was indeed coming out of it. I could wave my putty arms and open my fried eyes. The throng murmured from the bottom of their barrels. Through a doorway. Door slammed behind us. Sits me on the bed, holding shirt bunched in left hand. Glimpse of a big brown fat fist floating toward my face. Turned with it. BAM, with rockets and red glare and so forth. Hang on the edge of the world. Breathe in, breathe out. Stretched on bed. Undoing of buttons, undoing of belt. Sandals off. Secret giggling, tucked way inside of me, saying, But sir, we hardly know each other. Hoist naked and carried and put down thumpingly on the tile floor. Cool tile. Bathroom. Thunder of water into the tub. Very strong flow. Fills fast.

Hands grasping again. Take a deep and stealthy breath and let it all out and take another. Out, take another and the cool water closing over me. Hold breath. Legs all up-bent, jammed against faucets. Big hand pushing down on the middle of my chest. Aimless thrashing of arms. Okay. Let some of breath out. *Boink*ing of bubbles in tub water. Face probably a foot under water. Hold the rest of the breath but with mouth open, back of throat closed. Eyes half open? Yes. Wavery brown face above me, parched hair. Heavy pressure of hand gone from chest. Brown face further away. Brown face, brown chest, red pants. Hold entirely still. You can do three minutes, McGee. You claim you can. Don't let the chest start those involuntary heavings, trying for air.

At the very last moment, he turned very swiftly and left the bathroom. I resisted the urge to come lunging up out of the tub. I put my nose and mouth out into the air, into the sweet, delicious, beautiful air and lifted further, breathing deeply, until my ears were out. I heard him talking. "He's coming around fine, thank you. Just fine. I'll tell him you asked." A man answered, and I heard the door close, and I sank back to the same position as before, but this time good for three minutes more if need be.

I don't think the inspection lasted more than ten seconds. But I remained under. I sneaked up for air finally, then went under again. That little turn ahead of the slow-motion fist had softened the BAM just enough. Play it safe, McGee, or the bear will get you for sure.

It took time and courage to climb out of that tub. He was gone. I tottered out and locked my door and sat on my bed. I lay back on my bed. My head had begun to ache, the whole left side of it where it had been hit, twice by him and once by the stone of the terrace.

. . . When I left his room he was just fine. I should have stayed with him. I guess he must have decided a cool bath would make him feel better. He got in and . . . passed out again. I blame myself for this. I thought he was perfectly all right . . .

Impulse and opportunity. The sow bear had had a chance at me and didn't take it.

What now, hero? Rescue the maiden. How? And did she want to be rescued, to be jolted miserably upon her caudal end against the silver-worked saddle of the rescuing knight as they hie away into the sunset?

First find the maiden fair. No. First identify that little tune he kept humming as the tub was filling. Bum-de-dum-bum, bum-de-dum-bum, BUM BUM BUM BUM BUM. Oh, hell. Of course. "On, Wisconsin." Also any high school which happened to steal the tune. On, Shamokin. On, Poughkeepsie.

Get up! Why? So he can get another chance to kill you, stupid!

18

AT five minutes of noon, I finally discovered that the Brindles had gone out, that they were not in the hotel. Everybody asked me how I felt. I said I felt rotten. I said it had been one of those long mornings.

There were two cabs drowsing in the shade, apathetic about any chance of midday trade. I asked if a great big young man with long white hair had left while they were there. The second driver knew—a dollar refreshed his memory. He remembered that they had taken a taxi. Yes, it had turned left out at the end of the hotel driveway.

The other driver shrugged, pointed a thumb skyward, and said, "Maybe the tram."

It has happened before. It happens to everyone. That curious miracle inside the skull, when a hundred bits and pieces suddenly stop endless movement and become fixed in a pattern. This was the far end of the world, measuring from the United States. Any incident in a foreign country would receive police attention, professional inspection.

This was still part of the United States, but due to the strange channel of authority, it was part of the impenetrable bureaucracy, lost in committee structures within the Department of the Interior, left to the indifferent mercies of civil servants who have learned, soon after receiving their first rating, that survival depends on always giving the impression of taking action on controversial matters, while actually merely moving papers from desk to desk.

There were doctors in Hawaii and a doctor in Samoa who would confirm mental problems, depression. People around the yacht basin at Honolulu would have been made aware of the problem. Tom Collier would verify, if necessary. There would be a very slow pickup by the news media here, and whenever news is stale, coverage is meager or nonexistent. Depressed heiress to treasure fortune jumps off a Polynesian mountain after prior suicide attempts.

I laid a five-dollar bill upon the palm of the driver and asked him how quickly he could get me to the tram station on Solo Hill. He was under way as I pulled the door shut, saying that it would be no time at all. He was very good. Though he went sideways up a good part of the hill road, he did not lose momentum or traction. I was out of the taxi as the final shriek of brakes and rubber ended. The dark red car was not waiting in its slot. I stared along the down-dangle of cable and up toward the summit, and I did not see it in motion against the blue harbor or the far green slope.

My larcenous acquaintance took my five-dollar bill and gave me two, and went through his no-change charade.

"I think some friends of mine are up there."

"Yes?"

"A very big man. As tall as I am, but a lot heavier. A very brown face, bald in front, long blond hair. With a young woman."

"Oh, yes. A big, happy man. Laughing."

"Are they up there alone?"

He looked at some kind of record on the inside wall of his cubicle. "Right now, I think, yes, there are nine. Your friends and seven more."

I tried to exhale completely, to calm myself, but I could not empty the bottom third of my lungs. Too much adrenalin was making me shake and sweat. I knew that if they put the two of us out in the middle of a field, I might just be able to take him. But this was not a time for pride, for noble games, for a test of skills. I looked around and saw that my driver, evidently reluctant to give up a customer who was making a good day for him in a slow season, had parked in the shade in the turnoff. On request he unlocked his trunk. The lug wrench was the most suitable. It was an L with a short base, with the socket on the base. He looked at me with alarm and disfavor as I tried it on. It fitted down the right leg of the shorts, and with my shirt worn outside the shorts, the socket end, hooked over my belt, was concealed.

"This is not a good thing," he said.

"What thing?"

"That wrench."

"Wrench? I asked you to open the trunk so I could see how much luggage you can carry in there. Remember?"

"How much luggage?"

"And I handed you this ten-dollar bill for your trouble. Sorry! I didn't mean to drop it. I suppose that if a man wanted to steal a lug wrench, he could grab it and shove it out of sight while you were picking up that bill."

The smile started slow and became vast. He bobbed his head. He slammed his trunk. "As you can see, it is a big trunk. Lot of suitcases."

"Thanks for showing it to me." He had a merry smile. With filed teeth and blue tattoos, he could eat you, still smiling.

I strode back to the platform. I could see the red speck of the returning car moving down the jungle green across the harbor.

"How many aboard?"

"Who could know?"

"Can you ask the man up there?"

He tapped the phone box on the wall beside him. "Not working. In the rainy time, it doesn't work."

I had left the monocular in the room. I saw a battered old pair of binoculars on a crude shelf behind him. He gave them to me willingly. I looked at the trademark. Eight-power Bausch and Lomb. They were a long way from Rochester. They had been knocked just far enough out of true so that when you got them into sharp focus, they felt as if they were suction cups, pulling your eyes slowly out of the sockets.

It seemed at first that the car was jammed with people, and my heart sank. But as it drew closer I was able to count heads, in silhouette, looking through the car from front to back. They were moving around, window to window. I made it five for several counts and finally four. Leaving five at the summit—the Brindles and three others.

Two large, loud couples got off, speaking pure Texican. The attendant wanted to hold the car, waiting for more business. I must have given him a strange look. He backed away, shut the door, and sent me off.

If the fates are kind, I thought, the three strangers who remained on top will be out near the little thatched shelter. It is near the steepest drop, facing the open sea. Due to the contour of the hilltop, it is out of the line of sight of the television studio. If the fates are in a sour mood, the strangers will be watching the educational film monitors, and already Howie Brindle will have come pounding in, roaring and weeping, pointing back up the path, trying to find the words to tell them what his poor sick wife had done to herself.

The trip was forever. The car had to be moving more slowly than ever before. Soon it would stop completely. At last it came to its pause just below the terminus, then was hoisted slowly up to come to rest inside the slot where it rested and waited.

There was no one on the platform. The attendant turned and cupped his hands around his mouth and yelled up the slope, "Car ready! Car going!"

I sprinted. I held the wrench in place with my right hand. I went around the left side of the television station on the walkway, leaped down all the steps at the end, stumbled and went to my knees, skinned the heel of my left hand, came up running. Three people were hurrying down the curving walkway between the pipe railings. I thrust past them. An old tourist hissed at me . . .

Beyond the last upward curve, the little round pavilion came into full view. Big Howie was bending over something. He seemed to be alone. He looked like somebody bending over, tying a shoe.

"Brindle!" I yelled from fifty feet away, coming on fast.

He popped up and spun. Pidge was outside the pipe railing, on her stomach on the outer edge of the slope, legs hanging over. Her arms were wrapped around one of the vertical lengths of pipe that supported the railing. He had been taking her arms from around the pipe. Once they were free, she would have slipped over the edge, skidded down through shrubbery, started spinning, then bounced, sailed, bounced, sailed a longer distance, bounced, sailed out of sight over the lip of the final straight drop.

I had to be a considerable shock to him. He had drowned me and had come back and looked at the body to be certain, had seen the mouth agape, the eyes half open, the motionlessness under the tub water. Even in shock, he managed to move sideways, to give a hard kick at her face with his heel. It snapped her head back but didn't unfreeze her grip on the pipe. Complete terror turns on total strength.

Winded and dripping, I stopped short of him, poised for whatever he might try. He had no chance of sucker-punching me into another case of sunstroke. He began to bounce and grin. It reminded me of his tireless, cat-quick performance playing volley ball on the Lauderdale beach. Big, rubbery, loose-jointed bounding.

"Yay, McGee," he said. "Come on, baby."

Out of the corner of my eye I saw that Pidge had pulled herself up and was crawling cautiously under the fence.

"Run for the cable car!" I yelled at her.

She sprang up and went off down the slope like a track-team captain, sturdy legs almost blurring with the frantic speed. I sensed he was going to try to go after her, regardless, and as he tried to dodge around the pavilion, I pulled the lug wrench free and angled in from the side and banged him over the ear hard enough to make the iron ring. Half thud, half bong. He ran four more strides on macaroni legs, fell the way you are supposed to fall, rolled up onto his feet, shaking his head, turned, and ducked under the second swing. I had not expected to miss. The momentum of the too-heavy wrench carried me halfway around, and he hit me with his fist just under the last rib, right on the side. They hit like that with a swinging log to knock down castle doors. It knocked me six feet back, and it knocked me down, and it knocked the wind out of me. I got up like a shrunken old man, sucking air with a croaking noise, certain I would never be able to straighten up again.

He was almost to the television building, bounding along, white hair abounce, rubbery fat jiggling under the sweat-pasted fabrics. I ran half sideways, bent over and croaking, holding my right side together with my left hand, still clutching the lug wrench in my right.

Once I got past the building, I took in what was happening. The red car was too far down the cable for Pidge to be aboard. She had not gone down to the level of the car, but had gone up to the enclosure where the pulley wheels, a yard in diameter, turned noisily under the weight and stress of the dark and rusty cables.

She was on the far side of the enclosure, tense and waiting, knees slightly bent. Her face was intent. It was a schoolyard game. She hoped she was quick enough to stay away from him. The attendant was down on the platform, out of sight of anyone near the pulley station. He was probably watching the departing car. Or eating the rest of his lunch.

Howie stopped at the four-foot wire fence, looked the situation over, put thick pink fingertips lightly atop the fence and vaulted over it, and moved around the machinery to vault out again and thus herd her away from anything she could use as a barrier. I was laboring closer. She read his intent and ran along the fencing toward the corner. Howie trotted along inside the fence and then vaulted up onto the corner, standing atop the railing. It was on the down-slope side. As soon as she committed herself again, he could jump and catch her.

I used my laboring run for improving the velocity of the projectile. I put the tool way back over my right shoulder and held my left hand straight out. And then I hurled the lug wrench at him so hard that it spilled me face down in the grass. I never saw it hit him. Pidge told me later that it hit him in the back, just below the base of his thick neck. I sat up in time to see him leaning forward and waving his arms wildly. I saw the problem. He was too far off balance to be able to drop close enough outside the fence to grab it. He would land on a steep slope that ended in a drop to the cable-car slot, and he might very probably go over the outside edge of that, into a very damaging fall.

I saw him glance upward and outward, and then, with a surpassing, astonishing agility, he leaped slightly to the side and caught the outgoing cable, about an inch and a half in diameter, in his two hands. He swung free of the slope and quickly shifted his hands, turning himself to face back toward the hill, and I saw what he figured to do.

He could swing out and in again to drop and land in the car slot with no danger of going over the edge.

Two variables had to work in useful synchronization for him to land properly, the cadence of his back-and-forth swinging, and the outward velocity of the cable. He went backward faster than I expected. I heard a wild yell of astonishment from the attendant as the big man went by overhead, swinging. At the time he should have jumped, he was swinging outward. He was going to make his try as he swung back in, but when he did, he was just too far out.

I stood up and moved over toward the edge to see him better. The oscillation stopped. Howie was trying to look back down, trying to pick a place where he could drop into the jungle slope into thick brush and not too much incline. Maybe he saw a place he liked a little further down as the cable curved outward, away from the hill. With that chance lost through a moment of indecision, soon he was a tiny figure, high over the long roofs of the cannery buildings.

Pidge was standing beside me, shuddering and making a little rattling sound with each exhalation. I will always wonder what Howie was thinking. I don't think he was experiencing fear. I think he was just working it out. I saw him start swinging again, and then he doubled and hooked one leg and then another over the cable. He was too far away to see clearly, but I imagined he was hugging the cable to rest his hands. There was no decision he could make until he was at the lowest point in the slack. As long as he was able to rest his hands, there seemed no point in risking a possibly fatal drop into the harbor. He could stay with it all the way to Solo Hill and drop off just short of the cable station.

The attendant came churning up to the pulley enclosure, his face clenched with awareness of duty and responsibility. I did not know what he was going to do, and I don't know if I could have stopped him, or if I would have wanted to. He didn't unlock his gate. He climbed over. He braced himself and yanked one big vertical lever in one direction and shoved the other lever forward.

There was one hell of a shriek as the cable was yanked to a stop. I looked out there and saw the car swinging violently back and forth. An instant later I picked up the tiny shape of Howie Brindle, turning over and over, falling down toward the water. From that height, it would be the same as hitting stone. He hit about a hundred yards offshore from the canneries. He made a very small pockmark against the water. Pidge slid down onto the grass, then rolled up onto her hands and knees and threw up.

The attendant looked at me with a knotted brow and an attempt to smile. He shuddered and said, "Oops, sir." He closed his eyes and swayed slightly, rubbing his mouth with the back of his hand, brow furrowing again in thought. He could find no words to explain an error so instinctive and so horrid. He looked at me and said, once again, "Oops, mister," and hauled away at his big levers. The cable began moving as before.

Epilogue

IT was a warm and windy Bahama night, and *The Busted Flush* lay at anchor in the lee of a tiny island in the Banks shaped like a crooked boomerang.

I had Meyer crushed until he got cute and found a way to put me in perpetual check with a knight and a bishop. We turned off all the lights and all the servo-mechanisms that *click* and *queak* and we went up to the sun deck to enjoy the September night, enjoy a half moon roving through cloud layers, enjoy a smell of rain on the winds.

The deck chair creaked under Meyer's weight. "Are you really going to go treasure hunting with Frank Hayes?" he asked me.

He was giving me another opening. My friend, the doctor. Never too obvious. Therapy sessions delicately spaced. Any invasion of personal privacy still stung, however. Still hurt. I let all irritability fade away before I answered.

"I'll have to tell Frank no thanks. It was an impulse. Change of life style. And maybe get lucky enough to drown."

"Strange thing," he said, "the terrible contortions we all go through trying to climb out of our own skin."

"As a way to stop hurting, to try to stop hurting."

Okay. I had finally admitted it out loud. Chalk up one for Meyer, or for the poultice of time passing by, with infinite slowness.

Maybe I could get far enough away from it to believe nothing much had happened at Pago Pago. A young wife responded to treatment for deep depression. A tall hotel guest recovered from a slight sunstroke. A big young man, clowning around, showing off for his wife, had died in a tragic accident. A man from Auckland had eventually flown over to Pago Pago and purchased a fine motor sailer at a most reasonable price. Pidge could not have forced herself to ever go aboard it again.

Nothing much happened. We stayed there together, until all the knots in the red tape were untangled and retied, and until she felt strong enough to fly home.

Nothing much happened. I told her all about the life and times of Howie Brindle. We marveled together at there being such creatures in the world. We sighed, murmured all the words, made love in that concrete beehive, leased a little sailboat and found beaches without footprints and made love there too. We went to a *fia fia*, ate roast pig, listened to drums, locked eyes and laughed.

The world requires that one accomplish the little housekeeping chores, so after we flew back and I moved her aboard the *Flush*, I had my long and interesting chat with Tom Collier, retrieved Professor Ted's papers and records, and then had the conferences with Frank Hayes about the financing, the timing, the percentages.

"No big dramatic deal," I said to Meyer, breaking the long silence. "I thought it was some kind of crazy chemistry with that girl. Hangover from the time she stowed away and I took her back to Daddy. Or involved somehow with gratitude toward Ted for saving my life in Mexico. It was all too good there in Hawaii with her. Made me suspicious. Nothing is supposed to be that good. Ever. Tried to blur the impact with a few ladies."

"I couldn't help but notice."

"And comment. I remember. Then I think the worst time in my life up until then was when I knew she was alone in the empty Pacific with a monstrous . . . non-person with no motivation except boredom and impulse. I never ached so badly. I *knew* he was going to kill her, and I felt as if that was exactly what I deserved."

"Can I say something?"

"Why ask?"

"Because you have a very low boiling point lately and I don't want you to hit me in the head first and apologize second. Try this for size. You have this Calvinist concept the fates should kill her to punish you for all the rotten things you have done in your life. Of course you are not exceptionally rotten. Just average rotten, like everybody. Okay, so maybe the fates decided that killing her was clumsy and simplistic. Maybe the fates have a sense of . . . irony."

He was right. My first impulse was to strike out. Even at Meyer.

One tries it for size, hoping it won't fit. Together, aboard the *Flush,* it had been so absolutely perfect we had a superstitious awe toward it. We made bad jokes about the horrid adjustment problems of having a wife too young and too rich. We made bad jokes about her adjustment problems—about the three afternoon hours a week she had to spend in group therapy, trying to get down to the places Howie had broken and attempting to mend them.

Two people, totally, blissfully, blindly in love. And gradually it became apparent that there was only one person in love, and the other one was merely repeating lines which had once been spontaneous, going through the motions which used to be bliss. Excuses have a hollow sound. Lies have an earnest tacky melody.

Because of my size and visibility, I have had to become adept at following people. It was all too easy to follow Pidge, and be acidly amused at her amateur precautions. It took four of those therapeutic afternoons to track her to the grubby little singles lounge, to the booth where he waited for her. My first impulse was to say to myself that it could not be true. Only in television, in the worst of daytime television, does the handsome young psychiatrist fall in love with the lovely young patient. Never in real life. Please make it never. Don't let her fall in love with him. By a simple device I tuned in on that fateful line, that timeworn line as she said, "But I can't ever leave him, darling. I owe him my life."

Okay, the fates are ironic. The biter bit. If it fits, wear it. If you wear it, you have to laugh. Maybe it will go away if you laugh.

So I tried to laugh. For Meyer. For myself. For all young psychiatrists in love. God only knows how ghastly that sound of laughter could have become had not Meyer raised his hand and hissed at me. "Shhhh!"

Then I heard it too. That great rush of fish escaping a predator in the moonlight. With the stealth of burglars, we got the rigged rods and went over the side and waded into the moon pattern. I could still taste the laughter in my throat, exactly like vomit. On the third cast, something hit like a cupboard full of dishes and went arrowing off across the flats making the reel yell in an unaccustomed agony.

It was a long long time before I thought about Pidge again. Very long, for me. Almost a half hour, I think.